THE FRIZON

BOOK TWO OF THE THOMAS YORK SERIES

BOOKS BY SHIRLEY BURTON

UNDER THE ASHES
Book One of the Thomas York Series

THE FRIZON
Book Two of the Thomas York Series

ROGUE COURIER
Book Three of the Thomas York Series

SECRET CACHE
Book Four of the Thomas York Series

New in 2015
RED JACKAL

shirleyburtonbooks.com

THE FRIZON

BOOK TWO OF THE THOMAS YORK SERIES

SHIRLEY BURTON

*To Roy,
Shirley Burton*

HIGH STREET PRESS
CALGARY

HIGH STREET PRESS
Calgary, AB
highstreetpress.com
shirleyburtonbooks.com
First printing 2013

This book is a work of fiction. Names, characters, places and incidents are the product of the author's imagination or are used fictitiously. Any resemblance to actual events, locales or persons, living or dead, is entirely coincidental.

Printed in the United States of America
Available in eBook formats.
Design and editing Bruce Burton
Cover Bruce Burton, photo licensed Shutterstock.com.

Library and Archives Canada Cataloguing in Publication

Burton, Shirley, 1950-, author
        The Frizon / Shirley Burton

(Book two of The Thomas York series)
ISBN 978-0-9919531-2-7 (pbk.). —ISBN 978-0-9919531-3-4 (bound)
ISBN 978-0-9919531-7-2 (ebook)

Dedicated to my daughter Sara
for her spirit of adventure and her love of art.
And to my son Michael and daughter-in-law Janet
for their encouragement and love.

THE
FRIZON

ONE

Paris, France, May 2012

Rachel stayed close to the middle of the pedestrian mall, dodging customers from the shops as a bicycle passed through the crowd, splashing water on her from its fender.

Rain drizzled through the afternoon leaving Montmartre's ancient cobblestone streets glistening. Rivulets of rain danced on the terra-cotta tiles, and voices of vendors were drowned by the sound of water flushing down the eave spouts into cement troughs.

Rachel's footing was unsteady. She had no choice but to flee the scene of the murder on the hill. The shot she thought was meant for Thomas took another right before her eyes. She fled downhill toward their loft on Rue de Saules.

Panting to catch her breath, she stopped beside a window box overflowing with prosperous blossoms. Salty perspiration coated her eyelids from the humidity.

From her vantage, she could watch the full terrain up to the artist's hill behind her; scrutinizing the street and buildings for any sign of the killer. The man in black, who Thomas was now pursuing in the dead of night.

Her heart pounded in her chest, and the back of her throat was tender from panting and wheezing. She flipped her long auburn tresses and pulled her collar to her chin. In a quandary, Rachel wasn't sure whether to chase or run.

St. Pierre, the village at the bottom of the incline, was within two hundred meters and she could reach it quickly. Once more, she glanced from the top to the bottom, sensitive to pedestrian movements.

At dusk, it seemed safe to step out from the building alcove of the bistro–the point of her stake-out. Rachel calculated her next move as a tram passed, shuttling pedestrians from the Basilica. Its clatter and the clamor of tourist voices ticked like a pendulum, interfering with her concentration.

She stretched her senses for one more look; Thomas's physique couldn't be mistaken even from a distance. He would be unmistakable, six feet tall with broad shoulders and a noticeable limp from his old injury.

Where was he?

Life had been uncomplicated for Thomas and Rachel since arriving in Paris months before, transformed to life in Montmartre with new identities as Emily Warner and Joseph Harkness, in exchange for New York state evidence.

Rachel had adjusted to the community, inconspicuously blending into the passionate Parisian 'joie de vive', a new enjoyment of life. Before the sun rose most mornings, she walked the steep hill past the Basilique du Sacré-Coeur, and on warm evenings she mingled with real and pretender bohemian artists at the cafés.

For centuries the same walkways were home to masters and paupers, the brilliant likes of Dali, Monet, Picasso and Van Gogh.

Boutiques were tucked into weathered stone buildings, and colorful canopies fronted the painted dormer windows of studio apartments.

Their upper flat was diminutive but charming, with French doors opening to a scalloped wrought iron balcony. Garden boxes draped the railings, cascading in a dramatic kaleidoscope of nature.

Rachel didn't enter her loft entrance on rue de Saules, but found a shielded position a step from a bistro wall where she could scrutinize the entrance of Marie's flower shop, Le Magasin de Fleur.

The shooting was only thirty minutes before, but time was grinding painfully slow for her.

Tourists and buskers had been cordoned away from the taped crime scene on the hill, and the ambulance lights blazed across the wet buildings, exactly where she had been sitting with Thomas.

The echo of a siren squealed past with piercing tones beeping and droning, and blue strobe lights swaying over the hilltop.

Thomas wouldn't want me to go back to the scene. He'd trust me to find safety out of sight.

She struggled to grasp why the rifleman, perched on the steps of the church, would have targeted them.

And here in Paris . . . it doesn't add up.

She remembered at that moment, her sight line was drawn to a glint of light at the Basilica, with the sun reflecting from the rifle lens.

Panic welled inside. *Where is Thomas?* It rang in her head.

Shops were closing for the night, and her eyes followed Marie, watching her latch the wooden shutters.

At eight o'clock, the lights went out and Marie left through the back, her five-year-old bloodhound baying as she gripped his harness. Marie was singing the familiar French lilt that Rachel had often heard in the evening from her loft.

Through the clouds, the sky transformed from pink to a fiery orange sunset, then to moonlight as the humidity of the afternoon was reduced to a cool breeze.

Rachel unlocked the door leading to her unit above the flower shop. The hallway lamp was dim, and she knew there were twenty-eight steps. Counting each one in the darkness, she dug into her bag for the wooden key fob. She fumbled in the drawer for the flashlight but stopped, thinking it would reveal her presence.

Standing inside the door, she heard the quiet whistling of her own breathing over the silence.

What is ahead, and where is Thomas? And who was the gunman?

The feeling of being alone was loud and the shoulders of responsibility were heavy. Rachel felt her way to the king bed by the balcony, and stayed motionless as she retraced her last 24 hours.

They'd been sitting at a bistro patio, soaking the sky and warm breeze; Thomas had gone inside for coffee.

Rachel couldn't mistake it, so close behind her head, the same tobacco aroma that eluded them in New York. The hair on the back of her neck stood up simultaneously with goose bumps covering her arms.

Her first instinct was to turn sharply and look for the offender. But she spotted Thomas sauntering back, followed by a barista with the coffee and pastries. Rachel leaned in to Thomas and whispered, "I'm not crazy . . . but I got a whiff of the cherry tobacco."

He stood erect and craned through the tourists.

"You're sure?"

"Of course." She shot a glance.

"Don't worry, babe," he said, "My antenna is on alert . . . he must have been close!"

Setting out to track him, they trekked the hill to Montmartre's tobacco shops, paying off with a store that sold the same cherry Marnier brand that day. The clerk recounted a tall, slight man with reddish hair, and freckles peppering the bridge of his nose. He thought it odd the man wore a heavy wool beret in this mild weather, with his collar pulled up.

Returning to the outdoor café, they discussed the dilemma, convinced their past couldn't have found them, that the witness program was secure in moving them to Paris from New York.

Using their real names, the stranger calmly approached Thomas and Rachel at the hill while they sipped coffee. He wasn't threatening, but walked to their table like an old friend, curious and at ease.

Rachel's eyes were tight, reflecting on the horrific outcome of the evening, certain only one shot had been fired.

Agonizing through the night, she was tossed into reality by waking flashes of the bizarre events. At 1:00 a.m., she inched the double doors open for a breeze, and minutes later heard scratching from the kitchen door. Her hearing was acute to the slightest movement, and in the darkness the handle turned, followed by slow deliberate steps toward her bed. Her heart pounded.

Keeping her eyes closed, she hoped the intruder would not see her squint to follow his moving shadow.

She felt body heat standing near her, then he staggered and collapsed on the bed.

"Thomas! Oh, Thomas!"

She heard his whimpering and moaning, and reached for him, the relief so consuming that tears streamed on her cheeks.

"Thomas, are you okay?"

He hadn't spoken a word.

"Please say something to me."

His face was buried on the pillows, exhausted and too weak to sit. In less than ten minutes, he raised his head and mumbled, his eyes still closed but his humor intact.

"I'm alright, Rachel . . . it's not smart to use the narrow lanes running between the streets at night. I'm deathly sore, but expect to live. I'll explain in the morning."

She found her way to the washroom for a warm wet cloth to wipe the blood off his face, and he was already asleep when she leaned to kiss him on the forehead.

Listening to his breathing, she leaned on one elbow against her pillow and watched the moonlight land on his face.

Rachel's body was tense with fear, and she couldn't bring herself to sleep. Lingering by the patio door, she held back the lace curtain to see the street below.

A gas lamppost reflected on the street, and she watched in silence for an hour, afraid Thomas had been followed, apprehensive that trouble might lurk outside in the shadows. Exhausted, she took refuge next to him.

At 3:15 a.m. a noise awoke her. Through the patio window, it was the silhouette of a man, his profile barely visible.

Was it my imagination or was he rubbing his knuckles?

They woke before seven from the noise of Marie opening her shop and the bustle in the street. She got up to peer outside, but the night's shadows had been replaced by sunshine and singing birds.

Must have been my imagination.

Rachel returned to check on Thomas but heard the shower start. The water ran a long time and she assumed he was cleaning his wounds.

Still in her clothes from the night before, she sat on the edge of the bed, patiently waiting to see him in daylight and tend to his injuries. When Thomas emerged, she held back her horror at the damage, his right eye swollen shut and his face scratched with purple contusions distorting his chiseled cheeks. He dabbed at a lip gouge with a crimson stained washcloth.

"If I'd known last night how blackened you were, I'd have used ice packs on the swelling." Rachel rinsed the washcloth and dabbed his wounds with disinfectant.

Easing onto the plush cotton mattress, Thomas pushed his pillow against the headboard with his good arm.

"Good morning, babe! I guess I have some explaining to do. But please . . . right now I need extra strength aspirin and a strong coffee."

"Are you broken?" she asked. "You limped from the bathroom with your right arm against your side."

"My ribs might be broken . . . maybe my wrist too. We'll find a walk-in clinic somewhere today." He winced and pursed his lips.

Rachel shook her head. "You won't be walking anywhere today! I'll check with Marie and find a doctor willing to make a house call. A bit of financial gratitude should bring one easily enough."

Thomas didn't need convincing.

"How about that coffee or I'll fall back to sleep? Rachel, feel the bump on my noggin. It's possible that I've earned myself a concussion."

He'd been there before.

TWO

Dumfries Castle, Scotland, July 2004

Eight Years Earlier

The Scottish morning was humid and the still air hung over the countryside. The North Sea fog was burning off in the valleys, and the quaint, sleepy village of Dumfries was unsuspecting.

Rene left his room with a roll of paper under his arm. With side by side doors at the Dumfries Arms Inn, he knocked at the room shared by Robbie and Dodger. The stench of stale cigarette smoke and beer oozed out the door. The three men had played cards late into the night, then Rene went to his own room.

"Up and at 'em, lads!" Rene tried to arouse the two while scooping garbage off the table to spread the map.

"Here's the layout, but we need to go through things one more time."

Dumfries Castle was an awe inspiring edifice of the 17th century, miles from Glasgow in the lush countryside. He had considered July to be perfect for this job. It was the busiest month, with daily coach tour groups from London and the continent.

Robbie, the older of the two men showed little patience. "We've got everything down pat, don't waste your breath, Rene." He was six feet tall with an imposing frame, and his thick brown hair and wire glasses drew attention from his facial scar.

There was already tension when the third man spoke.

"I checked today's groups. A coach is to arrive at 11:00 a.m., a load of German tourists. And this company is known to be punctual, so no room for error." His cigarette dangled.

Rene interjected, "You're wrong, boys. The last minute check is the most important. The slightest slip and we'll be caught. One more time through, I say!"

Watches synchronized, they worked through each detail again, another full hour refocused on the plan.

"Don't carry any identification." Rene reinforced.

At 10:15 a.m., the three men exited the hotel and walked two blocks watching for the right vehicle. They apprehended an unlocked Volvo and Rene started it as the others got in. They zipped their lightweight jackets and stuffed their black leather gloves.

The tour coach for the castle was already at the Dumfries terminal, punctual as expected. Rene tucked the stolen vehicle tightly behind as it pulled to the road.

At the entrance, an attendant waved the bus to a passenger drop-off zone, but Rene was held at the gate and diverted to a lot two hundred meters from the door. Within minutes a second diesel coach, from London, fell in behind the Dumfries bus.

"We didn't plan for this," Rene grumbled, "but we are still on course."

The grand foyer bustled with tourists and the three blended easily into the crowd, staying close as the prattle of visitors drowned out their conversation.

"Did you hear me, Robbie?" Rene asked, his hand cupped to his ear.

"Barely."

"I hadn't thought about noise," Rene said. "We should've anticipated this." A detail man, he was embarrassed to admit he'd miss anything.

The young lad poked him. "A horrible shrew at the door demanded I put out my cig."

Rene just barked, "I told you about that before."

With scant attention at opening hours, it was time to make their move. "It will take those two groups half an hour to reach the Madonna." Robbie said.

They each put on leather gloves and entered the corridor toward the armed guard.

Rene's finger was to his lips as they walked in silence. "Robbie, you take him." He said, then snapped, "Now!"

From behind, Robbie gripped his muscular arm around the guard's neck, tightening his embrace until the man released his strength and collapsed on the floor.

Robbie dragged the guard inside the room, out of sight from the door, and returned to the guard's spot to watch the hall. He pulled the velvet rope stanchion across the entranceway.

Voices were now heading toward their room, and with a job to be finished, Rene and the lad continued unfazed, lifting Leonardo da Vinci's 'Madonna of the Yarnwinder' from the moorings, into its case.

A trickle of tourists was at the stanchion, and an anxious voice leaned in and shouted. "Hey there, young man, what are you doing?"

Robbie intercepted the woman with his hand in the air, and Dodger walked across coolly. "Don't worry, this is a routine drill on our wired security system."

Dodger removed a sign from his bag and hung it on the stanchion, "Exhibit Closed for the Season".

The art world was shocked again and the painting disappeared from public eye, out of circulation pending a clandestine sale three years later.

THREE

Paris, May 2012

Marie set out her painted galvanized pails with fresh spring flowers and Toby loped to each one, inhaling the fragrances. The delivery truck came early to her loading door every morning with boxes of supplies that she carried to the cooler. Bundles of crimson roses were put aside for the night walk, for strolling between tables of lover's duets at the top of Montmartre.

At 6:00 a.m., Marie was outside watering the window boxes in her garden apron when Rachel came down. Toby greeted her first and she reciprocated with a rub. He leaned his weight into her side, forcing a heavy paw on her shoe to prevent her from leaving.

Toby was a pure-bred black and tan bloodhound obsessed by smells in his small world. He was well-known on the street for his gentle nature and the big heart in his tail. His eyesight was questionable, but a prodigious hound nose made up for any shortfall. Finding a scent was always his reward, as with any bloodhound.

"Marie, where can I find a doctor able to make a house call? Joseph fell off his bicycle on the hill last night and I want to be sure he doesn't have a broken rib. Of course, I expect to pay an extra fee for the special service."

"Perhaps *I* should come and look–I used to be a mid-wife you know." Marie offered, and Rachel had difficulty covering a smirk, wondering how those duties could apply to Thomas.

"No, thank you Marie; that is so kind of you. Joseph is asleep right now, but if you could call for a doctor, I would feel better."

Rachel stayed on the stone walkway, admiring the vibrant floral displays, while Marie got on her phone in the back of the store. On her third call she made the arrangement, and satisfied with her accomplishment, she beamed a smile at Rachel.

"Docteur Rousseau will stop on the way to his office. He cured my gout a few years back. Shouldn't be more than about twenty minutes. That is good, non?"

"That is excellent. Marie, you are so kind to us."

Rachel tilted her head and kissed Marie's cheek, at the same time stuffing a generous donation of euros into her apron pocket.

Dr. Rousseau arrived at the loft with heavy footsteps on the staircase. Rachel greeted him before he had a chance to knock. From the kitchen, the doctor could see Thomas on the bed, unable to prop himself for a proper greeting.

"Merci, merci. Dr. Rousseau, it is good of you to come on your way to your office."

The doctor tipped his hat politely at Rachel but focused across the room at the patient in distress.

He took Thomas's blood pressure, then shook his head in disapproval. Each eyelid was pulled up, one at a time, the irises confirming a concussion.

"I see you took a crack to the head, young man."

The doctor's hands continued down Thomas's face, finding a bone chip fragmented from his eye socket, and continued to poke and grip every joint and muscle.

"Monsieur, you should have been advised to attend a hospital at the time of your injuries. It is more difficult to treat injuries after this interval of time."

Thomas smiled, his teeth bared. "Yes, I've been told that." He looked at Rachel.

Dr. Rousseau continued with the examination results.

"I can set the wrist here, but I fear you have several broken ribs. If they're not set properly, the lungs could puncture, which will be much worse. The lacerations have been left too long—one needs stitching and the rest I will bandage to avoid infection."

"Dr. Rousseau, I can't stand or walk. I can barely catch my breath, so stairs will be impossible. Please do your best to set my ribs here. I'll come to your office next week and you can send me for x-rays to see how they are mending. Whatever fee you wish, please." Thomas pleaded.

The doctor was in thought for a few minutes, and reluctantly turned to Rachel. "I'll give him an analgesic, and you will need to assist me."

"Of course, Doctor Rousseau. Whatever I can do."

"Well, we need a hard surface—the kitchen table will do."

The two struggled to elevate and move Thomas. His pain was aggravated when they lifted him onto the table and eased him flat on his back.

"Rachel, apply gentle pressure while I set the bones, I'll tell you when and keep ventilating him with this oxygen bag—slow rhythmic massage. I'll use my fingers to find the bones then flex them into place . . . I'm injecting a mild anesthetic now."

Thomas's eyes closed and his body went limp and eased into slow medically controlled breathing. Rachel wiped the doctor's brow with a white towel from her linen closet.

"You are an excellent nurse and I know Joseph will be fine. Ah, this is good, much better than I had expected."

"I used to watch MASH and their make-shift surgeries." Rachel amused herself.

Thomas began to stir, and in time opened his eyes.

"Young man, you are lucky! One of these ribs was only millimeters from puncturing a lung. You were right to insist on not walking."

Rachel propped Thomas to a painful sitting position. The doctor wrapped the ribs with strips of white cotton webbing, and laid Thomas in a horizontal position on the bed.

"You will spend as much time as possible flat on your back, young man, or you'll end up in the hospital."

Rachel knew it would be a challenge to follow that order. "A cup of coffee before you leave, Doctor Rousseau?"

But the doctor looked impatiently at his watch. "No thanks, I'm already late for my office."

"May I ask what your fee for today will be?"

She wanted to be generous, but had no idea what fees doctors charged in Paris.

"One hundred euros is fine." The doctor replied.

Rachel handed him twice the amount, which pleased him immensely. He thanked her and gave her a card with his address in the city.

"And Madame, please give him these; Thomas should have one every six hours for pain. Due to the concussion, you will need to make sure he doesn't move around too much, and no lifting."

"Good morning, handsome!" She burst through the door. Surprise! Two pastries and steaming Starbucks."

She stopped with a stern look.

"*How* did you make it over to the sofa without my help?" she admonished.

"I was tired of being bedridden. Ready for a wee walk . . . do we still have that old walking stick?" He adjusted his arm sling and stuffed a pillow behind his back.

Rachel nodded and pulled over a chair. It was time to quiz him.

"Before that . . . it's time you told me what happened the other night. How *did* you get beaten up?"

Thomas scrunched his eyes at her. "Let me have one of those pastries first?" He sat up slowly.

"Okay . . . I'm ready. At the Montmartre bistro, I did see the cherry pipe man approaching from a tavern. Not in a hurry, but definitely fixed on us, and calm and friendly. I've thought of the story Daniel Boisvert told of retribution toward Lewis & Roch's law firm in New York, so meeting Daniel here was bizarre. But it doesn't make sense anyone would have reason to kill Daniel. At least not *now* and not in Paris."

"Thomas, aren't you curious *which* Daniel the shooter was after?" Rachel asked.

He stared at the ceiling.

"The moment I saw the red laser pointed at Daniel's head, everything ground to slow motion. My first instinct was to see where the shot came from. Then, I looked at Daniel on the ground, his eyes were closed with no blood, but a distinct dark wound on his forehead. I assume it was fatal but I don't know.

"With sirens on their way, I took off toward the Basilica, focused on the figure running ahead of me. My night vision is good and I kept pace at first."

Rachel was transfixed, impatient to hear it all.

"It was drizzling and I slipped on the cobblestone on a narrow step, but adrenaline kept me going. The gunman knew I was there but he had such a head start, I had to be creative by cutting through terraces to close the distance. His footsteps then stopped and there was silence. I paused to listen, but from the roof above, he landed on me, agile like a ninja, pinning me spread-eagled on the ground with my face to the stone.

"When I regained my footing, he had the upper hand. He was dressed in black with a turtleneck sweater, jeans and a French beret, but I couldn't see the detail of his face in the darkness. I felt maybe a mustache or a beard.

"I shook him off once more and he bolted; for a moment it was unclear who was chasing whom. He must have stepped into a doorway and when I went past, he pounced again, kicking at me. That's when he broke my ribs."

"You should have stopped, Thomas. Just taken off."

"I was angry! I threw my best punches and he stopped to get his breath. He said his business wasn't with me—just to keep my mouth shut about Daniel. We apparently got in his way. He lunged again, this time with a switchblade, but I dodged and fell to the ground.

"I was drained of my strength and he stood over me blocking the light. He warned us to stay off his radar. In a few seconds, he blended into the plaza and I lost him. My senses told me not to chase a man with a knife."

She sighed. "I'm glad you took the advice." She rose and paced a circle. "And your injuries?"

"I couldn't get air into my lungs. Every breath brought a searing pain to my chest, with my body like a dead weight. I couldn't focus. My balance was off and with my eye swollen shut, I inched downhill. What kept me going was you, Rachel. Seeing that you were safe.

With confinement to the loft for more than a week, Daniel knew exercise was essential, and was anxious to stretch his legs outdoors. He was fitted with an air brace for rib support. Rachel suggested a venture around Paris, convincing him the Champs Elysees would be easy distance.

Rachel eased him down the hill to the Abbesses metro. It was a quick fifteen minutes to downtown.

She was intrigued with the art displayed at Montmartre but was ready to explore the galleries.

They entered the luxurious lobby of the Warwick Hotel near Avenue George V. Breakfast would be Rachel's treat, a sampling of opulence, minutes from the Arc de Triomphe and the Louvre.

They didn't see the man in the lobby when they entered, but he followed them discreetly to the lounge, sitting two tables away and facing them within earshot. He ordered a coffee and Le Monde, a Paris newspaper he used to shield his face from view.

Within minutes, Rachel was restless, her heart set on a gallery they'd passed. "Wait here, Thomas—I'll pop across the road and be back in ten." He nodded and clicked his phone for a news app.

"I'll be right here."

Thirty minutes passed and Rachel hadn't returned. Thomas drummed his fingers on the table, watching lounge patrons come and go.

The stranger was still at his table behind his paper.

Uneasy with her absence, Thomas went to the street, then walked to the corner, stepping up on an abutment where he hoped to spot her through the maze on the Champs Elysees.

The man followed him out and watched before placing a cell call. He hesitated with the phone to his ear, then returned to his yellow Citroen and blended into the traffic.

Ten minutes later, Rachel left a gallery on the other side and wended her way through the traffic, beaming when she reached Thomas. He reached for her hand.

"Would you believe, Thomas . . . I got a part-time job in a gallery!"

"Shouldn't we have talked about that before you applied? You're my right arm. Staying low-key for a while doesn't jive with this." He rubbed his bruised jaw to draw her attention to possible dangerous encounters.

Rachel countered, "It's only Saturday and Sunday afternoons. We can handle that, right? At some point our funds will run dry and it's nice to bring some income. A little boost to my self-confidence too."

She searched his eyes. "I want you to be happy for me."

"If that is what you want, we'll give it a try," Thomas conceded.

She reached into her handbag for a brochure. "Also . . . there were flyers on a table in the gallery. *This* one caught my eye."

Thomas was distracted, but thumbed through it, an estate auction in Rouen on Wednesday. The catalogue described exquisite antiques and art, clocks, armoires, statuettes, porcelains and candelabras.

Rachel tilted her head to see his reaction, but his face was pale from his discomfort.

"We can talk about this later," she added. "Time to get *you* home. Let's get a taxi from here." She stepped to the curb and whistled.

At they pulled up, Marie and Toby poked their heads out. Marie was concerned. "Si bon, you are on your feet. Docteur Rousseau was excellent, non?"

"Yes indeed. Thank you for arranging it."

Rachel obsessed over the Rouen auction. Searching train times on her iPad, she noted that from Gare Saint-Lazare, they'd be at Rouen in 90 minutes. She circled the brochure's highlights, the fortress where Joan of Arc was tortured in 1431, and Gros Horlage, the sixteenth century astronomical clock.

"Thomas . . . I start at the gallery on Saturday. Could we then take a few days away and go to Rouen? I adore French clocks, and if I can't find one at the auction, we can check antique shops. A few days in the countryside would do us good. Rehab too!"

She spread the maps on the coffee table.

Seeing her passion, he simply nodded. "You'll persist until I forfeit any objection . . . so let's do it. Maybe a B&B."

Rachel added. "And we could go on from there; it's a short train ride to Giverny, home of Monet. The gardens are beautiful, and open to the public. We need French culture."

She giggled realizing she hit a weak spot, and brought over her wine glass to snuggle into him on the sofa.

"Do you think your ribs will be up to the adventure?"

Rachel's first weekend at the gallery gave Thomas time to get caught up. He was walking better and his bandages were gone, but he sported nasty scars and his eye had changed from purple to yellow.

Rachel took the mid-morning bus to the Champs Elysees, leaving Thomas on his own. He opened the laptop and the temptation to check on news in America was too great. New York's papers continued to report on the Sanderson case, with some sentencing taking place. Lewis & Roch was in financial trouble, with the firm operated by an audit firm at the behest of the courts.

The online Gleaner in Ely brought a smile, with an ad for Butler's Eatery citing the best cheeseburgers in town. The social column promoted a lunch at the Odd Fellows' Hall, the knitting club providing woolen quilts for the homeless. The best item was an image of Lieutenant Jamieson receiving an award as Captain of the Ely police.

Ah, that's another life.

Down deep, Thomas missed that life and yearned for another caper like it. Despite the risks, he thrived on danger.

But he reminded himself that Rachel deserved a better life. He was no longer the man from New York, but now a different name and person, settled in the alluring city of Paris.

The authorities changed my name, but that's all. People might call me Joseph Harkness for the rest of my life, but I'm still Thomas York inside.

His thoughts wavered between past and present. The bruises were fading but the sense of revenge for the shot fired at Daniel was driving him.

FOUR

Rachel carried her valise and Thomas his old worn satchel. They caught the early subway from Abbesses Metro stop and arrived at Gare Saint-Lazare train station at 7:00 a.m.

They settled on the second class fare for the sixty mile trip to Rouen. The platform number wasn't announced until fifteen minutes before departure causing a last minute scurry by passengers, many with oversized bags under their arms.

Passing through farmland and vineyards, Rachel contemplated how artists would have such passion for this country with its bold and brilliant landscape colors.

Rachel was immersed in a magazine of Monet's works and photos of Giverny's transformation. The Japanese bridge and lily ponds were like a pastel dream. It seemed like minutes before they whisked into Rouen.

She had booked a B&B with full breakfast at a three-story home near the auction. Envisioning a quaint rustic cottage, instead they climbed to an upper garret on the third floor.

Hot water was available nights from eight to nine and mornings from six to seven, in the shared washroom in the hall.

Grey clouds pushed across the drizzling sky, and Rachel recalled Marie's assertion to do on a rainy day the same things that she'd do in the sun. With coffees in hand, they strolled down the Rue du Gros Horlage, past the historic clock toward the antique shops on the narrow streets.

"We can't stop now, we'll miss the preview." Rachel said.

An imposing limestone warehouse dominated the block, with tall columns aspiring to the roofline. A uniformed doorman guarded the glittering leaded door, accented with a polished foot plate and exaggerated brass door handle.

In a wrought iron frame, a sign with a hand-painted script advertised the event.

Aux Enchères Immobilières / Estate Auction

Rachel gripped his arm. "This is it, Thomas!"

Paying ten euros for the exhibit catalogue, they walked into the hushed mezzanine and exhibition room. They followed arrows past rows of furniture and tables cordoned by stanchions with red braided tassels and gold ropes. Rachel slowed to inspect a clock, and they were firmly nudged from behind by staunch patrons urging them to keep the queue moving.

It wasn't pleasant being there, and Rachel was feeling pressure.

"I'm sorry, Thomas, for dragging you here. It was *supposed* to be fun, but it's so oppressive I don't want to stay any longer. Can we leave?"

"No problem, babe . . . you're not alone. Take *that* exit door. We'll head to the shops to find your perfect clock!"

It was a typical Tuesday, with antique stores swamped by tourists hoping for a piece of history. Every cranny in the first store was packed with dusty treasures and Rachel was enamored by the centuries represented. She purchased a gold rimmed 1800s teacup from Limoges, southwest of Paris.

In the adjoining shop, the mantel clocks were in poor repair, and Rachel contemplated a porcelain figurine of Marie Antoinette with her skirt opening to a rotating mechanism. Disgusted with its condition she took Thomas's arm, resigning to postpone the excursion.

Outside, a hand-painted sign at the end of narrow alley caught her eye, pointing toward a shop in the shadows.

"One more, Thomas, please? Then we'll call it a day, I promise."

The door creaked and floorboards sagged. Rachel lifted her head to smell the mustiness of years of history.

An overhead bell brought an old man from behind a curtain. He raised a monocle to his left eye to see them from across the room. Hunched over, his feet shuffled to greet them and he spoke in broken English.

"Bonjour, Monsieur et Madam. What are you wanting today, jewelry, or paintings of Monet's house perhaps?"

The man was anxious to please. His shop was overstocked and overlooked, as tourists bypassed his twisted alley.

"Or a fine set of plates, with different scenes of Giverny?"

Rachel was polite but direct.

"I am looking for a special French clock, but I don't see any here." She was tired and turned toward Thomas, who was already at the door.

The grand monsieur called her back. "I have the item of your search. It belonging to my great grand-père, but he's gone and I have no children for an heirloom. Come . . . please. I've been keeping it just for you."

Rachel burst into a polite laugh to hear such an old line from this custodian.

"You are not without charm, Monsieur. Yes, I will wait to see your clock."

No-one else entered the shop and Rachel felt the stress from the old man's attention. Standing beside him, she noted it odd that he wore expensive jogging shoes, out of place in her mind.

The old merchant disappeared to the back and unlocked an old cabinet. With his weathered hands, he removed a brilliant gold Boulle Inlay clock by Frizon of Paris. He carried it to the light without a word, placing it gently on the counter for Rachel's inspection.

Thomas came to the counter. The clock was spectacular. Overwhelmed by its beauty, Rachel softly touched the gold crown, gilding and intricate brass feet. It was exquisite, standing two feet in height.

He was nervous about handing it over, his voice quivering.

"I'm afraid it will be expensive, many euros for you. There's a gold plate mounted on the back of the inside casing; its etchings indicated it was made in 1725. My father's own grand-père was immensely proud of it. He was a jardinier, toiled in Monet's garden and grounds at Giverny. I have a key somewhere in the old desk . . . you will need that."

Thomas thought the man's story was far-fetched, even suspicious, and noticed too the shopkeeper had forgotten his hunched back.

Rachel's heart pounded in anticipation and looked to Thomas to take over the negotiation.

"How much is expensive, Monsieur?" He asked.

The man's shoulders raised, his eyes opening wider.

"You see, it's in perfect condition, so . . . a premium. Enough that I won't starve in my old age. But you look like a man who doesn't turn his nose at a good investment. Few people come in my lane anymore and I may not have another customer looking for a clock."

He spoke in a low whisper.

"One thousand euros."

"Monsieur, how do we know the story you tell is true? Not meant to be derogatory, but we have only met you, and the tale of your gardener at Giverny is difficult to swallow. We wouldn't want to purchase an item with questionable ownership."

"Everyone in Rouen trusts a Bouleau. Ask around and you'll find I'm an honest hardworking man and I drive a fair bargain."

Bouleau flushed, offended with the remark, but continued to persist with the sale.

Thomas needed more information. "Is it well known that you have a clock from Giverny?"

"Non, non. It has been in the back . . . the same place since my father died. Years ago thieves ransacked my store but didn't even see it."

He peered intently through the monocle, calculating his opponent once more. Thomas looked back in silence, then reached out his hand.

"Well Sir, you drive a hard bargain. I don't know about clocks but this one appears to be worth what you are asking. We will do some research on its background."

Thomas dug into his wallet for enough euros to conclude the purchase.

The eyes of the old man lit up. "I'll find newspaper and a box to wrap it safely for you." He shuffled behind the curtain.

Rachel caressed every curve on the clock.

"Oh Thomas, it is truly beautiful. I'll repay you from my gallery earnings . . . I promise. Thank you so much."

He kissed her forehead.

Their stroll took them across a canal. Standing at the bridge over the Seine River they discussed taking a candlelight cruise. Instead, they continued their walk stopping at a quaint restaurant for dinner. Their riverside table gave them a view of the canal boats that were lit up like Christmas.

Parked across the street near the riverbank, a man sat low inside a yellow Citroen, certain not to be seen.

In the morning, before breakfast, they advised the house matron of a change of plans, to move on to Giverny. She pouted that there'd be no refund, her policy.

Thomas didn't object but continued to the breakfast room. "Rachel, I'm starved."

She poked him and smirked, then realized the landlady was standing in hearing range. "Eggs benedict, fried potatoes and orange juice, please."

The matron huffed and disappeared to the kitchen.

The clock was packed securely in Rachel's case and they felt anchored to it. If one wasn't watching, the other was.

Midpoint to the depot, a man accosted them; Rachel recognized him from the auction house. The sight of him made her squeamish. His greasy hair was parted in the middle and a wiry mustache covered his tobacco-stained teeth.

"Monsieur, Madame, you must wait!"

Thomas didn't like his tone or the scenario, and he took Rachel by the arm to go ahead.

"Monsieur Bouleau made a good sale to you of the old Frizon. But it was a mistake; he should not have sold it to you. I will pay you the same for it." They walked faster and the auction man was keeping up.

Thomas shook his head with irritation as the man persisted.

"I *must* have it! I never knew he kept it in his shop, we searched before . . ." Sweat beads were on the intruder's brow and his pitch higher; he knew he'd said too much.

Thomas interrupted, "I'm afraid I don't know what you're talking about. You must be mistaken, Sir, and we have a train to catch."

They continued their pace.

He shouted after them. "I will pay you a generous bonus for your inconvenience. I beg you, Sir, I can't go to my boss without it. You'll regret this!"

"And who is your boss? I have no idea who Monsieur Bouillet is and I don't know what a Fruz is? And if you continue to harass me, I'll call a policeman."

"My boss is not a patient man." He resorted to yelling.

"Nor am I, I assure you." Thomas's face was flushed.

Another man in a similar uniform limped over to the first. They spoke and pointed toward Thomas and Rachel, then turned back toward the auction house. Thomas thought they'd given up and waved down a taxi.

"To the train station, quickly!"

Once in the back seat, he looked behind to see an older brown Renault-made Le Car, weaving in traffic trying to catch them. Rachel gripped the suitcase on her lap.

The traffic ahead on the narrow street was blocked by a delivery truck, and a rookie crossing guard waved to halt traffic for the truck to worm back to the street. Horns blared in unison as impatient drivers mounted the sidewalk with their small cars.

Forced to a sudden stop, Thomas shoved a clip of currency over the front seat to cover their fare.

"Rachel, go now! Take the sidewalk uphill past the truck. Don't worry, I'll be right behind."

When he was sure she was safely ahead, he jumped from the car before it lurched forward, rammed by the brown Renault.

He didn't know what to expect beyond the truck but saw that Rachel had stepped into an alley entrance to wait.

"Quick, down to the end of the alley," he said. "Take the direction against the traffic movement . . . there, I see a bus ahead, get on it! I'm right behind you. Stay down from the windows."

Thomas was panting, running as he spoke.

Onboard the bus, he saw Le Car passing through the intersection, slowing to look into the alleys. He leaned back, satisfied.

"We've lost them! No one in Rouen knows where we live in Paris. We can go home and figure this out; then with the clock hidden, we can return at our leisure."

His arm braced her shoulder.

"We've agreed on that, Thomas, but won't they be looking for us at the Rouen train station?"

"Exactly! They *will* look there, so we'll go to the airport instead."

A hotel was ahead, with cars queuing at the main entrance.

"Next stop, Thomas." She pointed at the limos and he understood.

The yellow Citroen pulled in behind a pair of limousines. The driver didn't exit his vehicle, but waited for Thomas and Rachel to establish their fare and depart from the hotel's driveway.

It was dusk when they landed in Paris. Thomas hired a taxi to St. Pierre Cathedral and they walked the few streets uphill to their loft.

Thomas settled on the living room couch, perched over the laptop on the coffee table. Searching for 'Boulle Inlay Clock' and 'Frizon of Paris', he pulled up a description, 28 inches tall. That seemed right.

Rachel lifted the Frizon from the case and centered it on the table, inspecting every corner with a magnifying glass. The meticulous etchings and hand painted designs were immaculate, with intricate brush strokes in gold leaf.

The door on the back was sealed shut with corrosion built up over the centuries. She dabbed a liquid rust remover with a Q-tip to remove rust particles.

With a deep breath Rachel inserted the key from Bouleau's desk. It turned easily.

She gasped. "Thomas!"

The inside of the case door was plated with gold, and at first glance the visible workings had a gilt serrated wheel.

Her eyes widened as she looked inside.

Behind the wheel, on a gold plate panel was a breathtaking painting, an intricate oil of the Giverny pond in a space no larger than twelve inches square. Shivers went up her spine.

"Monsieur Bouleau said his great-grandfather was a gardener for Monet at Giverny estate, but why would this be here? Also . . . the clock was made in 1725 but Charles Monett wasn't born until 1850 and died about 1930. This must be a forgery!" Rachel was presenting logic she didn't like.

"This must be a forgery," she repeated.

Rachel inspected every wheel and bolt, paused when one of the front brass legs slightly turned. She tried the other with the same slight movement, and hesitated as they each seized.

They could break if I pressure them.

Thomas called from the laptop. "Rachel! Good news! This clock is worth four times what we paid!"

Rachel stood over his shoulder reading the Frizon's description, its size, case and movements, gilt, year and markings. They had found a treasure.

"Whoa!" She raised her hands to celebrate.

Thomas was still suspicious.

"Something about Bouleau though . . . did you see his jogging shoes? And at the door, he had lost his hunched back and monocle. I hope this story pans out, otherwise we know who to look for."

Rachel was perplexed. "I noticed, but it doesn't mean he's guilty of anything. If we run across him again, we'll have more pointed questions."

"We need to check the gardener story." He scratched his head. "Our next trip to the countryside needs contemplation. And the men from the auction house are sure to be on the lookout for us."

His thoughts jumped around. "How did they find out so fast from Bouleau? I hope the man is safe. For now, we should document it with lots of close-up pictures and find a secure place for the Frizon. A space of twelve by thirty inches would do."

As an art student, Rachel had majored in European art and found this to be right up her alley, knowing every work the impressionists had ever done, names and sizes, including Charles Monett.

Their hasty departure from New York in the witness protection program allowed no final contact with their family or friends. Rachel longed to talk to her sister but it would be against the rules and good common sense. Many nights, she reminisced about the times in university rooming with her sister, sharing their secrets and dreams.

It was different with Thomas. She couldn't tell him all her secrets but tried to be as honest as she could. He had become the balance in her life.

Thomas missed his elderly father in Florida, who would be wondering why he hadn't heard from him. His friend Martin

Sproule promised to keep tabs on his Dad, but absence of the heart left a huge void. He calculated when enough time had passed, he'd make a discreet phone call to St. Petersburg.

"Rachel, we may have stepped into a deep puddle, and it's not going to be easy to get out. We should stay away out of Rouen until this has died down. I don't see how they could find us here in Paris; we didn't sign anything or give our names to anyone, did we?"

Thomas looked up and she was concentrated in thought.

"Well, the B&B was registered under your name and that won't show up anywhere," she said. "We did purchase the catalogue at the preview but paid cash, so nothing there, and we didn't use train reservations."

A look of fear flashed on Rachel.

"Thomas . . . the art gallery. I left my new name on the job application. You don't think . . . ?"

"For starters you won't be working there anymore. Don't set foot anywhere near the gallery! Did you leave an address?"

His voice was firm and made Rachel more at ease that he'd protect her at all costs, find a way out if she needed it. She trusted him with her life.

"I put down St. Pierre and they didn't ask anything further."

She felt guilty for letting her guard down, and there was no use saying she was sorry. He knew.

Rachel's afternoon was engrossed in Monett's history, as a man, not a painter, finding that he had a penchant for intricacies and rarities. The Frizon would fit into that scope.

There were rumors of a romantic past with his mistresses, two of whom he eventually married. His first wife, Clarissa, died at an early age giving Monett a son and two daughters. The French love a romance, and fabrications survived three or four generations with embellishments never substantiated.

Lives of Monett's family remained obscure. As a tribute to impressionist arts, a museum was built at the town of Epte. Over time, the museum needed space and a structure of glass and white stone was built into a limestone cliff. At night a strobe light stood like a beacon on the hill.

Rachel pulled data about Giverny back to 900 A.D., finding the area was considered a valuable archeological find, with Neolithic statutes and monuments discovered between Giverny and Epte.

Monsieur Bouleau had bragged that his great-grandfather was a Giverny gardener, but that was impossible for Rachel to confirm. Piecing time frames, she suspected Bouleau at about seventy-five years, maybe more.

Thomas and Rachel concluded they'd get information at the Epte museum, relying on local folk lore more than thin historical records.

"When can we go, now that you're retired from the Champs Elysees gallery? I see from your French National map that there's a morning train from Saint-Lazare to Rouen and Le Havre."

Rachel was impressed. "Sounds simple enough. We'll get off at the town of Vernon, and from there it's only five kilometers to the museum gardens at Epte. We could take a local bus, or rent bikes . . . or even walk?"

She rattled on with her plans. "Think it'll be hard to find a guest house or inn? From ads on the train schedules, it looks like we'll be in Vernon overnight."

"We'll take our chances when we get there. No friends, no names, no family." He didn't mean to sound blunt, and saw her head turned toward the balcony, suddenly silent.

Thomas bent over her and saw teardrops forming; she looked up and the flood gates opened.

"Will I ever see my sister again, Thomas?"

"Of course you will. I promise you it will happen within a few short years."

"I'm sorry, Thomas, for the tears. The auction people have gotten under my skin and I'm distracted."

She looked at him for understanding. His mind was on the risk of their identities.

FIVE

Zurich, Switzerland, January 2009
Three and a half years earlier

Life in Paris hadn't been difficult, but there was a new prize in Rene's sight. He called the two others to meet him at the café on Rue des Dames.

"Robbie, four years on the lam and we've never been suspected."

He resisted gloating, and had reason for his renewed confidence.

"I've been studying the intricacies of museum security systems and I've found a jackpot for us."

Robbie had always looked up to Rene and trusted his acumen, but was still cautious. "We don't need the money, Rene. I've been trying the straight and narrow, and now safely playing the other side with two years of security management."

Rene knew it would just take Robbie a moment to contemplate it.

Robbie picked up again. "But it wouldn't hurt to talk, and it might even help if I can play both sides. What's it about?"

Rene nodded.

"Call the Dodger, and we'll meet here Friday morning, eleven sharp."

Dodger was a lad in his mid-twenties, bordering on malnourishment. His walk was brisk, sliding on a skiff of snow that blanketed Paris's sidewalks. He arrived early at Rene's designated boardroom, a cluster of three chairs in the café, a block from his flat.

"Well, here we are again—the three musketeers. We make a darn good team!" Dodger laughed and lit a cigarette.

Rene picked at him. "Kid, lay off those! Every tidbit you leave behind has your DNA!"

"This one's already lit, I can't waste it."

"Enough! You're lollygagging like women." Robbie had seen it before with them.

Rene summoned coffee for their table.

"To business now," he started. "It's a private Zurich museum with millions of euros in impressionist paintings. The collection is owned by a wealthy Austrian family, and they have neglected security upgrades, using antiquated alarms."

"How soon would we do it?" Dodger asked.

Rene continued, "Hold on! I've identified four specific works to lift. I spent a few weeks in Zurich surveying the museum. It's a cinch."

Robbie interrupted, "Do you have a plan mapped out, Rene?"

"I do . . ." Rene laid out the drawing he had sketched of the villa, and with his index finger he traced the trail of their routing."

Dodger pressed again. "It's excellent but when do we go?"

"This weekend!" They both turned.

"Yes, it is short notice . . . but that works best to keep us focused."

He pulled a black market Visa card and counterfeit passports from his case.

"These have the same photos as last time but new names. Robbie, book us one room at the Ambassador? Say it's a single for you, to avoid later detection. On Thursday morning we'll leave. It's a seven hour drive and we'll check in by late afternoon, so guarantee the room. We'll do the job Friday morning."

Zurich was beautiful in February, a mecca to skiers heading to the Alps. The influx of tourists would bode well for the musketeers, easier to hide with ski jackets and balaclava caps if needed.

"What time on Friday, Rene?"

"Their doors open at 11:00 a.m. and we'll enter fifteen minutes later, when staff are settled at their posts. I'll brandish a pistol to keep the guards at bay, and the two of you will need to move quickly to get the four impressionist paintings in the cases. Five minutes max. I've examined the room several times; the works are all in close proximity on the inside wall to the left."

Early Friday, Rene drove to the Zurich airport and picked a parked vehicle to confiscate from the long term lot. He was back by 8:00 a.m. and parked behind the hotel, with snow packed against the bumpers and plates.

At 10:00 a.m., they walked to the back. Dodger wheeled the stolen car to the unloading area in the front of the museum and left it unattended. Three in a row, they strode through the front doors.

"Pull down your face mask," Rene said. "Ready set go. Five minutes!"

Rene's gun was out. "Hold it right there, Monsieur. Stand still and you won't get hurt."

Robbie covered the overhead camera.

With duct tape, Rene covered the guard's mouth and secured his hands as Robbie and Dodger collected the four paintings.

The three strode out in three minutes and ran for the unlocked car.

Robbie shouted, "They're too large for the trunk!"

"Get in, we'll just go and hope for the best."

A second guard emerged from another wing and ran into the street, firing shots in the air. "Arretez! Arretez!"

Four blocks away, they pulled into a Petrol station and transferred Monet's 'Poppies' and Van Gogh's 'Blossoming Chestnut Branches' to a stolen van.

Sirens were closing on them, and in panic they fled, leaving the last two paintings in the stolen car.

The van disappeared onto Bahnhofstrasse, Zurich's main street.

"Musketeers? More like Stooges." Rene snarled at his cohorts' bumbling efforts leaving two paintings in the parked vehicle.

SIX

"Rachel, in France, we *have* to be Joseph and Emily a hundred percent, even alone, or we're prone to slip. Look how easy Daniel found us here–it could happen again."

She nodded and tried to enunciate slowly, "Joseph . . . Joseph. I'll use it more till it's natural, but it's so easy to fall back to Thomas."

"I'm afraid of the consequence with so much happening, we have to be committed to our new lives." Joseph said.

She felt defensive, sensitive he was lecturing her, but she knew he was right, they had to change.

Emily. She thought about it and said it out loud, "Emily."

She continued to pack, trying to think of everything: soap, shampoo, knife, granola bars, fruits and nuts, wire, whistle, matches, personals and basic clothing.

Joseph laced his hiking boots and tied two sleeping bags to the backpack. She watched him work, thinking how handsome he was, his light brown hair lit with golden streaks in the sun. His shoulders were broad and he had rolled his shirt sleeves to below his elbow. The large scar on his forearm stood out on his tan and she noticed how muscular he was.

Protection of the Frizon was their immediate concern, and they brainstormed for a secure location. Emily tapped the floor for loose boards and inspected behind a kitchen dumb waiter, but both could be obvious. The kitchen pantry had a stone floor, with the bottom shelving too wobbly to support weight.

Joseph crouched to the floor and ran his fingers along a brick wall behind the shelf, peeling down some wooden slats. He pulled out a crumbled brick, then pried it with a screwdriver, moving more bricks.

They shrouded the Frizon in a linen tablecloth and nudged it into the opening. With cement and mortar from the coal bin, Joseph edged the bricks into place, covering them with a layer of repaired slats.

Smug about their resourcefulness, they opened a bottle of Saint-Émilion.

The alarm chimed at 6:00 a.m. and Rachel fixed a cheese omelet and strawberries with brioche.

Toby and Marie were outside watering plants when Joseph and Emily left hand in hand toward the Abbesses metro.

The train to Vernon was forty-eight minutes out of Saint-Lazare, and Emily was making travel log notations of distances between villages and landmarks.

At the Vernon Tourist Kiosk, Emily asked for directions to Giverny on foot.

"Use the Grande Randonnée footpath, five kilometers on an old railroad track converted for pedestrians. You'll enjoy it." The operator opened a map with rest spots and hiking trails to the ancient Tourelles Castle.

They settled on a bench in the town center to consider their hiking options, agreeing it to take a few hours at the Giverny compound, then back to Vernon in the afternoon.

"Emily, if we become separated, we need a rendezvous spot back here. See anything?" Joseph asked.

"There . . ." Emily pointed. "That building on the hill with the pink roof, it was advertised at the train station, as an inn." She raised her hand to protect her eyes from the sun.

Joseph strained to see it. "Might be more than a kilometer . . . are you okay with that?" He waited for her answer, but she was snapping photos of the Epte train station on her phone.

The walk was physically demanding and they ground to a stop at an old stone inn on the pathway with an outdoor patio.

"Time for coffee," Joseph insisted. "Remember, we're on vacation!"

Enjoying the sun's warmth, he flipped through Emily's photos, lingering on the image of the Epte station.

"Emily, look here, in this picture." He zoomed it. "A man on the platform is watching us. See his eyes, they're directly on us? Strange."

Emily looked and agreed. "Who do you think he is?"

"Maybe one of the weasels from the auction house?"

Her thoughts flashed to the Rouen trip and the security of the Frizon.

"Somehow they knew what we looked like." She blurted, "Or even worse, who we are!" The consequences flashed before her.

"Joseph, at the preview we did pass the security entrance, and I bet they have footage of us."

He thought and added, "My premonition . . . it's about more than the clock, but who would want it so badly? Bouleau had to know about the painting, otherwise there'd be no reason for the harassment."

Emily stiffened.

"Joseph, don't look! We're being followed . . . in the shadow of the overhang. And now he has a colleague."

The men were in a heated exchange, and an outlook man was pointing toward Emily and Joseph.

"Emily, let's stay on the path and see their next move."

"Wouldn't it be better to elude them?" she urged.

Tourelles Castle was over the next hill, foreboding in its black masonry and weathered by centuries of elements. The castle wasn't open for public viewing, yet a sign showed three walking paths.

The longest loop would take several hours, but most tourists chose the short route marked in yellow. They paused to consider whether to take a route, or to continue to Giverny. Five people were ahead and the pair of figures behind.

Stopping by some thickets for shading, they looked back toward the station. The men had disappeared.

Thrashing in the bush alerted Joseph, and as he turned, one of the men jumped, knocking him to the ground. The other was behind Emily with a knife to her throat.

Joseph studied the scene, considering a karate move, but stayed back fearing retaliation against Emily. She gasped and heaved, then succumbed to a cloth doused in chloroform. Her legs buckled underneath and the heavier of the two men took a firm grip, dragging her from under her shoulders.

Joseph bellowed at him, "No! Leave her alone!"

He shouted back. "Don't move and do as I say."

The second man put a burlap sack over Joseph's head while the first tied a blindfold over Emily's eyes. He was close enough she could smell the filth and grease on his hands. He knotted her hands behind her back.

Joseph's voice was muffled. "Don't hurt her—if you do, I'll hunt you down!" He knew he wasn't in a bargaining position.

"Please!" He added, falling to his knees.

The castle path was wide enough for a group of tourists, built for wagons in past times. A Peugeot sped in to pick her up, wrangling on and off the path. Emily was hoisted to the back seat and her backpack tossed into the trunk.

Joseph couldn't see she was unconscious. He hollered in desperation.

"What do you want? *Please* don't take her."

His voice pleaded, but they ignored him and tied his hands with hemp rope. The path was abandoned by tourists in the late afternoon, and the attackers were confident they could yank and prod him in the open.

Joseph heard the roar of the Peugeot fading as he was poked and pushed toward Giverny. Meticulously, he counted the steps they took. He estimated his inclines and kicked stones to the right and left as he was able, leaving a directional pattern in the dust.

Joseph felt helpless but not defeated. He had to find her.

Who's going to look for me in the darkness near Giverny? I have no idea where they've taken Emily. I have to take control of the situation. Think. Think.

Half an hour later, the ground evened out to pavement.

A voice Joseph hadn't heard before approached them. "Maurice, what has taken you so long? Take him to the basement to the cold storage area."

The man named Maurice grunted an acknowledgement and nudged Joseph.

"Watch your step and keep your head down. The ceiling is not for a tall man."

Joseph stumbled to the bottom of the staircase, pressing his shoulder against a concrete wall to maintain his balance. Still wearing the sack, he was thrust inside, toppling onto the cold floor. He was sickened by the thud of the door and the dreaded click of the lock.

The steps of two men retreated up the stairs and a heavy door slammed behind them.

Will I ever get out? I have to save Emily.

He struggled and shook the sack from his head, assessing this to be a storage basement of a museum or a winery. The air was musty with a fragrance of oak, but spoiled by a putrid smell like paint thinner.

The room was dark, and overhead a bank of windows was open to improve the circulation and ventilate the fumes. His roommate, a curious mouse, scurried for refuge.

A water canteen hung on a hook halfway up the side wall, and a grey woolen blanket was folded in the corner, dirty and saturated with remnants of mouse droppings. The full moon offered light, enough for Joseph to set a plan in motion.

With his hands bound, he writhed to reach the Swiss army knife in his shorts. A sharp pain shot through his shoulder and he knew he had damaged it.

Grappling with the knife, he sawed at the wrist bindings and warm, sticky blood complicated it.

Finally free from the bonds, Joseph surveyed the air vents at the top of the twelve foot walls. He peered through an opening to the outer room, examining a long pole on a hook, used to open the vents. He looked around for other potential resources among the crates and drums, pallets and makeshift wooden shelving. The work tables in the center were heaped with clamps, measuring tapes, stretchers, rubber mallets, and bins. The kind of tools he liked.

The labels were too far to read and his limited French comprehension wouldn't help, but he suspected flammable chemicals.

A burst of frenzied voices erupted from the floor above and he stopped to listen. It was loud and argumentative, and he couldn't decipher anything in the fury, except the words *Monett* and *Towers*.

Emily's safety was at risk, and staying here long wasn't an option. He focused again on the hook and speculated the distance to the draft window.

Patting himself down, he inventoried his hidden pockets for tools and spread his meagre supply on the floor, the twine and D-ring next to his belt.

The chloroform had turned Emily's legs to rubber and drained her of her fight. She recalled someone approaching her from behind and placing a cloth on her face, then her memory became spotty as her feet were dragged in the dust.

A cloth band had been tied around her eyes and she remembered the stale cigarette smoke in the back of a French mini, then the sound of Joseph's voice yelling to save her.

The Peugeot sped on the narrow road and after a dizzying circle it became silent.

Treading up the tower steps, the men scraped and bumped her on the walls and mid-way they stopped, panting with exhaustion. The chloroform was dissipating and her senses awakening, as the odor of perspiration and garlic emanated from one of the men. She longer for fresh air.

Tightly bound, Emily was dropped onto a rotting musty blanket, and a basin of fresh water placed in the corner.

The carved oak door shuddered as it slammed, and a wooden bar was jammed in place. She was relieved the footsteps were fading, but also hoped they'd return to release her.

Emily dragged herself to the wall and rubbed the knotted blindfold on the coarse surface until it loosened. It was dark except for the moonlight and her eyes adjusted as she examined the enclosure.

Dire thirst from the chloroform drew Emily's eyes to the cool basin, and she wobbled to it. She wriggled to loosen her tied hands, without success, then climbed onto a bale of hay under the turret to survey the lands below. Giverny was in the distance and she wondered if Joseph would be there, or looking for her. She needed to send a signal.

Perhaps a white flag or a carrier pigeon.

The vision entertained her and she jolted back to reality.

She looked to the distant ground; jumping was out of the question.

Her fingers fumbled searching in the gravel debris for a shard sturdy enough to hack at the ties. Cutting her wrists brought the attention of a rat inmate smelling blood.

The walls of the tower had withstood three thousand years, with barnacles and moss planting their roots centuries ago.

This musty smell is from previous tenants left here to die.

It was a haunting reality, sharing an eerie sensation of historic figures who perished here. She had to keep thinking. With one more slash and a yank to her wrist bonds, her hands loosened.

Emily rested her chin on the sill, focused on the yellow path below. Nightfall came and she resorted to the floor of cold stones, afraid of disease from the rotten blanket. There was an aspirin in her shorts and she dared a gulp from the basin as relief from the chloroform's after-effects.

A beam of sunlight shone through against the wooden door, highlighting a rotted key lock beside the latch. Emily squatted at the door and squinted through. The hole was big enough for two fingers but she couldn't reach right through.

On the outside, the door was held shut by a two by four, inserted into a metal bracket that prohibited the door latch from opening.

I just need a rod or stick to push the board upward off the gauge.

She started with her corduroy belt and continued threading various items through the hole, without success.

A rat came, then another, finding her leather boots irresistible. Emily watched them wondering where they came from and went.

Taking the laces from her boots, she looped one around her belt buckle and tied a granola bar to the other end. She poked the crumbling granola piece through the hole far enough to rest on the lever on the other side. Her hope would be that the rats would attack it from the other side, and that their weight would pull the belt down to release the lever.

She waited and watched and finally the lace jerked, with a tug.

Steady footing, girl. Easy, easy . . . bingo!

The lever clanged as it fell and the door swung open. She inched down the stairwell, and near the bottom she lost her footing and tumbled the last six steps. Freedom was so close and she longed for fresh air as her lungs had inhaled the dank moldy air for too long.

Making her way through the bushes and thistles, she reached the town path without drawing attention. Some currency bills and a railway ticket were still sewn in her lining.

Refusing to accept defeat, Joseph picked at his door lock with the wire coil in his supplies. Using the mini flashlight, he needled the tool until his fingers were raw.

One more try. Just one more.

Clink! He yanked the door open.

Joseph inspected the labels on the drums and found one that would work. He filled an empty soda bottle with a combustible fluid and stuffed a roll of cheesecloth in its mouth. He ascended the stairwell to the ground level and stopped before opening the emergency door, determining that it would set off an alarm somewhere.

Gingerly, he set the bottle on the floor inside the door and lit the cheesecloth, then opened the emergency release bar for his exit. Within seconds a pop and whoosh induced a shrill pinging, followed by barking guard dogs.

Joseph ducked into a thicket to catch a breath. Smoke was seeping from the seams of the exit door and two fire emergency vehicles wheeled in front. The red flashing lights left Joseph vulnerable and he moved slowly from bush to bush.

An older brown sedan raced in followed by a black sedan. A stocky, disheveled man went into the building, and moments later, a man in an elegant blazer.

"Get the dogs, Maurice, and find him!"

Maurice wasn't used to handling the German shepherd guard dogs. Harnessing them on long leads, he bumbled and tripped along, afraid of losing them.

The dark black sedan pulled up beside Maurice and yelled. "Let them go, you idiot. Just follow them."

In minutes, Joseph was trapped and cornered by the dogs.

"Maurice, tie him up and get him back to the basement, out of sight."

"Can you help me with the dogs, Monsieur Tourneau?"

"No, I have to deal with the fire department. We can't be fully exposed by having the basement searched." He jumped into the black sedan and sped back.

The fire hoses already breached the premises.

Maurice struck Joseph on the back of his head and shoved him toward the path. "You stupid, stupid man," he said.

Joseph hoped for another plan before sunrise, but instead was asleep on the floor. He awoke with searing pain in his shoulder.

Sitting up in the darkness, he heard voices and heavy steps on the stairway. From outside his locked door, they switched on his overhead bank of lights, momentarily stunning his vision.

There were two men and a woman, and Joseph recognized Maurice's voice from the night before.

"This is strictly room. No board, Monsieur Harkness." Maurice sneered. "And too bad . . . and you must be hungry!"

"Maurice! That's not the way to barter for a Monett! Go fetch Monsieur some breakfast, one of the baguettes from this morning. We need him to cooperate with us, not to be our enemy."

A young, stocky woman in dungarees stepped boldly from behind the two men, her prematurely grey hair in a bandana.

"I see you have found your way out of our bonds last night. You were a naughty boy toying with matches. You were lucky the farce was confined to the hall. Do you wish to volunteer cleaning the soot?"

"I'm a die-hard boy scout, your ropes were amateur." He said without making any reference to the charred hall.

"You are from Paris, Monsieur Harkness? That is what your papers say. Why did you go to Rouen?"

Staring with her hands on her hips, Monique waited.

"Yes, I'm from Paris. My friend and I were hunting for antiques in Rouen and found a lovely mantel clock and we were pleased with the artistry and craftsmanship." He tried to sound genuine to placate the woman.

"Do not fool with me, Monsieur. No one goes looking down the lane to see Bouleau and comes out with a masterpiece without a mandate. Have you searched the clock and thoroughly examined it?"

Maurice returned and removed the heavy metal pole from the door, holding a tray with the half baguette, a slice of brie, some red grapes, and lukewarm black coffee.

"You may come out now, Monsieur Harkness," the woman urged. "It is more pleasant to talk without the door between us."

She pointed at a milk stool near the large tables. Maurice set the tray beside Joseph.

"I don't see any reason to labor over last night's incident. In return, I expect your co-operation." Monique spoke calmly.

The lapse in conversation was his opportunity to inquire about Emily.

"Where is my friend? I need to see she's alright. And why do you behave in such a barbaric manner, tying people up and throwing them into dark rooms? You expect to negotiate poorly under these circumstances, I presume?"

"Monique, he shouldn't talk to us like that. We have the girl. He should be punished for starting the fire." Maurice blabbered.

"Yes, Maurice, we do have the girl, but he has the Monett. Which do you want? Stop thinking with your mouth you buffoon." Monique admonished.

Joseph continued, "If the Monett is all you want, why don't we discuss this civilly? We paid one thousand euros to Monsieur Bouleau, however we've learned the clock is valued at well over four times that amount. What is this talk about a

Monett? I know nothing about a painting, perhaps you should check your sources."

The three negotiators looked at each other in surprise and bantered in a heated dialogue in French. Monique's piercing grey eyes were fixed on Joseph, in an attempt to determine if he could be toying with her or was bluntly honest.

"Monsieur Harkness, we were having a nice conversation, why do you ruin it with your foolish question? We can make your life difficult and I'll warn you not to attempt your brain strategy. I will not accept that. I will *not!*"

Monique was standing inches from Joseph's face and spit sprayed on him with her last affirmation. A red rash rose on her face, fed by anger.

The man standing at the back in woolen pants and jacket stepped out from the shadows.

"Monsieur Harkness, Monsieur Bouleau told us of the Monett. He tells us his great-grandfather was once a gardener and the clock, with the painting, was given to him for safe keeping. Do not deny the truth. The reckless old man knew there was a painting inside, but didn't know it was authentic."

His voice was calm and firm. "You see, the clock belongs to the museum. The existence of the Monett is not well known but is highly demanded by black market art dealers. These merchants are unscrupulous and will stop at nothing to achieve their ideals."

Monique jumped into it.

"These dealers will kill us as easily as they will kill you, so we are on the same side. You give us the Monett and we can keep it underground well preserved for the future of the art world. The time to reveal an undiscovered Monett is not now. It has no purpose but it will bring out a hoard of seedy characters."

Joseph listened, wondering what use *he* was to any of the parties wanting the clock. Once he revealed its location, both he and Emily were erasable as they could identify the perpetrators.

It suddenly hit him. *The legs—there's something in the legs.*

"I know nothing about a Monett." Joseph asserted. "Are you saying you work for the museum and are only interested in the preservation of art, Monsieur . . . ?" He hadn't yet heard the man's name.

"I beg your pardon, Monsieur Harkness, please call me Alexandre. Last names are so unnecessary. I'm sorry if I have misrepresented myself, and yes, I do share in the museum's objectives."

"I see your position more clearly now, Alexandre. The one thousand euros means nothing to me, Monett painted a lot of beautiful pictures I can't even bring to memory. But my friend, she means the world to me. I'll negotiate her return in exchange for the clock. Do you agree?"

A tenuous smile crossed Alexandre's lips, enjoying the satisfaction of his capture. But Joseph was not what they assumed. He had experience and training to outwit the three blind mice as he silently mocked them.

"Monsieur Harkness!" Alexandre was adamant, shouting now. "The directions to locate the Frizon, please! And don't leave out one detail."

"I am sorry, Alexandre, I will need to be the one to retrieve it. You have my friend, so that is security enough. It's hidden at an inaccessible place." He was confident he could be cheeky without reprisal.

Maurice, Monique and Alexandre congregated to converse. Alexandre was in charge of the kidnapping, Monique the tough and ruddy one, and Maurice appeared to be nothing more than a loyal lookout with aspirations in crime. His nose was crooked from previous poor encounters.

The deliberation concluded and Alexandre spoke gruffly. "You will go, but Monique will be as they say in America 'be our eyes and ears.' You must remain in her sight. And remember at all times . . . she is more than adequately armed. Understood?"

Joseph countered, "The Frizon will not be released until you give me Emily back. And Monique will not touch the clock. Those are my terms."

Alexandre and Monique exchanged looks of disagreement.

"As he says, Monique." Alexandre shrugged with a grunt.

"From here you will be taken by car to the train station. The slightest adverse hand movement and you will be wearing handcuffs."

Maurice returned the hood to Joseph's head.

THE FRIZON | 55

SEVEN

Emily saw the train station ahead and a farmhouse with lights burning on the rise of the hill. She questioned whether Joseph could be there, but urgency prevailed and she headed for the train platform.

She boarded and took a seat in the corner where the lighting was turned down for sleepers. A man and woman chose seats near her. She nodded off in spells as the train ran through Vernon and Rouen. At midnight it arrived at Saint-Lazare in Paris, and she hopped the metro to the Abbesses station. Gas lit lampposts dotted the uphill incline.

Emily sensed she was not alone; in this situation she should use the roof ladder behind Marie's shop to climb to the loft. She scurried up a back walkway to the street above and then plied her way through an alley. The voices were more distant, and she climbed to the loft."

In the stillness of the room her imagination was acute and she thought she heard the clock ticking. Daring to peek out, she spied the pair down the block watching in both directions. The woman was on her phone.

Thank goodness they don't know my address.

Emily took a flashlight and a chisel, and crawled into the pantry. In forty minutes the bricks yielded, and the Frizon was there, ticking. She brought it out, reasoning that it must have been nudged inadvertently to trigger the pendulum.

On the center of the table, she carefully unwrapped it. In the darkness she didn't take her usual time to admire it. Using only moonlight, she gripped her fingers around one of the feet and a tiny dab of oil turned it.

Emily loosened and removed the first front leg and with a magnifying glass she examined the socket. The end of a rolled parchment protruding from the cylinder.

Poking a quilting needle into it, she was stopped by an obstruction. Twisting and easing, the rolled paper loosened, and with the rounded tip of her needle she removed it.

She was enthralled. The first page was out, yellowed and brittle. Her hand shook as she unrolled it, a hand written document, the Certificate of Marriage dated 1869 between Charles Monett and Angelique Sauliere. She retrieved the second parchment, the Certificate of Birth for Gilbert Sauliere, son of Angelique Sauliere and C. O. Monett.

This is an astounding find, an amazing discovery

Emily rolled the scrolls up and placed them on the coffee table. She noticed the altered spelling of Monett, different than the master Claude Monet, and considered it more than a coincidence.

I suppose it's possible this is a forgery, maybe even a copy of one of Claude Monet's works. Somehow, we need to find the Sauliere to answer the question.

Returning to the pantry, she placed the Frizon back into its temporary vault and re-mortared the bricks.

Emily's pulse accelerated. Without anyone hearing her words, she boldly stated her determination.

"We may have to give up the Frizon to get Joseph back, but I'll not part with these scrolls without a royal excuse. This is actual undiscovered history, another secret of the world."

Emily ran a hot shower, allowing her thoughts to play randomly. As grim as the situation might be, she speculated at the irony.

The kidnappers negotiating for my safe return in exchange for the Frizon. Ha! They have greatly underestimated me.

Emily dressed in a navy suit and heels and left her apartment with a large brown leather catalogue case. She had cased the street throughout the night and the couple had gone.

She took a taxi to the Swiss Bank in La Defense, the main business district in Paris, and an hour later was back in Montmartre without the case.

A thought hit her coming back.

Toby, of course. His bloodhound intuition. .

Occasionally, she did play hide and seek with Toby, and he always bounded to her hideouts in the alley. She could take an article of Joseph's clothing for it. But asking Marie to part with Toby for a day wouldn't be easy, the two being inseparable.

Changed to her casual wear, she rehearsed her speech for Marie, deciding to plead on her compassion. Marie's voice was below, chatting with Toby.

Emily was fine dealing with kidnappers and murderers but would be nervous dealing today with Marie.

"Marie, how are you this fine day?"

"Très bien, et vous?" Marie replied cheerfully.

"My dear Marie, I have a great favor to ask of you."

Marie smiled and waited for her to begin.

"Joseph and I were in Giverny yesterday on a hiking trip, but were separated in Epte and he didn't meet me at our rendezvous. Perhaps he fell somewhere and could be trapped or injured."

"Good gracious, poor Joseph."

"Marie, I would be grateful if Toby could come back with me today to find Joseph. I promise to take the best care of him, he is so precious."

Emily saw anxiety on Marie's face, torn between tortured feelings and the painful thought of separation from her best friend.

Marie reserved her reply for a moment.

Kneeling beside Toby, Emily talked to him, whispering in his ear. He leaned his head against her knee and she massaged the velvet edges of his ears until his eyes began to roll. She had a sinking feeling, ready to accept that Marie was searching for words to let her down lightly.

Emily closed her own eyes and said a prayer of hope. It was the only lifeline she had to rescue Joseph.

"Toby would have fun doing the work he was bred for." Emily admonished herself; she was pushing Marie too much.

"How long would you be? I can't spare him for long." Marie regretted the words as soon they were out.

Emily simplified the challenge. "I will leave this morning and should be back tomorrow afternoon. I'm sure with Toby's help, I'll locate Joseph quickly."

"It will be hard for me, but if it brings Joseph home, I know Toby will be a good help. Get ready and I'll prepare his snacks and canteen."

Marie looked at Toby with adoration, and Emily wondered if it was such a good idea. She gave Marie a long hug and escaped up the staircase to collect her backpack, waiting by the door.

She returned to the shop in minutes. The unsuspecting Toby waited with his work harness, his tail wagging. Marie had a sack of food, snacks and a wine bag full of cool water ready to go.

Toby was confused as they walked toward Saint Pierre station. He let out a painful bay, pulling to turn back in an attempt to abort the mission. He had a short memory.

Shortly after noon, they arrived in Epte and headed on foot down the path toward Giverny. She noticed the same farmhouse, this time with a man and woman in the field working the crops. An open-stake truck drove by hauling hay, and Toby barked.

Emily pulled Joseph's shirt from her bag to give a scent to Toby. She thought it would be prudent to rule out the farmhouse area, and called out to the woman.

"Bonjour!"

Emily waved and hastened up the dusty road toward the sowers, with Toby's nose to the ground and his ears dragging in the dirt.

The couple rested their seed driller and advanced a few steps to greet them. The farmer was a burly man of fifty-five years, and his was wife slender and sunburnt, about forty-five with a wide-brimmed straw hat. They spoke English.

"Bonjour to you as well. Can we help you? Are you lost? We heard your dog."

The man didn't take a breather between sentences.

"Perhaps the hound is in need of water." His wife took a pail to the wagon and poured cool water onto an enamel plate.

"Is he friendly?" Her hand went to pat his head and his tongue found the plate before it was on the ground.

Emily bragged, "Oh, he is the friendliest. Thanks for the water, we are grateful. I'm not lost . . . but my friend is. Did you happen to see a man being pushed or dragged on the path yesterday afternoon?"

They didn't answer, and she continued, "You have such a panoramic view from here. By the way, my name is Emily Warner." She extended her hand.

"Pleased to meet you, Emily. I am Henri Sauliere and my wife is Madeleine. I'm afraid we haven't seen such a man."

Emily was stunned as she processed his words.

The names . . . the same names from the certificates.

The Sauliere appeared to her as a simple hardworking family and her instinct told her they couldn't be mixed up in something sinister. The story would have to wait.

"I'm sorry to look surprised. You see I was reading something recently and that name was 'Angelique Sauliere'. It's a small world to have such a coincidence."

The couple exchanged darting looks. Madeleine stepped forward, urging Emily by the elbow to come and join them in the house for café and fresh baked bread. Emily wanted to accept but couldn't leave Toby unattended.

"Merci, merci! Your invitation is kind. But you see, Toby is a borrowed tracking dog and I can't let him out of my sight for even a minute."

"Non, non! The dog is welcome inside. He doesn't wander in the kitchen, does he?" Madeleine was amused.

Emily gave a laugh, imagining Toby's head in a flour bin. She reassured Madeleine he was obedient and their demeanor became more relaxed.

The aroma from the baking was wonderful and Toby's nose became active.

"Toby, sit!" Emily raised her hand and he stayed with his paw on her foot under the table.

"Would you mind, Madeleine, if I feed Toby as we talk?"

A basin was set by the door and Emily filled it with one of Marie's food packets.

A loaf of homemade bread, fresh from the oven, was placed a cutting board with pots of creamery butter and homemade raspberry jam. Madeleine brought a trivet for the coffee pot.

Henri was waiting to raise the issue again.

"Now Emily, you have more to tell us, I could tell by your face when I introduced myself. Whatever you say, we keep within these doors." He was insistent.

Emily was up against a wall of time, and desperate to solicit their support to find Joseph.

"You're right, I do have a story to tell you, but it is urgent that I find my partner first. My friend, Joseph, was taken outside of Epte, and I have returned in search of him. I don't know who the kidnappers are."

Madeleine tensed up and went to the phone.

"We have three sons, Stefan, Philippe, and Felix; they will come to help us search for your friend. I'll call for them."

The full family turned up and agreed to join Emily's impromptu posse, led by Toby. The boys were strong and burly like their father. Henri carried a rifle, Stefan a pitchfork from the barn and the other two had baseball bats. Madeleine carried two cast iron pans.

The farmhouse gang paraded over the hill like a comic troupe. It was funny to her. "I wouldn't want to come up against such a fearsome gang." They didn't seem to get her American humor.

Toby knew he was being readied for work, and leaned into her shoulder. Again she unfolded Joseph's shirt for Toby to sniff, and in minutes he was set to go.

They walked the Grande Randonnée route toward the Tourelles Towers where Emily had last seen Joseph, and on the path, Toby found the scent. He was in the lead, stopping only to circle for a stronger hold on his trail. Becoming more fixed on it, he bounded faster. Emily quickened her pace and the ensemble followed.

A commotion ahead brought them to a halt and Emily moved to a treed area to watch the delivery entrance of the Museum. A hooded man was jostled and thrust toward a waiting Peugeot at the road. It had to be Joseph. She unhooked the harness.

Joseph heard Toby's yelp but kept a firm stance as Maurice shoved him up a flight of steps.

It was now closer, and he deliberated that his break should be at the car when his abductors would be at ease. Maurice constantly poked him with the revolver butt, but Joseph allowed it without showing his annoyance.

Although he couldn't see, he knew that enjoyable sound, a familiar baying and barking. It happened nightly when Marie left the shop. Mostly it was welcome relief that Emily must have escaped, that she'd be the one with Toby.

Maurice told him he was three meters from the door and to step down to a cement landing. A passenger door was open and he was to climb in.

The howling was closing in on them but the kidnappers hadn't yet figured it out. Then the voices with Toby became clearer to them, and they fired a shot.

Joseph stiffened.

Monique took a firing position from behind the Peugeot and Maurice mumbled to the others, unsure if Joseph should go back down the stairs or into the car. Before Maurice made up his mind, Joseph flicked the hood off.

Toby's ears flew above the wild grass, his lanky legs thrashing in all directions, and in seconds, Joseph was decked, landing flat on the concrete, with his hands tied behind.

Maurice recoiled, sensing the dog could be vicious and that he'd be attacked as well. Alexandre disappeared in the melee.

Weapon drawn, Monique found a sheltered position, unclear about what happened; then she fled on the path. Philippe and Felix spotted her on the run and took off in chase.

Toby held Joseph on the ground, his arms folded on Joseph's chest, claiming his prize, excited and proud. Stefan, the brawny one, held Maurice's neck with the tip of his pitchfork against his face. There was no resistance as Stefan grasped and tied Maurice's hands.

Amused at Maurice's dumbfounded look, Emily thought of the wildebeest in Africa. The aimless male wants his own herd of females and picks one female, expecting her to wait while he chooses a second. Returning with a second, the first was gone; that was Maurice's look, realizing Emily had escaped.

She rushed to Joseph and knelt as Toby washed his face. Joseph took ownership of him. "It was our bloodhound who saved the day!"

Emily sobered.

"Joseph, these are my friends, Henri Sauliere, his wife Madeleine and their sons. Stefan has the pitchfork."

She pointed back to the path. "There are the other two, Philippe and Felix, bringing the woman back this way. There's a long story to tell, but first, how do we take care of these thugs?"

Madeleine answered. "Philippe, go now, get the Police Capitaine at Vernon, he'll want to hold these ravisseurs for questioning. We can start with that."

She didn't notice Philippe whispering to Monique and her scowl of disapproval.

Anger was growing on Philippe's face; Emily noticed it but let it go.

There was new energy in the kitchen as Madeleine and Emily fixed a hearty cassoulet and gratin. Henri and Joseph conferred over coffee; both were hungry, and impatient to hear Emily's story.

The best of times had taken place here with good food and conversation. But none as special as today.

Tureens of food lined the sideboard, with loaves of warm bread and Madeleine's own butter. Before the men dug in, Madeleine turned to her husband.

"This is truly a day to be thankful."

Henri closed his eyes and gave thanks for new friends. No-one commented, and the ravenous crew delved in.

Toby stretched by the door, sprawled on his side. His bowl was empty and water dish dry, his eyes closed tight.

The Sauliere were wide-eyed, their heads turning to Emily. She breathed deeply, allowing time to pick her words.

They were speechless as she re-lived her ordeal in the tower, and their camaraderie grew stronger as they laughed with her about her tale of the rats and her ingenious escape.

Emily turned to Henri. "Do you know a Monsieur Bouleau in Rouen?"

Henri flinched.

She continued, "I purchased an antique Frizon clock from him a few days ago."

"I believe I've heard the name, perhaps from my grandfather. Please go on."

Henri and Madeleine gasped when Emily revealed the existence of the Monett painting.

Joseph hadn't heard the next part, and she spoke most directly toward him as she described the parchment scrolls in the clock, the Marriage Certificate of Charles Monett and Angelique Sauliere, and the Birth Certificate of Gilbert Monett.

Henri stood and paced, then reached for Madeleine's hand and held it tightly as tears welled in his eyes. Emily gave them a few minutes alone, and Philippe hugged both his parents.

"Do you know what this means?" Henri asked. "My great-grandfather shouldn't have lived in disgrace. The tale told to me as a child was that Angelique, my great-great-grandmother, was a mistress to Charles Monett.

Apparently both families were opposed to the relationship, however they secretly eloped. She was later sent to Normandy to live in poverty, and died with consumption in a poor house."

'I'm so sorry your great-grandfather had such a difficult time, Henri." Emily said.

"The child, Gilbert, was my great-grandfather. And the Bouleau name? Yes, they took him in. The name you mentioned from Rouen is the same. A piece of art was in trust with their family for the Sauliere. It was to be preserved for Gilbert without falling into greedy hands."

Henri went to the hall bureau and opened a leather album. "This tin plate portrait is of Angelique with Gilbert on her knee. She was beautiful, but sad eyes gave her away. Monsieur Bouleau must have confessed his part to unworthy ears. But now, to avoid falling on the ears of ruthless men, there should be no mention of the clock.

"The Epte museum inherited many of Monett's works as well as other French impressionists. A portion of the gardens was purchased from the estate for the purpose of a museum. A wonderful new glass structure was built into the hillside. We don't wish to claim anything, other than our heritage."

"That is understandable." Joseph said. "It's a disgrace so many years have passed, and we can't be naïve about the situation. There are many unscrupulous dealers in the black market."

Madeleine added, "You should know, thugs have raided us before searching for lost paintings."

"Do you suspect these kidnappers are involved with art dealers? Then who are the good guys?" Emily interjected.

Joseph asked Henri, "Do you have any legitimate connection with a museum that would genuinely want to resolve the case of the Monett?"

Madeleine looked sharply at Henri. "What about Monsieur Tourneau? One time he suggested that someday he'd have a generous gift for us. I've thought that to be an unkind thing to flaunt over your neighbors."

"Did you say Tourneau?" Joseph was startled to hear the connection. "He was one of the men at the museum basement when I tried to escape!"

"There will come a time for him to prove his ethics." Henri said.

Emily quickly developed a bond with them. "Your family shouldn't live umbrage. We'll find a way for the museum to recognize your parentage."

Exposing her vulnerability to the Saulieres, Emily inwardly felt naive to have trusted so quickly.

On the train back to Paris, she explained to Joseph her journey home from Epte.

"It was midnight when I got to the loft. There was a couple following me. Although, I evaded them, I worked in the dark to retrieve the clock. When we first examined the workmanship and artistry I noticed give in the legs. This time I massaged the joint with oil until they loosened.

"A piece of paper protruded from one of the cylinders and I unraveled it. There were two documents from 1869, a Marriage Certificate to Angelique Sauliere, and a Birth Certificate for Gilbert".

Again she looked at Joseph. "Gilbert Sauliere is Henri's great-grandfather . . ."

Emily, Joseph and Toby were on the 9:00 a.m. train home in the morning.

Joseph surmised, "The thugs know about the Frizon, but not about the certificates. We'll keep it that way until the investigation is concluded. All they want is the painting."

Emily agreed. "The Saulieres and I were speculating on the kidnap motives. Bouleau said the clock was in his family since his great-grandfather's time. He wouldn't have sold it if he'd known of its contents."

"But the men from the auction said Bouleau told them of the Monett." Emily pondered. "Maybe they were testing you, Joseph."

He nodded. "I don't trust the lot of them. This started at the auction house when we were caught on security cameras. Now they wanted to exchange the Monett clock for you, Emily, so someone had knowledge of it."

"What's most important right now is that the clock and documents are safe in Paris."

EIGHT

Sao Paulo, Brazil, May 2009

Three years earlier

In the ten months since the Swiss heist, their activity had been careful and inconspicuous.

The Monet and Van Gogh wouldn't be marketable so soon after the robbery, and the risk was too great for them to reveal themselves even to an underground buyer. Carrying on unsuspecting day jobs in Paris, they hungered for more thrills and another payoff.

Dodger got the first call. Rene had summoned them all to meet again at the restaurant by his place. He hadn't reached Robbie, but Dodger came right away.

Rene started with small talk, asking how Robert was doing, then Dodger interrupted and came to the point.

"Rene, is it too soon for another museum that would be quick and safe? Surely, it's in our blood. We'll never be able to stop, at least not unless we fall into the cracks and get arrested."

Rene hesitated, he wanted Robbie in too.

"I have a small cache tucked away; and if Robbie will be in on this too, we'll be having a vacation in Sao Paulo. He didn't answer my call though."

Rene got up to find a barista. "Call him, Robbie; see if he can join us. I need another coffee."

A disgruntled Robbie walked into the café and pulled a bistro chair to the patio.

"Where's my coffee?"

"I'm not your servant." Rene laughed and Robbie hailed a server.

"This will stretch your imagination, boys, but the swoop and go will be in Sao Paulo, Brazil. It's tropical and beautiful this time of year. Not a beach holiday though; it's highly industrialized and we'll need suits and ties, gentlemen."

"What is the catch?" Dodger inquired.

"We've been hired by an underground art dealer to bring back two Picassos. The ransom is a hefty million euros and we'll get ten percent of that off the top, plus whatever else we take from the Museum—that's the bonus. I've identified four paintings that we can either sell or process for forgeries. Two Picasso's, a Renoir, and a Segall. This will take muscle; it's a nighttime break-in using equipment. Can you boys deal with that?"

"When's the next flight out of here?" Robbie chuckled.

"It will take me three days for passports, IDs and documents. I'll travel on Saturday to Buenos Aires and connect to Brazil on Monday, and you'll both change in Washington, DC, arriving on Sunday. Three of us arriving from France would be too obvious to piece together. And Robbie, book one room at the Tivoli."

Sao Paulo was sweltering in tropical temperatures when Robbie and Dodger checked in. The manager upgraded them to an executive suite with two bedrooms and three queens.

Rene joined them in the morning and surveyed the city from their 19th floor, an expanse of high-rise buildings.

Dodger checked his list. "Rene, I'm going out to try to buy a crowbar and a car jack."

"Careful who you talk to . . . oh, and burlap and tape to wrap them. Dodger, I want you to study the photos of the paintings; you'll only have minutes to make the snatch."

Rene tossed night vision goggles to the pair. "We'll be going in under darkness, early in the morning. Nobody will be in the building other than patrolling guards, and I can derail the security system in an instant. We don't leave anything behind. I rented a local truck as our getaway."

Rene laid out the rules again, then ordered steaks, fried mushrooms and a six-pack of Brahma beer.

By 8:00 p.m. they retired but were dressed again at 2:00 a.m. Rene hadn't slept.

The truck puttered toward the outskirts of Zurich at four o'clock, in a surprising amount of traffic. Using the museum's service lane, the truck turned into the vestige of the rear loading dock. The lighting was poor, and the men scanned the back, finding a heavy aluminum door set on traditional moorings.

"Over here, Robbie . . . your crowbar!" Dodger whispered. He maneuvered the pick into a worn area of the upper hinge.

"I can hear the hinge easing from the jamb." Dodger said. A final yank heaved the door ajar, and with the car jack they forced it the rest of the way.

Rene didn't move. "Stay here. I'll disarm the system." He inched toward a web of laser beams stretching across the width of the floor.

"Ahoy, boys! It's clear."

In minutes, Robbie and Dodger grabbed the five paintings in minutes, with no resistance from the mountings.

They placed the works into the back of the truck, and Dodger took the wheel, heading for Rio de Janeiro. They'd be there by 9:00 a.m. with time to arrange shipping and abandon their tools before their overnight to Paris.

Seven days later their sealed shipment arrived and cleared customs in Frankfurt, labelled as imported luggage and leather goods, and destined for a shell company in the city.

With 28 million euros from the sale of the Renoir, the three made a pact, a trust arrangement as blood-brothers, not with blood but with rings.

Three sterling silver rings were designed, each with a raised triangle, and a portion of a sword. When the three rings were together, the emblem would be complete.

The pact was a commitment to sacrifice for each other at whatever the cost. Never to deceive or betray.

NINE

Robillard sat at a high table in his third floor office, looking down slightly on the chairs reserved for guests.

Adjusting his monocle, he inched his nose to the surface of the canvas spread before him, barely touching it. The lighting needed adjustment and he held a strong magnifying glass to observe the contours and colors, then the underside.

The stone building was once a tenement and was being renovated to become the gallery and offices of a new museum in Lyon. Designers were submitting bids for their unique salon creations, and mechanical contract work was already underway to build the foyer.

Monsieur Robillard returned from his inspections of the foyer. He had made snide criticisms at every stop, demanding nothing less than the most superlative quality to astound the world's art community.

The marvelous gala and exhibition would be only six months away, and red ribbon ceremony invitations were already couriered to elite socialites of France, political diplomats and wealthy patrons and prospects. Robillard was contemplating members of Europe's royalty for the press coverage they'd attract.

Lyon, between Paris and Marseilles in the Rhone region of the French Alps, has an architectural core visible in its vibrant art, fountains, and ancient churches. It is renowned for its famous rich cuisine, as the gastronomic heart of France.

Holding international honors, the restaurant Exquis in Lyon is the prized jewel of the revered epicurean Toussaint Denis-Brault, one of the world's top chefs.

As the pinnacle of dining, Exquis was equal to Robillard's lofty standards and rewarded his stalwart guests by holding a standing reservation on the second Tuesday of every month.

On this occasion he arrived with a substantial art dealer from Los Angeles.

The reservations ritual was common in his circle, rarely with refusals as the high price for such disrespect would be greater than the cost of the meal.

The menu was always orchestrated by the chef himself, balancing aperitifs, digestifs, soups, entrées and decadent desserts. The preset menu was delivered course after course by a troupe of waiters, to the dining room filled to capacity.

"Sam . . . may I call you Sam!"

"I prefer Samuel."

"Samuel, you are in for a most extravagant dinner. I dare say it is unparalleled anywhere else in all of Europe."

Opening aperitifs were Saint Veran 2001 and Saint Joseph 2006, followed by sumptuous creations, each a work of art. Tonight's menu would not disappoint Robillard.

Soupe aux truffes noires
With plat cree pour l'Elysee

Quenelle de brochet, sauce Nantua
Granite des vignerons du Beaujolais
Canette de Bresse rotie a la broche
Selection de fromages frais et affines
Crème brulée à la cassonade Sirio
Delices et gourmandizes
Petit fours et chocolats

The extravagant meal was spread over four hours, allowing Messieurs Robillard and Wentworth to discuss the great impressionists and specific works coming up at Sotheby's and Christie's auction houses. It began with cordial small talk, and progressed to a debate about forgeries ending in negotiations.

"I have a prized collection, sealed in a bank vault, back in Los Angeles." Wentworth said. "Of course, I display a few replicas in my boardroom and residence."

Wentworth was a tall man, with dark hair and telltale grey at his temples, and always dressed impeccably in a black silk suit.

If Samuel Wentworth thought the dinner to be a free cordial invitation, he was badly misled. There was a price.

Robillard showed less dignity and reeked of opulence and arrogance.

"I pride myself on an insatiable appetite for the great masters. I negotiate for the best and, of course, arrange only for superb forgeries to hang in my new museum. The tourists and local visitors have studied them with pretend intelligence, but no one has ever found a flaw in my reproductions. They must be given back to the public so why not make a profit on a few forgeries too." He laughed alone.

A seasoned man, Robillard was about fifty years of age with thick wiry hair, and he came to the Wentworth dinner with a day old beard and unruly mustache. He was known to foes as an ogre, a man with a temper, self-important, and greedy. By his victims, he was remembered as a dangerous man with a wary future, and endless capabilities.

The conversation of the odd couple moved to the masterpiece offerings and possessions of Mr. Wentworth.

Robillard's manner took a turn and he flexed his position, with a sudden demand that Wentworth donate a pair of originals from his private vault to the Lyon Gala.

"Monsieur Wentworth, you must understand, I am a man with an undeniable passion, an insatiable hunger to succeed in the art world. You see, my name should become synonymous with the great collectors of Europe."

"I *will* achieve my goals, but I assure you, your collections could only increase with your cooperation with me and the ideals I represent. You would be naive to fly back to America without coming to agreeable terms." Robillard shed any remaining politeness.

Mr. Wentworth's face was pale, with a nerve twitching under his eye. He had already lost his pawn without knowing the game had begun.

"Monsieur Wentworth, I will offer you an original undiscovered Monett in exchange for a pair of paintings of your own choosing, accepting of course they must be original masterpieces from the great European artists."

Robillard slid a piece of paper across the table before continuing.

"Here are some suggestions. This Monett has been hidden from museums and art dealers for over one hundred years. It is painted on gold plate on the back of an old Boulle Frizon."

He watched Wentworth's face, hoping he had instilled a degree of fear. "I will need authentication and seal of ownership from you within seven days. I'll wire a notarized photograph of the Frizon on your return to California with the validations." He paused and watched Wentworth's face.

"Your answer tonight before we part company, yes?" Robillard's volume was drawing the attention of other patrons.

Wentworth tried to appease him and look for a way out of the unexpected predicament. "I'll need to discuss this with my insurance agent and my attorney before I can give you an answer."

Robillard's face became crimson and his voice now boisterous. "Did you not hear me? I said we will have an agreement tonight! It will be midnight in forty-five minutes. I have connections around the world, where you'd least expect, and you'll be under surveillance wherever you go. Your future bids on art pieces will be interfered with, I'll see to that! I do not work alone, Monsieur. I work for some devious and immoral people."

Robillard pounded his stiffened index finger on the table. Unmindful of other patrons, it gave Robillard power to allow Wentworth to cringe in embarrassment.

They were both unaware of the gentleman at the next table, entertaining a lady in a business discussion. Robillard had noticed the man's hand was bruised but didn't give it further thought.

Arriving in Paris with the homesick pup, Emily and Joseph trudged up the hill toward the flower shop. Marie was in the shop and once in his sight, he bounded forward, his ears flying and legs in all directions.

"Ah, you have been recovered, Joseph!" Marie laughed but her eyes were on Toby. He stood in front of her, a paw on each shoulders, licking her chin.

"I don't think's it's me you're so glad to see." Joseph said.

Emily flattered Marie. "Thanks to Toby, we had no difficulty finding Joseph at all. We are so grateful to you."

"Well, bloodhounds are bred for that, so I guess it is good to put him to work. I didn't think I'd miss him as much as I did. He always sleeps in my bed, and without him I had a restless night."

Marie continued to rub Toby's ears. "But I am glad we are all home now."

Joseph said, "Marie, tonight we'll celebrate by dining at Montmartre, all four of us. Maybe a steak for our hero. What do you say?"

Marie's face flushed, graciously accepting.

Joseph and Emily were oblivious to the man watching from the boulevard through a pair of binoculars.

Alexandre remembered from Joseph's license in the backpack that he lived at Montmartre, and watching the street, it was easy to identify where they lived.

Back at Epte when Joseph's escape was orchestrated, Alexandre slipped onto the train before the French police arrived. He'd received orders from Monsieur Charest, on behalf of Robillard, to search their Paris loft for the Frizon.

It was simple. "Return with the clock or I will find someone else who will. We have a buyer for the clock, so have it in Lyon by midnight tomorrow."

Packing a revolver in his belt under his jacket, and a pistol strapped to his calf, Alexandre watched them. The lights in the loft were turned down; Joseph and Emily joined Marie to walk up the hill.

The bistro at the top had outdoor patio tables with evening linens and candlelight, in the open air where Toby could join them. Gas lanterns were lit and minstrels serenaded the street with harps, flutes and fiddles.

A man in a turtle neck and a beret blended in to the sea of bistro tables beside the art displays. From a distance, he was able to watch the threesome dine. The dog was of no consequence.

He knew Alexandre had been dispatched to search the loft, but calculated Joseph and Emily's cleverness.

Alexandre, you fool, you're clearly on a wild goose chase.

Joseph and Emily avoided Marie's personal questions but diplomatically pried out Marie's family history from Basque Country in the south of France. She had never married but enjoyed a full life with faithful friends. Every Christmas her widowed sister visited her in Paris, and Marie longed for those visits throughout the year.

The door to the loft was an easy pick for Alexandre and he was confident enough to turn up the lights. The loft was completely ransacked, every rug, drawer, nook and cranny. He wanted to leave a menacing message.

But his failed mission for the clock brought a rush of adrenaline and fear. In his fury he tossed a chair through the patio window. The explosion of breaking glass echoed below and a voice yelled out that the police had been called.

Alexandre took up a post in the alley. He would blend in as a bystander when the police arrived, and afterward, would take one of the women at gun point, Marie or Emily, and bargain for the clock once again.

All did not go as planned for Alexandre. Three hours later he watched the troupe approaching in the distance. Toby was in the lead, and picked up Alexandre's scent from Giverny. He charged toward the alley, barking an alert, with Joseph and Emily behind. Marie followed cautiously and tensed up at the sight, with Toby baring his teeth to defend her.

The reflection of Alexandre's revolver caught Joseph's eye and he lunged at his arm and wrested it to the ground. Emily moved quickly to pick up the gun, holding it on Alexandre.

"It's one of the three blind mice." She announced with recognition and insult.

"The Frizon will be the death of you," Alexandre growled. He spit in Emily's face. She retaliated, slapping his face and with a memorable kick to his shins.

Joseph held him by the throat with an arm twisted behind his back.

"Marie, you can release Toby now. Please go into your shop and phone the police; then stay there until I come for you." He was calm and firm.

Walking to her shop door, she stepped on shattered glass and looked up to their balcony.

"He has broken your window, Joseph."

Joseph tightened his grip and spoke into the culprit's ear.

"Who sent you here?" Joseph was shouting and people on the street were starting to gather.

"I'm a dead man without the clock so what's it to me to tell you that?"

Joseph answered without thinking. "I might be willing to negotiate if you are interested in a double-cross; besides you owe me for the window."

Alexandre relaxed his resistance. He watched Joseph's face to see if he meant it, and seemed ready to discuss the idea. A true con with no morals, thriving on self-survival.

"You don't know who you are up against. We'll both be dead." He said.

"I see the police coming uphill. I need an answer. Now! I can still give you a chance to run." Joseph offered the bait.

"Okay, okay!" The fish was hooked.

Joseph continued. "Be at the western edge of Lycée du Parc outside the Interpol building at Lyon noon tomorrow. Otherwise, you'll return without the Monett and explain your failure and learn your fate. And I'm sure my attack dog and I can track you down if we need to."

Joseph gave him a shove, forcing him to fall to the cobblestone.

"Blasted American!" Alexandre cursed and panted, running through the darkness of the alley to the terraced roofs.

The police interrogated Joseph and Emily about the apartment robbery asking if they'd seen the man before; they hadn't. He instructed them to visit the station in the morning to provide a statement and a list of stolen items.

The officer ripped off a sheet with their case number. "We'll post a man in the area for the rest of the night in case he returns."

TEN

Paris Museum, France, April 2011
One year prior

Rene sat with his coffee while he played with a brioche and jam. It was the same café near his apartment where he used to meet Robbie and Dodger to plan their heists.

'Le Parisienne' the local French newspaper in Paris was on the table, and he looked at the front page article for the third time.

THIEF ABSCONDS WITH FIVE MASTERPIECE

Paris–A lone thief breached the security system of Les Arts Musée last night. Police have described the robber as wiry to have maneuvered through the air tunneling system. A witness saw the burglar's ascent from the roof ventilation unit. The laser control system and visual panels were disarmed, and two patrol guards were overtaken by chloroform. The masterpieces taken include Picasso and Matisse estimated to be £86 million. The heist was well-planned, however, one grainy photograph was taken in the building. If you can identify this person, please call Interpol.

Rene stared at the picture. Overwrought with rage, he raced home, jumped in his car and sped across town to the 8th Arrondissemont.

Taking two steps at a time, Rene bounded to the third floor flat and pounded on the apartment door.

"Dodger, you son of a gun, open up!"

Opening the door slightly, Dodger looked sheepish. Rene kicked in the door and grabbed him by the collar.

"We have an agreement! What were you thinking, you imbecile? Mon dieu!"

The two struggled. Dodger was thin and wiry. He landed a powerful fist and Rene reeled and collapsed.

"Calm down, Rene. Listen to me."

"There's nothing you can say to mend this sacrilege of trust."

Rene barged out of the room and retreated to his car on the street below. Moving the car out of the direct line of Dodger's window, he made a call to Robbie but it went to voicemail.

Minutes later Dodger left on foot. Rene almost missed his exit. He was dressed in a tweed sports jacket with his hair combed back.

"What's he doing, dressed like that, he's never owned a jacket before?" Rene grunted.

Dodger crossed over the bridge on foot and met with another man who'd been waiting. The older gentlemen handed Dodger a portfolio then shook his hand. Rene snapped some quick photos. He zoomed in to see the face of the older man.

"Confound it! That's an Interpol Agent."

ELEVEN

She shook her head. "What are you thinking, Joseph? You're not really going to give him the clock?"

Without answering, he asked. "Is it still in the wall behind the pantry?"

"No, Joseph." He was surprised.

"Where is it?"

"In a safety deposit box at the Swiss Bank in La Defense district. I have an access key, a security code and I've memorized the box number. The documents are all there too."

"My clever girl, you've made this much easier storing it at a bank! Now it's secure, we only need to toy with them using a safety deposit box."

"Taught by the best." She smirked, relieved he wasn't annoyed.

"I am certain Alexandre is the tip of the iceberg. I suspect our clock has already been offered on the black market. It's not the clock we need to protect right now, it is Alexandre. He is a mouse, manipulated by the Pied Piper, but he will lead us there."

"Joseph, are we are in deeper than we can handle? When we left Albany, we were given an Interpol contact." She fretted. "Maybe it's time to call."

"Granted, Interpol may be interested in delving into the art dealer's black market, but I know we have the upper hand regarding the clock." Joseph mused.

"You're a freight train looking for an accident." She regretted her word choice.

"I'm sorry Joseph, I didn't mean to bring that up. I was only playing with words."

In New York, Joseph's car had been forced into a train collision, erasing his memory for months and requiring a long return to rediscover and regain his life.

"It's okay, babe, that was another chapter. And if it hadn't been for that, we wouldn't be here in the most romantic city in the world." He put both arms around her. "I wouldn't have found you."

She sighed. "I'll see if Marie has a broom and dustpan to clean up this mess. The tiniest shard of glass can get into Toby's paws."

With the cobblestones groomed and the glass swept from the balcony, they flaked out on the sofa. Emily was anxious.

"Okay Joseph, spill your plan, I'm all ears. It's easy to see your wheels are spinning." She sat up with her arms crossed.

"The Interpol headquarters is an intimidating place to convene. If Alexandre comes alone, we can trust him to lead us to the art dealer. That would be too naïve; the black market is wide-spread and intricate. But if he returns with back-up, a sharpshooter could take us out easily."

Joseph took a breather and a sip of coffee.

"Emily, it will be best if you're not with me, but watch from a distance. I still have a bullet-proof vest that's hardly been used. I'll take it to Lyon."

"So far, I'm not liking this much." She was stern and he knew her concern.

"I'll make an inquiry, by phone, this morning to the Interpol number," he said. "It's the direct line they gave me in New York.

The call was picked up on the second ring and the man spoke gruffly with a French accent.

"Hello, please identify yourself?"

"My name is Joseph Harkness. I was given this number, in the event I needed help. I understand we are under low level Interpol surveillance in Paris."

"You should refer to me only as 'Agent Yves'. Clarify your situation."

"My friend and I have stumbled upon black market art thieves who are tailing us. We purchased a valuable clock in Rouen and since then we have been chased, kidnapped, and beaten. Last night our home was ransacked."

"What do you want me to do? Normally, we don't do babysitting."

Joseph was angered by the affront. "I thought you would be interested in breaking into this art ring. It has international repercussions. I'm sorry to have disturbed you." Joseph was prepared to hang up.

"Where are you meeting up with your sting? I will come and make an assessment, but no further promises."

Disgruntled, Joseph gave the agent his plan for the meeting with Alexandre and his boss. The call ended abruptly from the other end.

"Okay, please back up and run through this in basic steps." Emily wasn't clear on the outcome.

"You'll have a cell phone and the agent's number with you," he said. "If anything goes awry, call him immediately. We'll catch the turbo train to Lyon tonight and get a hotel near Interpol. Alexandre will meet me, but I won't bring the Frizon. If he wants to work undercover, I'll return with him to his boss. They won't harm us until they have the clock."

"Joseph, we have all morning in Lyon before your meeting. Can't we meet with your Agent Yves beforehand and get some cover for the rendezvous?" Her face was tight.

Joseph looked pained from her lack of confidence.

"I suppose, if only for backup, we could use a marksman."

Agent Yves agreed to meet at a café a block from Interpol's headquarters at Lycée du Parc, surrounded by international venues and ultra-modern buildings. Joseph and Emily arrived early waiting inconspicuously at a table.

The agent surprised them, catching Joseph off-guard when he appeared. Joseph jumped to his feet, his chair falling to the ground.

He tightened his fist ready for a fight at the slightest move, his face tense and angered.

"I am sorry, Mr. Harkness, I have misled you. As I told you on the phone, your movements have been monitored since removing a concerned threat. I trust your bruises have healed." Joseph was still incensed.

Yves was medium build, about thirty, with a distinguished groomed goatee. He wore a black turtleneck sweater under a corduroy jacket. Joseph was pleased when Yves rubbed his still bruised knuckles.

Flabbergasted, Joseph turned to Emily. His hands were in the air and he could hardly speak. "This is my assailant on Montmartre the night the rifleman fired from the Basilica."

Emily was angry now too. "Why did you shoot an innocent man? Daniel gave us a great deal of help and probably saved our lives a few times. You must have a whopper of a story to condone your behavior!"

"All I can tell you is that a threat was removed. I didn't say the man you refer to was killed nor have I said he is alive. I am not at liberty to explain; it's not your business."

Joseph ranted again. "You could have talked instead of beating me!"

Yves listened to the events of the last few days, the existence of the Frizon and Joseph's daring plan. But they held back the existence of the scrolls. Yves held his chin in thought, then tried to deter Joseph from the proposed scheme.

Joseph was adamant. "My instincts supported me through the worst of times, and this is the pinnacle of a network of black market art dealers infiltrating museums across Europe. Don't tell me Interpol has no interest in this underground faction. I understood the mission of your organization is preventing and fighting crime! Am I wrong?"

Yves couldn't help but smile at Joseph's passionate plea.

"You're an admirable student of the internet I see. These decisions are not up to me. I'll ask my superior for permission to attend as an advisor, but I don't promise anything more."

Yves stood and without another word walked away. Joseph was sure he detected more than a passing interest from the agent when told of the Monett.

Alexandre was at the rendezvous site in Lyon five minutes before noon. Pacing, he lit a cigarette as he evaluated the rooftops across from the park. The sunlight struck a glint of glass from the rooftop. He squinted to examine it and his muscles relaxed.

Yves set up a vantage point on the Boulevard de Stalingrad, with a view of Alexandre and a clear sound download from Joseph's wire. With a telescopic rifle lens he swept the rooftops.

Finding the spot where Alexandre had directed his attention, a lone marksman was focused on the meeting site.

Joseph parked his rented Fiat nearby and walked toward the site. Alexandre glanced discreetly into spaces where his cohorts were waiting. It was obvious Joseph was not carrying the clock, but it was not apparent he was wired.

The man on the roof stepped back and lifted a pair of binoculars for a closer look at Joseph.

Alexandre was agitated, then became explosive.

"Where is the clock? What are you doing? I thought we agreed on terms!"

"I did not say I was bringing the clock. I said we could negotiate." Joseph pulled a small tape recorder from his breast pocket and replayed it.

Alexandre sullenly nodded defeat, "I trusted you and assumed you would give me the Monett. You intentionally duped me."

His whine was intended as a distraction, but his distressed glance to the roof was a giveaway.

Joseph looked upward. "And you me."

Alexandre lowered his head as Joseph continued to grill.

"Where would you be taking the clock if you had it right now? I understood your boss has a buyer and you're given a limited time to weasel it away from us. Is that not true?

Alexandre replied, "You know my back is against the wall. Why are you doing this?"

His frustration aggravated his nicotine craving. As he pulled a pack of cigarettes from a pocket, his sudden hand movement prompted Joseph's reach toward his pistol.

"The clock is in a safe secure location, in a safety deposit box. There is no need to tear my place apart. You'll accompany me on your return to Rouen and we can discuss this with your boss."

Joseph pointed at the glimmering glass. "Furthermore, wave the sharpshooter off the roof!"

Alexandre realized he had been exposed. "I need to make a phone call."

Avoiding Joseph's stare, he spoke in a low voice to the man on the roof. But before he'd instructed the accomplice to disarm, Yves was on the roofline and surprised the perpetrator with a blow. With a gun to his head, he led the culprit to the stairwell.

"I presume you're connected through the Rouen museum. I will need names and details, Alexandre."

"Okay, okay, quit the crapshoot. Yes, I worked with my partner, Monique, at the Rouen museum. But you need to understand—we work undercover, sometimes for the museum and sometimes on our own."

He fidgeted, looking over his shoulder.

"Can we move to a location not so open?"

Joseph nodded and they crossed the road to the café where he and Emily had met with Yves.

Alexandre persisted. "My boss is here in Lyon. But I'll need protection, I know too much. How are you going to help me?"

"How are you at farm work?" Joseph asked. He had a specific thought in mind.

"I'll do whatever I have to, just to stay low until this all comes down." Alexandre agreed.

"What were you to do with the Frizon?"

"I am to meet my contact at 2:00 p.m., then to go to an arranged location. He is waiting for the clock."

"Have you met your boss in person before?"

"Monique told me the head guy from Lyon had been to the auction house in Rouen, but I met him only once when he had a meeting with Charest."

Emily was snapping pictures from her vantage of every move the two men made. Listening, Yves kept the telescopic lens in place.

Joseph's cell phone rang and it was Yves.

"Interpol needs more information before determining Alexandre's use as a go-between. They want specifics of his job and his Rouen connections and details of the kidnapping–who planned it and what he knows about the art dealers. Tell Alexandre he *must* postpone his meeting!" Yves demanded.

Joseph turned his attention back to Alexandre, who had lit another cigarette and was getting edgy, balancing from side to side.

"Alexandre, who ordered the kidnapping?"

"It came from the Rouen auction house. I was given direction by Monsieur Charest to meet with Maurice and Monique. Maurice knew nothing, he's a total dimwit. Monique on the other hand–I don't trust her but she is a bulldog with key access to the museum basement. I was to bring the clock back to Rouen to Monsieur Charest, who was filling an order for the guy in Lyon."

Joseph said, "Since you're already in Lyon, wouldn't it make sense to meet with the head man here instead of going back to Rouen? This man Charest is not thinking straight. The 2:00 p.m. meeting must be postponed. Call your contact and make another twenty-four hours delay. He has no reason to deny your request other than simple impatience."

Alexandre pulled his cell from his pocket, but hesitated. "I don't know the name of my contact, it will be whoever answers the phone."

He punched in the number. "Monsieur, I beg your patience. I have apprehended Monsieur Harkness and I'm negotiating for the Frizon. I need to postpone my appointment with you until 2:00 p.m. tomorrow to allow their courier to arrive in Lyon."

Alexandre waited as silence continued at the other end.

Joseph stood close enough to Alexandre to hear the conversation, and Yves listened on the transmitter. The contact's throat cleared. His voice was gruff.

"This does not please me. Alexandre! You need lessons in following orders and respect for punctuality. There are many other people involved; you are not in a position to bargain. I *am* displeased. I will consult and call you back."

The receiver was slammed in place.

"Alexandre, come with me, we're not finished with our questions. Remember our agreement from Montmartre that you would assist us in a double-cross? I intend to hold you to that promise."

Joseph put his hand on Alexandre's shoulder and nudged him toward the car. He dialed Yves as they walked.

Yves told Joseph to take Alexandre to the Le Jardin Hotel at Place Charles Hernu. A room was registered under the name of Simon Walker.

"Give the desk clerk one hundred euros when you ask for the key. The rooms are soundproof and we use this one as a safe hideout as it's wired. Stay with Alexandre and use cuffs if you need to. I'll be in touch. Gather all the information you can, any previous dealings with museum art theft or forgeries.

"Don't worry about Emily. I'll ask her to return to your hotel and wait for me to call her."

TWELVE

Rouen Auction House, France, May 2012

R ene was on a rampage. "What went wrong?"
He commiserated over several bottles of cheap wine.

After following Dodger for several days, he tried again to contact Robbie to see if he could offer clues about their wayward partner. Still no answer, so Rene drove across town to Robbie's boarding house.

Driving slowly passed their favorite eatery, he stopped on the pretense of asking if the barkeep had seen Robbie. He couldn't believe his eyes.

Robbie and Dodger were at a table for two, laughing and swilling beer. Rene marched over and forcefully, he flipped their table over.

Dodger yelled out, "Hey, calm down Rene! If my memory is correct, it's a year since you last called. Do you expect us to put life on hold and wait for you to decide what we do and where we go? As a matter of fact, I've got myself a security job of my own. Informant fees pay my rent."

"Does your employer know you moonlight?"

Dodger laughed. "I was testing out the museum's new unbreakable security system. So what, if it gives me a nice stash on the side. It was a one man job. You jealous, big man?"

"So these rings mean nothing to the two of you!"

There wasn't an answer and Rene stomped out.

For the next few weeks, Rene tailed Dodger between Lyon and Rouen. Robbie met up with him once a week and they seemed to have a plan.

Dodger took a room in Rouen within walking distance of the auction house, and Rene watched until he thought the way was clear to install a transmitter in Dodger's room.

Frequent calls took place between Robbie and Dodger, both deeply involved in producing forgeries of stolen art bringing in a heavy payload. The filtering base was the auction house.

When Dodger wasn't playing with his paints, he worked on security assignment, with Interpol.

"Impossible! How could he get into Interpol? Must be an informant, or a security guard."

Rene took an early train to Lyon, and waited in a rental car outside Interpol's building watching for Dodger's arrival. Dressed again in the sports jacket, Dodger passed through the secured entrance without difficulty and walked a flight of stairs to his meeting.

Within minutes, Rene entered, stating through the glass, he had evidence vital to a current investigation. He was provided a Visitors tag and directed to an office on the second floor, Room No. 204. He was aware security footage would monitor every step.

Walking down the hall, he saw Dodger down at the end. The door at Room 202 was ajar and Rene slipped inside. The reception desk plate said 'Recruitment', and adjacent was a row of three offices, the first one labelled 'Yves Deslorme'.

The clerk invited him to take a seat.

"Hello," Rene was at his best. "I would like to apply for basic recruitment for field work. I have many years of security experience in my resume. I'll take whatever you can give me."

She handed him an application. "You can use that office to fill this your form. She directed him to the Deslorme office.

At the Rouen auction house, Roger Garnier finished his overnight stake-out. He was bloated from too much coffee and his clothes were rank with cigarette smoke. He cranked the car windows down for in the fresh morning air, then turned the engine over of his red 65 Isetta, getting a quiet backfire sputter.

During his Interpol training, he'd been assigned to cases interlinked through museum thefts. He'd now been assigned to watch the Rouen museum, suspected of processing illegal counterfeits created in the museum.

When the auction house had been closed for renovations, Roger installed a hidden cabinet in the rafters, shielded by a sheet of plywood, and on rare occasions he visited the rafters to store certain canvases out of the museum's sight.

Roger had become brash in helping himself to information in Charest's files, knowing exactly when and where shipments were going.

He was careful to work at night, or when he was sure Charest was out of town and the warehouse was vacant.

The twelfth floor room at Le Jardin Hotel was hot and stuffy for Joseph and Alexandre. The windows and blinds were closed and it radiated stale cigarette and cigar smoke from past sessions. Joseph ordered a bin of ice with Evian water and a bottle of Uberach whiskey. If he could loosen Alexandre, the answers might be more generous.

In their confines, Alexandre revealed he'd taken a Picasso forgery to an auction house in Paris and delivered heavy, oversized crates from the museum to a warehouse in Normandy.

He confessed to crating and smuggling a painting to the U.K. and carrying out illegal jobs for Monsieur Charest's boss. His immediate direction always came from either Charest or Monique.

"Tell me about Monique," Joseph demanded. "Where does she come from, and where is she now? I heard bail was posted for her within hours after the kidnapping charges were laid."

"I met Monique two years ago. She was with an employee from the Epte museum, a plain looking man, wide shoulders and muscular arms. I don't recall the name . . . I've only seen him once or twice from a distance. One time when I took the crates to Normandy."

Alexandre stopped to gulp the whiskey.

"Then Monique was with another man. When he handed me the shipping papers, I saw that he wore an excessive silver ring. It was ornamental with a raised emblem."

"Who is this other man?"

"He appeared from time to time. First name was Robert, but I can't tell you anything else about him."

Alexandre paused.

"The few times I saw him, he was wearing a disguise. I heard he did undercover work."

Joseph stepped away from Alexandre to call Emily. He had a list of questions for her to google. More about the ownership of the auction house and the Epte museum, and catalogues of art showings in the last two years.

"Joseph, are you alright? I don't like being in the dark like this, but mostly I miss you."

Emily suspected the phones were tapped and carefully called him by his alias. She sounded lonely and forgotten.

"Don't worry, babe. We're close to finding the kingpin in Lyon; it sounds like a racket. Alexandre is safe with me but I bet his friends are looking for him tonight."

She was uneasy with the plan.

"Don't you think this is bigger than you can handle as a lone wolf? Did Yves suggest a plan?"

"Emily, I haven't discussed this new information with Yves, but I'll do that when I ring off. He wouldn't have sent me to this interrogation room if he didn't have some interest, besides listening to everything that takes place in here. Probably even this conversation, Emily. So you see, I'm not a lone wolf."

Yves rang back seconds later.

"Sounds like you want to talk to me; I couldn't help hearing. I've gathered incriminating material here at Interpol about the guys you are playing with. Don't take this too lightly, Joseph. We lost an agent last year trying to get into this same ring, and I took his loss rather personally."

The news leveled seriously on Joseph.

"I'm sorry to hear about your agent, Yves."

Joseph lingered at the bathroom mirror splashing his face with cold water, before it hit him. He stopped short, and looked at the door. Alarmed, his hand shot around to the revolver in his back belt.

It wasn't there; he knew it was on the nightstand. Now only a door between himself and Alexandre, who he knew could be holding the gun at the door.

Bracing himself, he kicked the door wide open. Alexandre was standing within a few feet of him with the revolver aimed at his forehead.

"Was this a test of my loyalty?"

"I trusted you, Alexandre," he said, and a karate chop brought him to the floor.

"Haven't you learned yet?" Joseph asked. "Remember the loft? You have to smarten up if you want a future in crime."

Alexandre pulled himself up, and this time Joseph handcuffed him to the radiator by the window.

"Always determine the consequences of your actions!"

Yves called Joseph moments later.

"You, along with Alexandre, will be meeting with Monsieur Robillard. He is organizing a major art exhibition in Lyon. Robillard has been actively recruiting important paintings from around the world and is known for his unethical and ruthless behavior, so use caution.

"I was privy to a recent meeting he had with an American art collector and I heard the word Monett. This would fall into place with the information Alexandre gave us."

Yves paused but Joseph was waiting for more.

"You'll be wired and I'll be in a marksman position. I'm not able to expose myself. Emily will be our lookout. But I'm curious . . . since you don't have the clock with you, what are you offering to Monsieur Robillard?"

Joseph thought, then replied, "Perhaps Emily can go to Paris to retrieve it early tomorrow." Referring to Rachel as Emily was still awkward to him and he hoped it wasn't noticed in his inflection.

Yves agreed. "It would be best then if I shadow Emily. Everything rests on the safe delivery of the clock. I'll contact her and make the arrangements."

At 8:00 a.m., Emily stood in the hotel lobby waiting for the airport taxi with the empty suitcase at her side. Assessing her surroundings, she was confident her presence in Lyon had gone unnoticed. Yves was in his vehicle within sight of her.

Her plan would take her directly to the Swiss Bank then return to the Paris airport with the clock. Minimize the opportunities for interception–that was Yves's advice.

At the bank, she approached the safety deposit reception, entering her codes in the validator. A man in a black suit emerged for a formal introduction and escorted her to the vault. She provided her passport for identification.

Inside, she opened the empty suitcase, and with soft flannel she tactfully wrapped the Frizon for stowing, and locked the case. The Sauliere scrolls were placed back in the tray and returned to the vault.

Yves watched from a bench across from the bank, but picked out a man in a parked Renault with binoculars fixed on the door. Yves pulled up his jacket collar and walked through the bank's glass entrance. Emily was approaching the front door when Yves put his hand on her elbow.

"There is a back way out for employees. Come with me."

He pulled Emily toward the back, brushing past a floor manager who tried to detour them.

"I'm sure it's a false alarm but better safe than sorry."

Yves hurried her to a lane connecting to the parking lot. The first building had a rear employee entrance and the door was not snapped shut. Safely in the grand lobby, Yves left Emily to wait by the security desk. "I'll retrieve my vehicle and pull up front."

His yellow Citroen pulled into the drop zone and Emily quickly stepped to the curb and into the front seat.

"I thought you were going to stay in the shadows." Emily reminded Yves.

"We live on the edge and are adaptable to situations as they become modified. Flexibility is my motto. Are you unhappy with your airport chauffeur?" It was the first time Emily had seen a smile from Yves. She noticed he had a mischievous, boyish charm.

"Express service to the airport!" She called out.

"What made you become an Interpol agent? Do you have a family somewhere?" She dared to ask as Yves merged into heavy congestion.

"The less you know about me the better. IP agents generally don't have a family. It's much too dangerous and would leave the agent vulnerable. Why are you so curious?" Yves was uncomfortable about the questioning.

"I am coming to understand why a man . . . well like Joseph, can be driven to want to resolve crises. He's not happy spending idle time without risks and challenges. I've watched him growing restless in Montmartre. It's because he thrives on solving puzzles, but feels he's of less value when that's not the high point of every day. Do you know what I am saying?"

Emily regretted beginning the conversation, her feelings about Joseph should have been private.

"I don't even know why I am telling you this. Sometimes it is better not to say anything."

Yves shrugged. He had nothing further to say about Joseph, and remained silent to the airport. Emily stared out the window as buildings and highways flashed by.

She dwelt on how much Joseph meant to her, yet was willing to put himself in danger's path every day. Was she like the 'other woman' in a relationship, sharing Joseph with his determination to solve the world's problems? They had been so close, confiding their hopes and dreams. But his hunger for adventure was dividing them.

She felt sick Joseph was holed up with Alexandre in Lyon, and she didn't know when she'd see him next.

THIRTEEN

The meeting between Joseph, Alexandre and Monsieur Robillard was planned for 2:00 p.m. in an ancient part of Lyon above the Wine Caves.

Emily was with Yves when he parked his car in a nearby alley. Lyon's streets were narrow with shops opening onto the sidewalks, and parking was difficult. Street after street, the lanes were lined with wine shops, chocolatiers, cafés and boutiques.

Emily picked an obscure table inside a bakery where she would see Yves's signal, but not be seen. In the meantime, she would snap photos and behave like a tourist.

Joseph and Alexandre approached the entrance of the wine restaurant. Alexandre was smoking and showing his agitation.

A portly man of fifty-five watched Joseph's arrival from the street. His stride and appearance was impressive, wearing a mid-length leather jacket and an expensive grey Borsalino fedora. He removed a pocket watch from his jacket and peered over his spectacles at Joseph and Alexandre on the street, before moving toward the restaurant.

Joseph surveyed the street and avoided eye contact with the man, but instinct told him it was Robillard.

"Alexandre, don't look directly. A man a few doors down is watching us. Have you seen him before? I suspect it may be Monsieur Robillard." Joseph was loud enough to be heard but not draw attention.

Alexandre's cigarette was extinguished, but before he had an opportunity to take a look, Monsieur Robillard walked casually into their range.

"Bonjour, Monsieur Harkness!"

Robillard forced a wry smile below his mustache and tipped the fedora in acknowledgement. Joseph extended his arm for a handshake, and couldn't miss his ornate silver ring with raised emblem and blue sword.

"Please my friends, join me inside."

He waited for Alexandre to open the door, then led them into the inner sanctum. The restaurant's décor was left over from the 1980s, with heavy furniture, red velvet, and booths with amber glass fixtures over the tables. Daylight filtered into the glass front door and neon blue lights glimmered at the bar.

Joseph was cordial. "It's a pleasure to meet you, Monsieur Robillard, I've been looking forward to this."

Robillard was blunt. "Flattery is not necessary. This is purely a business meeting, Monsieur Harkness."

The trio marched through the wine bar to a spiral staircase in the back. Dim lighting below aided their footing down the iron steps.

At the bottom, Joseph looked behind and didn't see Alexandre, but another man was standing in the staircase.

"Alexandre! Are you coming?" Joseph beckoned.

In a warning tone, Robillard interjected. "Do not be concerned, Alexandre is being taken care of. You can rejoin him later."

Vintage cellars clustered out from the center room like spokes of a wheel, joining ancient passageways and a web of tunnels. The circular room had heavy wooden tables with areas for tasting tours. Black robes with red and white capes hung on a rack, reminiscent of pictures Joseph had seen of the Order of Beaujolais. He wondered if Robillard was trying create his own infamy.

Robillard held his hands high to be the center of attention. "Please have a seat!" He had already seated himself in a grand leather chair.

He turned to Joseph. "I see you are not carrying a package. That does have me concerned."

"The Frizon was safely deposited in a Swiss bank vault in Paris." Joseph didn't see any reason not share that.

"Don't toy with me, Monsieur."

Robillard's face was growing red with anger, his eyes attempting to pierce into Joseph's soul.

"I need to guarantee the safety of my friends. The Frizon is of little consequence to us. Yes, there is a small Monett painting inside the clock painted on a gold plate. But surely it is not worth this tirade of kidnapping and deceit . . . and your sharpshooters threatening our lives!" It was the confession that Robillard was waiting for.

"I did not ask your opinion. You already know I have a reputation for achieving success at all costs. I admit to a fetish for impressionist art, and when the Monett's existence came to my attention, I decided I must have it. Business transactions never constitute an exchange of currency, strictly favor for a favor or collateral for collateral. How do you plan to exchange this favor?"

He stopped and reached for a goblet. "Beaujolais, yes?"

Robillard selected a bottle of 2009 Moulin a Vent. He poured it into a chalice to breathe, and allowed them both to absorb the aroma before partaking of it.

Joseph brought them back to the business. "It's come to my attention through your own avenues that a buyer has already been found for the Monett. The Frizon belongs to my girlfriend, and it will be appropriate to receive fair compensation for the treachery your friends have put us through."

Robillard swilled the wine below his nose, inhaling the fragrance as he considered Joseph's words.

"What do you propose, Monsieur Harkness? Perhaps we can come to a meeting of the minds. Your boldness is curious."

"A reasonable exchange would be a Monett for another artist's work. You no doubt have something in your collection you value to a lesser degree. We both know the market price of the Monett has not yet been tested and it could be destined to remain unseen by the public. On the other hand, your collection has been valued. Surely there's an original lesser-known Picasso or Dali you could part with?"

Joseph was building his confidence and was pleased with his spur-of-the-moment negotiation.

Robillard practically choked before unleashing an evil laugh.

"Non, non! You are crazy!"

Joseph went on. "Take a moment and think about it. You make an equitable exchange for the Monett plus I understand that Mr. Wentworth, under duress, is providing you with two originals for your gallery."

He looked up hoping to see the shock on Robillard's face, but he was calm.

"You certainly have done your homework, Joseph. May I call you Joseph?"

"Let's leave things with a formal understanding, Monsieur Robillard. I will escort you to your vault collection and you will give me an original. Then you will accompany me to the front of the Interpol building on Boulevard de Stalingrad. If it makes you happy, bring along your own guard. The exchange will take place in the open. I don't wish to insult your integrity but you have already warned me of your reputation."

"You confuse me, Monsieur Harkness. You told me the Frizon was in Paris."

"I said it *was* in a vault in Paris. You don't expect me to play all my cards at once do you? I'll need time to make arrangements with my courier, besides it will be dusk soon and I don't like to make transactions in the dark. Would you be agreeable to meet a 9 a.m.?"

Robillard huffed and reluctantly nodded. He hesitated and pointed a finger.

"How do you know about Monsieur Wentworth?"

"You would be surprised where I have eyes and ears." Joseph couldn't resist the jab but knew his boldness could come back to bite him.

Yves was privy to the two hours of conversation between Robillard and Joseph, but Emily knew nothing. She watched Joseph emerge, with Alexandre keeping pace at a short distance.

Ten minutes later, she crossed the street, and the tension on her face was discernable to Yves who was waiting in the car. She lifted the suitcase onto her lap in the front seat.

"So Yves, are you going to tell me what went on?" Emily's voice was sarcastic and desperate.

"Everything is under control. *You* will be the courier to deliver the clock to Joseph at the Interpol building tomorrow morning. Robillard will be with Joseph and they will be carrying an artist's case."

Yves saw her frustration.

"Joseph will be with Alexandre this evening. Perhaps I could take you to a nice dinner and you can relax?"

Emily appreciated his compassion and sighed.

"That is gracious indeed. I'm sorry, I didn't know I was that uptight."

"Emily, the Frizon must be secure. Perhaps we could store the clock in a vault somewhere nearby, or would you trust it with me to lock it up at Interpol?"

"Yves, I promised Joseph I wouldn't let it out of my sight. I do trust you, but I gave my word and that means something. I can manage it under the table."

"Yes you can, but I was thinking of appearances."

He silently pondered the options. "I have privileges at some of the finest restaurants in Lyon, perhaps we could lock it in my trunk and park the car in view."

"I suppose I could be amenable to that." Emily realized Yves had cornered her with objections and he couldn't be dissuaded.

They drove for thirty minutes to the end of the Lycée du Parc. The culinary school would be Yves's chosen venue, with every meal a gastronomic affair from the head chef, Jacques-Francois Berthier. Reservations are mainly through connections, and Yves was able to make it happen to impress Emily.

They were shown to a candlelit table, window side, and Yves was transformed into a cultured gentleman, holding her chair and consulting with the steward for the best Beaujolais. He kept the conversation around the beauty of Lyon and the Cote du Rhone and Burgundy vineyards.

Emily's mind was on Joseph and what he'd be doing. She wished he could be here instead of Yves.

The chef's presentation was lavish, and Yves, accustomed to rich foods and fine establishments, polished a glass of wine as each plate was served. The menu was exquisite.

Bouillabaisse
Légumes à la grecque
Escalope de veau viennoise
Pommes sautées a cru
Tarte aux poires a l'alsacienne
Baked Brie with caramelized walnuts et apricots

Emily listened politely but kept a steadfast watch on the Citroen through the leaded window, and more than once she thought a pedestrian lingered too long near the trunk.

"Yves, someone's hanging around the back of your car." He didn't immediately acknowledge her concern and she was now agitated. Yves tried to distract her but she had an unsettled feeling something wasn't right.

Yves stood to look. "Ah, see there is nothing now. Please enjoy your dinner and let me worry about the security."

Joseph ordered breakfast and a pot of coffee at 7:30 a.m. to the room of Simon Walker at Le Jardin Hotel. Alexandre awoke, grumbling and protesting that Joseph was taking risks affecting his safety.

"Monsieur Robillard will *not* do as you ask, you know." Alexandre warned Joseph.

Joseph was calm. "We have anticipated he may deceive us into a detour, and we have our own deviation."

"Will you be bringing the painting this time?"

"It will attend the meeting, yes. But you have too many questions, Alexandre, that don't concern you."

Joseph went into the bathroom to hook Yves's wire under his collar, then called to finalize the details. Emily, with the valise, would have telephone contact with Yves, and from a reasonable range with his telescopic lens, Yves would watch for the signal from Robillard.

Yves had an art appraiser with authentication credentials nearby, and at the least suspicion of Robillard trading a forgery, he would be called in to make an inspection. He was a worthy informant who had worked on prior cases with Yves.

Joseph and Alexandre flagged a taxi to Robillard's caves a few minutes before 9:00 a.m. A doorman led them to the cellar, then through to a vaulted door. A second man was at the vault, and a third stood at the bottom of the staircase.

Insisting on privacy, Robillard went alone to the vault. He adjusted the humidity and dialed the combination as the others watched from across the room.

Inside were three tiered racks with coded pallets. He took down a rolled piece labeled DF4982 and carried it with care to the grand table and spread it out for Joseph.

Joseph examined it and looked up with displeasure.

"We negotiated for an art piece from one of the European masters."

Robillard glared back over his spectacles in disdain. "This is a Louis Mignon! Surely you have done your homework, Monsieur Harkness."

Joseph shot back, "I *have* done my homework. This piece was sold in Connecticut last October for a little over $500,000. The Monett will fetch between $40M and $80M in US dollars." He was annoyed by the attempted deception.

Robillard was reluctant to enhance it, but continued. "Well, I see you are more prepared than I anticipated. Since we are far apart on values, I propose perhaps that you would accept a Faberge egg, once in the family of the Czar. It is brilliant blue beyond description and encrusted with diamonds and tiny pearls. I purchased it a number of years ago for $10M." He tossed the Sotheby's catalogue in front of Joseph.

"Of course, it will need to be inspected and authenticated before the exchange. Please bring it out and we'll look at it. How do I know you didn't steal it?"

Robillard sneered. "You are a guest here, at the present, and that was an inappropriate question." Robillard did not move from the painting but signaled to a man in the shadows who retrieved a purple velvet box from the vault.

Yves waited impatiently for Joseph to exit the restaurant, remaining disciplined with his lens fixed constantly on the front door.

At the top of the stairs, Robillard halted abruptly and pulled his gun on Joseph, forcing him toward the back door with the velvet case in hand.

"We will take a short cut through the courtyards."

The art dealer gained a sudden air of confidence, nudging Joseph a few steps at a time while motioning to the man behind him from the shadows.

"Alexandre, thank you for misleading Monsieur Harkness for me. It will make today's transaction so much easier."

Robillard wanted Joseph to know he had been betrayed once again. Joseph looked at Alexandre's face and wasn't sure, even then, of his loyalty. Alexandre avoided eye contact, enjoying the complexity of his double-cross, aware his superiors couldn't keep it straight.

The trio left through the back alley surrounded by apartments, narrow lanes and alleys. Some tenants were on the balconies but none seemed interested in the troupe marching through with Alexandre in the lead.

'We're off to see the Wizard' played in Joseph's head and he laughed, wondering if bad guys see the same humor.

Yves heard enough to pick up on Robillard's deviation. At the end of the lane Alexandre disappeared and Joseph concluded it was either by deliberate choice or Yves's interference.

"You seemed startled your loyal man has left you alone in a bit of a fix." Joseph announced with amusement.

"He's like a hungry rat, to whoever feeds him best. He doesn't have any concept of loyalty, Monsieur Robillard."

It didn't faze Robillard and he waved his gun to keep moving. From a terraced roof, Yves took a calculated leap, landing square on the dealer, and yanked him to his feet in a choke hold.

Joseph clutched Robillard's jacket with both hands, shouting so loud that he was spitting.

"What do you propose to do, Monsieur Robillard? You have rearranged our rendezvous into total chaos. Your intentions are not honorable, yet you had no objective of legitimate exchange. Am I correct?"

Joseph glared at him from inches.

"I beg a thousand pardons." Robillard was wimpy and pathetic. "I must have the Monett for my American buyer. I concede you have outwitted me."

Joseph turned to Yves. "We will release Monsieur Robillard and negotiate directly with Mr. Wentworth."

Robillard spoke again. "I'll do whatever you ask; I've already catalogued the Wentworth pieces into my gala collection. What do you want?" He looked smaller and pale.

Yves stepped forward.

"Monsieur Robillard, you have met with eight different art collectors from around the world. On each occasion you demanded two masterpieces, using greed and intimidation in return for only one from your questionable collection. A rather expensive dinner for your companions. There's a microchip in the salt shaker." Yves couldn't resist the poke.

Robillard eyes widened with surprise but Yves wasn't finished.

"And likely you give them forgeries. I want to know about your forgery counterfeit operation."

Joseph listened and digested it, wondering how Yves had so much information, details they hadn't discussed.

Must be from the dead agent's past efforts.

Robillard tried a barter. "In exchange for giving you that knowledge, would you allow me to complete the deal for the Frizon to Mr. Wentworth?" His pocket watch was now open.

It had become Yves's deal now. "In part, you'll agree to accept only one painting of comparable value in exchange. That would be a fair arrangement don't you agree?"

"Agreed! We must go to meet your contact for the exchange before he leaves." Clearly Robillard withheld his commitment.

"Not until I hear Mr. Wentworth at the other end of your phone call."

Joseph offered his cell phone to Robillard.

Emily sat at the café where they met Yves days before. The server noticed her shoulder checks, curious who she was watching. He refilled her coffee from the hotplate and his staring made her uneasy.

Joseph and Yves left her with the prize piece, the Frizon, placing great risk on her. She resented the isolation of the past two days.

They hadn't asked if she was even willing to give up her precious Frizon. Then for the past two days she was practically hand-cuffed to the clock. It seemed unfair.

Emily glanced back to see the server, but was astounded. He was talking to Monique at the door. She toyed with the idea of leaving but didn't have a viable plan. Yves had told her to call in an emergency.

Monique's phone rang as she looked at Emily, but seconds later Emily was gone. She negotiated her way into a walking tour, but conspicuous with her leather case she crossed over to a small hotel wedged between shops. The entrance was unmarked with just a logo on the brass door's beveled glass.

The concierge stood up from behind the counter, and Emily pulled a handful of euros from her pocket for his cooperation.

"I'm being followed!" She waved her arms. "Please hide me here until my friend can pick me up? Quickly!"

He motioned to a door labeled 'Baggage' and opened his hand to accept her currency.

"There's a cushioned bench on the side."

Emily felt secure enough to call Yves, after all, this *was* an emergency.

"Yves, Monique is following me. Remember we told you about the kidnappers near Giverny? She was one of them. She has some connection with the museum and knows about the Frizon." Her voice was close to a breaking point.

"Come and get me! It's time for some backup."

"We are in a taxi on our way to the rendezvous right now. Where are you?"

Whispering her squatted location to Yves, she felt a little foolish. She bent to peek through the keyhole, watching as a man at the counter spoke to the concierge in rapid French.

The brass door burst open and Yves rushed the man, pinning him on the wall. They had an angry argument in prolonged French before Yves released his grip.

"What are you doing mixed up in this?" He shouted as he shoved the man out onto the cobblestone street. The man bolted and Yves looked to Emily.

She wasn't sure what had taken place, but knew Yves was covering something. They could get to that later.

"I am so glad to see you, Yves!"

"Are you alright, Emily?"

"I'm fine now."

"Joseph has gone ahead to the meeting sight."

Leaving the hotel, Emily surveyed the avenue for signs of Monique, spotting her still back at café.

Yves was walking quickly and Emily took a few running steps to catch up. He didn't react about Monique as he wanted to get back to the exchange.

Joseph was standing across the way with Monsieur Robillard.

"Hi, babe! Are you okay?" Joseph reached her with a tight hug, giving her some reassurance.

"I'm fine. But let's get this over."

Her smile was convincing.

FOURTEEN

Donated by a conglomerate of artists, the Epte museum was purchased as an open air forum established for the appreciation of the works of impressionism with many works from the Charles Monett collection.

Monsieur Tourneau, the museum's administrator, was adamant the painting in the Frizon be returned.

Tourneau's passion had selfish personal reasons, relishing the day of the unveiling when the work would become public. Tourism and membership revenue would increase providing a much-needed cash flow.

For his ego, it would bring accolades and fame to the often overlooked administrator, and to his curator, Monique Bedard. A healthy bonus would be returned to Tourneau for his genius.

Monique believed her mission to return the Frizon and Monett to the museum was above board, and had the brains and brawn to take on any man standing in her way.

Meeting briefly with Alexandre near the Robillard courtyard, they agreed he would act as her backup. She knew he was playing both sides but had no choice but to rely on him one more time.

"Pitiful to have an art convention in the concrete park, in front of Interpol." Monique thought to herself.

She was not interested in the Faberge egg and didn't care who ended up with the piece.

Joseph and Monsieur Robillard were joined by Yves's appraiser to determine the item's authenticity. The examiner was unassuming, in a rumpled overcoat and a government issued briefcase. He opened his case and withdrew some technical instruments.

Yves and Emily remained in the Citroen, watching, with the Frizon at her feet. She zoomed her phone on the informant and snapped a picture. She was curious about the sudden introduction of another new player. Yves hadn't discussed this.

She brought it up to Yves. "Should we be concerned? The examiner has a trench coat with his collar pulled up and a monocle. Does that description match anything, Yves?"

Yves squirmed. There wasn't time to answer.

Robillard's Faberge egg was evaluated first. With his magnifying glass, the examiner scrutinized every centimeter, noting a scratch and two missing encrusted diamonds from the gold cockerel.

When he was finished, he turned to Joseph. "This is not in catalogue condition, but it *is* from the Czar of Russia, you can tell from the miniscule initials here in the corner. It has historical value. I would estimate the value to be perhaps close to $3M at auction, or with museum grade repairs, maybe more." He removed the monocle.

The Interpol plan was to allow Robillard to take possession of the clock and then intercept him with stolen good.

Joseph nodded to the examiner and signaled for Emily to bring the clock. She left Yves's car and joined the melee of three, literally a meeting of pros and cons.

Approaching the table, her attention went to the examiner; she considered he was wearing a disguise with a fake moustache. She was right, there was a scar on his chin that couldn't be hidden.

She unzipped the circular opening of the case and carefully lifted out the package.

The velvet unfolded, falling gently beside the Frizon, now in a standing position in the light.

Emily's eyes were wide. *This isn't right. It's not my clock.*

She held back the horror and slowly unlocked the case door at the rear. The key didn't move smoothly like she remembered. *Maybe it had accumulated some rust.*

Emily knew something was very wrong. How could it not be her clock, it was with her constantly. This clock has signs of wear, with chips and fading. Mine was a perfect specimen.

She pondered longer, then turned sharply to Yves.

"I'm afraid, gentlemen, this is a forgery!" Emily stared at the Citroen and looked again at Yves.

The examiner approached the clock. After only a cursory study of the exterior and the interior painting, he announced to the group, "Yes, this could barely fool a novice. In consideration of the clock itself, it is indeed worth four thousand euros. But the painting is merely a good amateur's attempt."

Joseph was bewildered and shot a questioning glance at Emily. With a flip of her eyes, she gestured toward Yves.

However, all was not lost as Monsieur Robillard was moderately interested in the forgery and offered to negotiate.

Monique watched from the park and arrived to observe. She spoke up with a bid on behalf of the museum and Monsieur Tourneau, a surprising competitor to Robillard.

"I don't see what value a forgery is to either of you." Joseph couldn't make sense of it.

Emily continued to examine the clock. It had to be switched in Yves's trunk.

If she acknowledged this to be her clock, she and Joseph could walk away.

On the other hand, there's still an original Monett in the genuine Frizon and Yves must know where that is.

Yves must have located another Frizon in advance. I should never have laid my confidence with him. What now?

Genuine Frizons from the early 1700s in any condition were rare, and in those few hours the painting would have been copied onto a fake gold plate of the spare clock. The copy was excellent but not perfect, and Emily wondered if the examiner was also a forger and party to the scam.

"Who could have done such a thing?" Emily said aloud.

Monique was firm in her bidding. "Monsieur Robillard, I see ironically that I am negotiating with you for the forgery." I will give Monsieur Harkness one million US."

Robillard wouldn't lose it, on principle and reputation. "One million five and that is where I stand, if you wish to spend more for a forgery you will be thought an imbécile."

Monique turned to Joseph.

"You have sold your forgery to a fool. I suspect your flock of detectives knows the whereabouts of the original, and you are not off my radar. You are the cheese and the mice will come for you. Don't think for a moment you can walk away from this. An undiscovered Monett belongs to the world."

Joseph was off his game but one thing was certain, the check from Robillard would be a fraud as well. He didn't care about the money. It was now about cleaning up the mice and bringing honor to the Sauliere.

Emily walked over to Yves waiting in his car. "You double-crossed me! And who are you? I trusted you."

"You admire my work then, Emily? You are too trusting for this business. I have taken an oath of service to find the truth and make retribution. Think about that for a while and you will understand Joseph's trickery with Monsieur Robillard was a personal conquest.

"I will tell you this only once—the clock has a rightful owner. I'll continue to work with you while you delve into the black market organizations. We did lose an agent last year who was too curious." He showed little emotion.

"Where is the clock with the Monett?" She demanded.

Yves laughed. "You don't expect me to answer that, but I'll advise you when and if you need to know. You are not in a position to interrogate me."

The art appraiser vanished quickly. Monique had words with Alexandre, before Monsieur Robillard led him away. The fake Frizon was now Robillard's.

The exchange was humiliating to Joseph, and deflating. He remembered the night of his first contact with Yves, when Daniel was shot. It was the same feeling. Taking another run at Yves was all he could think about.

Emily said. "Joseph, we have to move on. For now, we must stay close to Yves until we find the clock. We are under surveillance by Monique, and Yves as well. As far as Monique and Robillard are concerned, they both believe we know where the original is."

Emily folded her arms under his, and tightly around his back.

"Together we will work through this."

Yves confirmed his reservation, mirroring Robillard's, again at the magnificent Exquis Restaurant, at Collanges-au-Mont d'Or on the edge of Lyon. He had the courage to call Emily to be his dinner companion, that she'd understand his reason.

He made his request formal. "I owe you this.

"You'll need an elegant disguise, Emily. There may be people in the room who would recognize us. Thus, I will be sans goatee and my hair lighter and shorter, and you should take similar precautions."

She needed convincing. "I am curious of the purpose of this invitation."

"Several Tuesdays ago, I sat at the table next to Monsieur Robillard and his American buyer. That is how I came to know of the Monett, before you and Joseph called. Let's leave it at that." His reply was curt.

"Text me with a location where I should pick you up tomorrow evening. The reservation is for 7:00 p.m."

After he rang off, Emily recounted the discussion to Joseph. "Perhaps there is another way in for us. A way back to the Frizon."

Joseph wasn't happy about Emily's suggestion to cut her hair. He adored her long auburn tresses.

"Perhaps a dye job and tie it up or something."

A compromise was agreed to cut her bangs and pull her hair up into a French knot.

They left from the Abbesses metro for the morning train to Lyon, booking a quaint hotel near the Soane River. Emily spent the early afternoon shopping in boutiques for an evening dress and Joseph took in a televised football game at a nearby tavern.

A rich blue indigo Chanel dress with diamond straps adorned the new Emily, her hem draped to mid-calf on one side and to her knee on the other, a style popular in Lyon.

Yves arrived at the hotel with a black sedan. He called Emily's cell and waited. Joseph came down with her and kissed her goodbye, then hailed a taxi for himself.

Emily was overwhelmed at the extraordinary Restaurant Exquis. They were welcomed by waiters with silver trays of aperitifs and canapés. The room began to move, the back swallowed up to reveal a rotating carousel and steam organ. In the opulence, they became unaware of their waiting time, and at last the great doors opened ceremoniously.

Yves was a true gentleman tonight, dressed impeccably in a Saville Row tuxedo. He ushered Emily to a table in the corner with romantic candlelight.

"I compliment you on your dashing new look, kind of a Daniel Craig likeness, clean-shaven and tussled hair. You've been watching a bit of James Bond, haven't you?"

"Thank you for the compliment, Emily. I do have my own bag of tricks and disguises." His face was slightly flushed.

The dining room was at capacity as it was every night. Yves surveyed the room. Monsieur Robillard and his guest were two tables in front, with Emily's back to them. Yves's view was clear.

He excused himself to the men's room and bumped Robillard's table knocking a napkin to the floor. Bending to retrieve it, he placed a bug under the table and apologized.

The sommelier introduced himself with a tray and two crystal champagne flutes, and in minutes was back with an exquisite Krug NV Grand Cuvee. To Emily, the meal was legendary, terrine de fois gras with seasoned rosemary toasts, steamed mussels and shallots in wine sauce, and mushroom rich veal stew. The pace was slow and methodical, ending with decadent desserts, cheeses and brandy.

Yves kept a constant eye on Monsieur Robillard. He was cordial to his guest and Yves deduced that the man was an Englishman from London, recruited as a contributor to the fledgling museum. The two men consumed a second bottle of wine, noticeably fortifying Robillard's confidence.

Yves listened intently to their conversation, and Emily did her best to avoid turning to see them. She kept an idle one-way chatter with Yves as a distraction, enjoying the venue and experience.

Emily closed her eyes, to marvel how amazing it would be to attend a gastronomique school under a great chef. She still needed a solution to fill the void created when they left New York for Paris.

Yves shattered the thought and her eyes opened. "Emily, will you make a few notes." He handed her a notebook.

"Sure, Yves."

"Write what I say: Nigel Baker; Wiltshire & Bradley Investments; Swiss bank transfer; Sotheby's storage vaults; Virginia; Renaissance, Cubism, Impressionists categories; Cezanne's 'The Card Players' $250M; Munch's 'Scream' $120M at Sotheby's in New York. I'll explain these later."

Yves kept his volume low.

Emily daydreamed again, speculating where Yves could have hidden the Frizon.

Must be Lyon, he didn't have time to go anywhere else.

Robillard's voice rose, this time loud enough for Emily to hear from the table.

"Monsieur Baker, many art dealers court me for an invitation here and you have been honored with this privilege.

Do you really think it would be good business for me to be so extravagant without a goodwill gesture from you?"

The rotund Frenchman couldn't be swayed from his focus and boldly announced his demand. "We have enjoyed pleasantries about exorbitant prices on the auction circuit, but I am here to ask you for your contribution of a Cezanne to my gala gallery opening."

Robillard's guest reacted with total astonishment and straightened his back in the chair.

"Well, Monsieur Robillard, this is a most unexpected turn of events for this evening." Baker swallowed hard with a gulp of wine.

"First of all, in my circle, a dinner invitation is a gracious gesture. I see you are not aware of that term. Secondly, are you asking to borrow one of my Cezanne's or are you testing the waters to see if I would have one for sale?"

Robillard's manners abruptly changed to arrogance. "You should learn to speak French, Monsieur. That English drone of yours is irritating me. I'm not a patient man. I ask for your contribution as a donation. I may be willing to exchange a newly discovered Monett painted on gold plate in a clock."

Robillard didn't hint that the new one was a forgery.

"Certainly its value would enhance your collection. In addition, I'll provide you with a superior forgery of any of the great canvas works you admire. I have connections in an art world you could only dream of."

Baker replied, "I am kept up to date in the art world. Surely if this were a true discovery, I would have heard of it."

Baker had found his spine.

"You don't expect me to take your word for it, do you?"

Robillard hadn't anticipated the rebuke in Baker's tone. He pulled a folder of photographs from his suit pocket and arrayed them on the table before his guest.

Yves smirked in disgust.

"What a numbskull? He is forgetting he's in a public place. Many a clandestine meeting takes place in this room."

Not privy to the banter, Emily gave him a confused look. "Was I supposed to write that down?" Emily chided.

Yves couldn't help but chuckle.

Baker stood up suddenly.

"Monsieur Robillard, I find this astounding. I thank you for the dinner, but do not hesitate to send me a bill as I do not care to have any obligation to you. Furthermore, you would be the last person I would collaborate with over a Cezanne."

Baker threw his napkin on the table and exited the dining room leaving Robillard with his mouth open in a room of well-heeled patrons.

Yves leaned to whisper to Emily.

"Well I didn't get what I was hoping for, that's for sure. There was no bait and catch here tonight."

Joseph's taxi pulled up just as Yves and Emily returned in the sedan. Joseph paid his driver and waved to Yves to hold up a minute.

"How goes the sleuthing?" Joseph laughed, partly from too much lager.

"Rather uneventful but I had a lovely dinner companion to pass the time. And you?"

"I checked out a bar looking for a football game and oddly I found the weasel Alexandre following me. I'm finding him somewhere between annoying and amusing. However, I had a drink or two with him and his tongue loosened quickly."

"What did you talk about?" Yves turned off the key.

"Monique thinks she has him in her back pocket. The two of them are connected with the auction house and are scheduled to pick up some forgeries to transport to Paris in the next few days. One is a Cezanne going to Robillard,"

Yves was interested. "I wonder what the connection was between Robillard's dinner meeting and Rouen. Do you have an agreement with Alexandre? Could you get the names of the forgery pieces being moved?"

Joseph was fast in his reply. "Alexandre will be in Rouen the day after tomorrow and I'll find him there. He has requested an informant's fee–I discouraged him from getting greedy. I'll come up with some sort of contra arrangement to keep him productive. I doubt he'll wander far."

"You will keep me informed, Joseph." It was a command, not a request.

"I'll keep you informed like you keep me informed. On a need to know basis!" Joseph snapped and they exchanged knowing glances.

"I'll trade you some details later for our Frizon. But I'll take my lady back now."

Joseph gently reached for Emily's arm, trying to be gallant.

At the St. Pierre stop, Joseph and Emily exited the bus looking forward to a rare evening at home. Toby spied them on the hill and bounded down in his manner.

"Welcome back." Marie called out.

"Marie, it was lovely, an excursion to Lyon and the countryside. It's beautiful, so much history. Anything exciting around here? No more burglars I trust?"

Marie reflected. "Now that you ask, you had a visitor yesterday. A man in a leather jacket with a toque or beret. He asked when you would be returning but wouldn't leave his name."

They thanked her and went to the loft. Emily ran a mental list, eliminating most geographically.

Joseph suggested a romantic walk up to the artists' village to view the displayed works for sale from young artists. Emily downloaded the memory card from her camera and brought along an extra one to be prepared for anything. Strings of miniature lights were already on for the night, adorning the rows of easels. A collage of bistro tables and chairs lured patrons in for a coffee, crepe or poutine.

Emily stopped at Evangeline's bistro. A young woman played Greensleeves on a magical harp, and with appreciative tears, she reached some euros down to her beret.

It was so long since they had privacy, they took their time sauntering on the hill, stopping to relish the sky and the stars over the Basilica.

"I've missed the sweet scent of your hair and my arm around your waist, Emily. I am sorry I haven't been more attentive of late."

Joseph took her in his arms and kissed her softly.

FIFTEEN

Nigel Baker phoned Los Angeles to speak with Samuel Wentworth.

The morning after the dinner calamity with Robillard, Baker received a call from Yves, requesting his cooperation in the investigation. At first, Baker was offended by the intrusion on his private meeting with Robillard. But learning of the past meetings, he came to a new perspective that he might be of help to Interpol. Yves correctly assessed Baker as a man of integrity.

Sitting across the desk from Nigel Baker, Yves waited to listen in to the call. He had spent the previous hour coaching Baker, rehearsing questions and foreseeable responses. The room was silent as Baker dialed from his office.

"Mr. Wentworth, allow me to introduce myself. I am Nigel Baker of Wiltshire Investments in London, England. We have a dinner companion in common by the name of Monsieur Robillard."

Baker paused, hoping to hear encouragement, but got nothing.

"I believe he may have coerced you into an extraordinary deal where you'd end up with a considerable loss. From another interested party, I understand you showed some moderate interest in the Monett."

Baker paused to allow Wentworth to absorb the context of his inquiry. There was still little response and he continued.

"Mr. Wentworth, I had a similar experience at Exquis, with Robillard trying to force me into an unfair trade. Would you be willing to assist me to track this man down? Everything will be totally above board and we'll deal with authorities. Otherwise, we believe he'll continue with similar scams every month. We are only two men, but many have been harassed."

After a pause, Mr. Wentworth spoke.

"Excuse me, Mr. Baker, how are you privy to my discussion with Mr. Robillard? You must understand, I have not met you before this call, and you suggest a preposterous scenario. But I *have* done a quick computer search on you while talking, and I concede your reputation is honorable."

Baker replied, "I understand . . . I have taken you off guard, Mr. Wentworth. The integrity of our museums and investment in collections is being poisoned by floods of forgeries, many creeping in unnoticed. Mr. Robillard would not have given you an authentic Monett as all he has is a forgery. I have this from a well-respected examiner who has seen the Frizon."

The silence was awkward, and Wentworth gathered words.

"I don't know what this Frizon is. Furthermore, my paintings are in transit, Mr. Baker. A man's reputation is sometimes worth more than his art collection. I have never swindled a client in my life and my friends count on that. The most valuable one is a Cezanne en route to a London art storage facility under sealed lock and escort, for delivery on Friday. I'll be arriving in London Thursday evening, and have a scheduled meeting with Mr. Robillard on Friday at noon."

Yves slid a note to Baker.

"Does the vault code 'Virginia' mean anything to you, Mr. Wentworth?"

"Yes, I have heard that somewhere, but I can't place it right now."

"I would be grateful, Mr. Wentworth, if you'd allow me to meet you on your arrival in London, before you meet Robillard. You will be welcome in my home for dinner. My wife is an excellent cook and I too have dined at Exquis."

"My curiosity insists I graciously accept your invitation, Mr. Baker. If you are able to meet my flight, it would make the best use of our time." Baker noted the details and their productive call ended.

Yves was generous in his praise, but also self-congratulatory. "That went well, Mr. Baker, you handle yourself with dignity. I have a partner who sometimes assists me. His name is Joseph Harkness. I'm certain he will agree to join us as a lookout."

"You have guaranteed no one will be in harm's way throughout these meetings." Baker reiterated. He didn't care that much, but for appearance sake he wanted to be proper.

Following the meeting at Wiltshire & Bradley Investments, Yves called Joseph to enlist his help.

Charest met to discuss strategy with Tourneau and Monique, mostly to lick their wounds after coming up empty in Lyon.

Charest shrugged to Tourneau that Emily seemed truthfully shocked the Frizon had been switched. Although she may not have the Monett, our best bet is to keep tabs on her until she leads us to her betrayer."

He turned to Monique. "I understand from Alexandre the Citroen driver was the one calling the shots. We have to find this nameless counterpart. Do you have a suspicion where the clock is now?"

Monique dared her opinion. "I believe it's still in Lyon, but it's pointless to search for it randomly. The third person of their trio will lead us there. I'll be running some forgeries to London for Monsieur Charest and will take Alexandre with me. Something tells me I will cross paths with these thieves along the way."

Monsieur Charest added more fuel. "Can we be assured the forgeries will not be traced? I'm not certain we can trust Alexandre. I have inside information a Cezanne will be delivered in London about the same time you arrive. If it's possible to intercept it, there would be a generous bonus for you."

Monique smiled in disdain. "Monsieur Charest, my focus is to find the Monett and take care of the transports. I doubt time will permit other such grand scale pilfering. Don't you have ethics, or is any piece of art bypassing you a huge injustice? As for Alexandre . . . I know how to handle him and, yes, he does play both sides but that is all the better for us. I can manipulate him at my pleasure."

Charest's face reddened in humiliation, and Monique knew she had gone too far with her opinions.

"I apologize Monsieur Charest. I said some things out of line."

"Monique you do have a sharp tongue, but I appreciate your candor. The shipment to London will be ready tomorrow morning. I've hired a club van and Serge will load it for you. We won't require an armed guard on this trip, as we do not have originals. I've marked your route on this map, and here are the manifests." The envelope was stuffed with papers.

Monsieur Tourneau rose from his chair to signal the meeting was adjourned.

"Monique I expect to hear from you on your arrival in London, and I will keep Monsieur Charest informed."

"I will call Monsieur Charest directly." She wasn't easily controlled by anyone.

Arriving in Rouen, Joseph and Emily headed straight to the auction house. With the London climax nearing, the stakes for the criminals had risen and they knew to stay under the radar.

They found an abandoned truck at the end of the lot with a view of the building. Monsieur Charest's Phantom Rolls was parked beside the familiar Renault in the freight bays. The garage door was open with pallets stacked on the loading dock, and metal steps led up to a steel door labeled 'Rouen Auction House'.

Joseph was equipped with a Q-Pro long range listening device to hear phone conversations within the building. Charest, Alexandre and the man they referred to as Serge were inside.

They lowered their heads as Monique's rental van pulled in. Her route to London, mapped out by Charest, would minimize checkpoints and terminal crossings that could detect their cargo or weapons. From Rouen she would take a country road to Caen and then to Ouistreham. The Channel crossing would take six hours to Portsmouth, then another two hours; eleven in all.

Monique's nature was to challenge. "Do you think it wise, Monsieur Charest, to travel in darkness on poor grade roads?"

"Just ensure the shipment arrives at the art storage facility in London by 9:00 a.m. tomorrow." Charest closed the issue.

"I'll need Serge to ride with the cargo and alternate with Alexandre," she said.

"Serge will not be accompanying you, I have another job I need him to do. I might ask Robert but he is difficult to find. Here, Monique, call me on this number if you run into any kind of trouble, and at the latest on your approach to London."

A hand written number was scribbled on the back.

Joseph and Emily decided they needed a car rental. Emily biked to the train station while Joseph stayed back to watch the auction house. He placed a GPS transmitter under Monique's van.

They knew the trip from Rouen to London would be tight. Joseph agreed to be the lookout for Friday's Baker-Wentworth meeting, coinciding with the arrival of the Cezanne and the delivery of the forgeries.

He watched and snapped pictures as Monique's van was loaded and left with Alexandre. Emily wasn't back yet and Joseph checked his watch.

The Rouen train depot was congested for the holiday weekend traffic, and Emily tried five rental agencies, with all economy cars and sedans booked. An agency proposed a special on a two-seater Vespa, and with no other option she accepted.

She muttered, "I don't think Joseph will be pleased."

The Vespa came with two helmets and rented leather jackets. She was back within twenty minutes, ten minutes after the van departed. Joseph was anxious but still laughed when Emily arrived on the scooter.

"Did you have trouble with your French?" He asked.

Joseph donned the jacket and helmet and Emily took the back seat with her arms around him.

"Tap me if you need me to stop. The van headed north and I have a good signal from the transmitter. Ready?"

"As I'll ever be."

In Lyon, Robillard was getting ready to travel to London, routing himself to Paris, connecting to a late flight from Orly. Along with his carry-on, he had a briefcase with a combination lock. In a leather artist's tube he carried the three small paintings he'd removed hours earlier from the cave vaults.

It was July 14, Bastille Day, a public holiday. Robillard couldn't find a taxi in Lyon, and the streets in the center of the city were closed to traffic. The fire brigade was in charge of festivities and crawled forward with red lights flashing and sirens blaring.

Robillard was edgy, and the stress was building perspiration on his brow. The background noise of the throngs cheering and singing became mute to the booming fireworks lighting the sky.

Continuing to weave through the sidewalk revelers, he worked toward the train station where he'd be assured of a taxi to the airport. His agitation increased as crowds pressed around him.

He was a pompous man, believing he was the kingpin of the art dealers' black market. If he didn't reach London for the 9:00 a.m. meeting, it would cost him his reputation, plus a vastly inflated profit.

Unaware of another man stepping in and out of doorways, he fought his way through the pedestrians. The man wore a cat burglar's costume with a woolen toque over his face, warm for the July evening, but acceptable with the mood of the street partiers.

The whirr of people was dizzying, and in the swarm, Robillard was tripped and bumped. In a panic, he held the briefcase close to his chest. Thinking he heard his name, he tried to hasten his step, his normal boldness dissipating.

As he passed a tavern's patio, two women ran from the partiers and looped a scarf around his neck to pull him inside. The man in the dark costume stepped out and pulled him by the elbow.

"This way Monsieur Robillard. I will take care of you."

He was relieved of the assistance but before he questioned the Samaritan, he was shoved into the alley.

"Who are you? And how do you know my name?"

With force, the man poked him in the chest and struggled for the briefcase. Robillard was off balance, but struggled to maintain his composure.

"It doesn't matter who I am, but it does matter who you are. You've seen me before but never gave me the time of day. You were always too busy in your treachery. You're despicable. No moral conscience, no compassion, and no integrity. I'll relieve you of your precious paintings now. I've listened to all of your conversations and I know about the forgeries churned out of Epte and funneled through the Rouen auction house."

Robillard was disoriented and his eyes shifted wildly as he listened.

"I know your codes and how you plan to proceed with the London shipments, so why would I need you? Think of me as an equalizer. I have all the information I need, and know about the forgery register in your vault listing your contacts. You will be nothing more than a blight in history."

Robillard's mouth dropped to protest, and the man pulled out a switchblade and it snapped into place.

"This is for my friend. Do you even remember Roger?"

"I don't . . ."

The pain was sharp and sudden, but Robillard didn't suffer as he slumped in the alley. The attacker removed his ID and documents and took a key from his pocket, then poured a bottle of whiskey on his body.

He wrenched the heavy silver ring with a raised emblem and blue sword from Robillard's finger. Slowly his rage began to ease, and he rejoined the merriment on the street.

SIXTEEN

Yves arrived in London in the afternoon with enough time to drive past Baker residence on the west side of Hyde Park near Kensington. Two vehicles were in front, and across the street a row of elm trees would be suitable for stakeout of uninvited strangers.

Yves wondered why a man of Mr. Wentworth's status would agree to such a swap. Wentworth was now aware of the Monett forgery and anticipating disgrace among his peers, his initial embarrassment had turned to anger.

Nigel Baker was in his early forties, smart and handsome, with no enemies. He'd inherited his father's fortune and made wise investments, diversifying in art and precious metals. At 5:30 a.m. daily, he jogged with his neighbor, rain or shine, and still achieved a rigid schedule of breakfast meetings at 7:00 a.m.

Yves researched Mrs. Eleanor Baker, born and bred in high society, with memberships in all the appropriate women's clubs. She was a few years younger and online social pictures showed her as attractive with blonde hair swept up with clasps. An organized woman, she planned each day by how much exercise she'd enjoy and the calories needed to maintain her figure.

Mr. Wentworth's flight from LA was expected at Heathrow at 6:00 p.m., allowing Yves and Baker time to meet it and return for an elegant dinner.

Wentworth stood at the baggage carrousel. He was easy to spot, tall, sixty years old, in a dark suit with a brown Buxton case.

Baker was accustomed to service at the snap of his fingers and he summoned a skycap to retrieve Wentworth's luggage.

Formalities were rushed and Nigel led his guest to a waiting limo at the curb. Yves followed as far as the door, then went to his own car in the drop-off area.

Yves followed them toward Kensington, about four cars behind to ensure there hadn't been a tail waiting for Mr. Wentworth, as his arrival in London would be well known.

Minutes from the airport, Yves noticed a black Daimler falling in behind the limousine, making the same turns. He decided to test his suspicion and entered the round-about in the passing lane until he was close to Baker's limousine. Yves slammed sharply on his brakes and veered right toward the next exit, forcing the Daimler off the circle.

The driver cursed at Yves, blasting his horn. He attempted to rejoin the chase, but in the congestion he lost sight of them.

By the time Yves arrived at the Kensington estate, the limousine was gone. The yellow Citroen was parked along the row of elms, and he waited fifteen minutes watching for any activity, then rang the bell at the grand front entrance.

Baker tried to be courteous with his broken French. "Bonjour, mon ami!" He was pleased to see Yves. "Allow me to introduce you to my lovely wife, Eleanor."

She looked like a goddess in her elegant black evening dress. Eleanor left her political discussions with Mr. Wentworth and came to the door.

"My pleasure madam, it is an honor to meet you. Your husband gave us ample warning of how exquisite you are, but I must admit you take my breath away."

Yves kissed the lady's hand and she blushed.

They dined at a circular table in cushioned arm chairs. Eleanor's table sparkled with crystal and glittered with polished silver. She had prepared a sumptuous menu with the main entrée, the finest baron of beef from Cambridgeshire. The men refrained from business discussions over the meal, then settled into the library with a Taylor's vintage port.

Monsieur Tourneau stopped at the Sauliere's farmhouse for an impromptu visit. Madeleine was hanging her wash on the line outside the kitchen. She wiped her hands on her apron and insisted Monsieur Tourneau come in; she would put on a fresh pot of coffee.

Madeleine stepped outside and whistled for Henri. He was in the barn milking cows, and he quickly washed and headed toward the farmhouse. On the back stoop he unlaced his muddy boots.

"Bonjour Monsieur Tourneau, we haven't seen you for some time." Henri extended his hand.

Tourneau looked at Henri's hands, holding back his feeling of disgust at the dirt and grime from his hard work. However, he managed a light handshake and a smile.

"I heard recently you might be aware of a Monett painted onto a Frizon clock. It's rumored it had been in the possession of Monsieur Bouleau in Rouen."

He watched for and saw the look of alarm between the pair, and knew he had struck a chord of guilt.

"Why do you ask us this?" Henri asked.

Henri reached to Madeleine and squeezed her hand, his impromptu cue that he would take the lead.

Tourneau replied. "Well, you can understand why it would be of interest to the museum. It is only right the museum benefit from such a piece of art. Monsieur Bouleau confessed he held the clock for safekeeping, therefore the ownership wasn't transferred and would still be the property of the Monett heirs. Do you understand my point of view?"

The kindness in Monsieur Tourneau's eyes dissipated.

Henri was firm. "I don't understand why you have come? We have nothing to say that would help you, Monsieur Tourneau."

"I ask you one more time. Have you seen the Frizon with the Monett?" Tourneau persisted, his posture now more rigid.

"Our answer is no, Monsieur Tourneau. Do you think we are thieves?"

Henri got on his feet to escort Tourneau to the door, controlling the urge to let his anger speak for him.

Tourneau realized he had sounded threatening, and tried to soften his approach, by inviting their cooperation.

"I apologize for my directness, Henri and Madeleine. I did not intend to sound sharp. You can imagine our excitement when we heard of the Monett. We are especially anxious to preserve it from unprincipled hands. If it does come your way, I will be grateful if you would notify me."

Monsieur Tourneau was in the yard by his car when Philippe arrived on his moped. He stopped beside Tourneau and they spoke.

"What are you doing at my parents' home? There's no need for you to come here, you know how to reach me."

Philippe turned his back to him and walked toward his parents, who were watching from the kitchen door.

"Papa, what did the man from the museum want? Did you tell him anything? I thought we agreed you would let me take care of any dealings with the museum."

"Come and sit down, Philippe. I have a story to tell you."

Henri led Philippe back to the kitchen.

"Papa, I know more than you think. The Sauliere name is mine too. I heard about the Frizon from Monique and I heard the tale of Angelique when Emily and Joseph were here."

Henri stopped him. "How are you acquainted with Monique? She's a criminal and was party to the kidnapping. I don't want any of my sons associating with her."

Henri pleaded but knew Philippe was a grown man and would make his own decisions.

"Papa, you're wrong to allow a man like Tourneau tell us what we can and can't do. We have lived a good life abiding by the laws of France and contributing to this country. We should be proud of our heritage."

He pounded his fist and shouted, "This family won't live under the thumb of the museum."

"Philippe, what do you propose to do? We don't mean to go behind your back. Monsieur Tourneau arrived here this morning uninvited." Madeleine spoke softly.

"I'm sorry Ma, I didn't mean to raise my voice. I know the Frizon is in Lyon and I believe I can retrieve it. And the less you know about my activities, the better for you. You won't have to lie to Monsieur Tourneau if he asks what I am doing."

Standing behind his mother's chair, Philippe leaned to give her a shoulder hug and a kiss on the cheek.

Philippe rode off toward the station on his moped with a backpack. Adjusting the pistol holster on his calf under his jeans, he inspected the tools he'd purchased at the detective store by the pawn shop.

He had done enough jobs at the Epte museum to learn the differences between forgeries and originals. The museum basement was a virtual warehouse of canvas, stretchers, paints and cleaners, with easels holding paintings covered with sheets.

It was in Tourneau's personal interest to turn a blind eye to the crated pallets, routing new art pieces to the basement, then on to the auction house. It wouldn't take a detective to assess a shop full of forgeries as each pallet was labeled in code.

When Philippe first learned Bouleau had the Frizon, he deduced it was being held on behalf of his great-great-grandfather. Years before, rumors of a Monett painting caused the Bouleau's family home and store to be ransacked, and the auction house never let the matter close.

Philippe rode the paved lane from Epte to Rouen, then the train to Paris. He boarded the Eurostar to London. Monique told him about the spoiled Frizon rendezvous. One day when she was out of the room, he checked her handbag. Finding a map, he photocopied her routing to London.

It was paramount Philippe dispose of Monique and Alexandre while they had possession of the Rouen shipment, but before the Wentworth meeting.

Strong and burly, he was more than capable of subduing Alexandre who was puffy and unfit from years of too much food and wine. Monique could be another matter.

Monique can hold her own in a scuffle. I'll catch her unaware.

For the two and a half hours of the train journey, Philippe rehashed the plans.

The Vespa followed the van to the channel crossing. Emily and Joseph found contoured ferry benches and slept with light sheets to avoid detection. Monique and Alexandre stayed in the museum van during the full six hours except for bathroom breaks and coffee.

Monique hadn't seen Emily since the fiasco in Lyon. Emily's appearance had since been altered for Yves's dinner event and she didn't expect to be recognized now. She ventured to the coffee shop, safely retrieving their dinner of double cappuccinos and cheeseburgers.

The ferry arrived at Portsmouth in darkness, and Monique's van was off first. Joseph relied on the GPS tracking to keep up as she picked up speed on the thoroughfare wending her way toward the storage facility.

The Q-phone picked up Monique's call to Charest. The three forgeries were packed in the back in two pallets measuring four by six feet.

The front palette panel was tacked lightly so the lid could be removed and exchanged with the Cezanne lid, as the original papers were glued and had to remain intact.

Charest updated their directions to take the A40 and exit at Greenford A4127, then the Harrow and Sudbury sign from the roundabout.

The phone crackled. "Monique, are you prepared for the security officer at the storage yard?"

Charest was over-managing her and fatigue from the trip left her with edgy nerves and a sharp tongue.

"No matter how many security guards you lined up, there would never be one who knew the difference between an original and a forgery. It'll be a snap. We're on schedule and will be at the site first thing in the morning. Alexandre and I are going to pull over and grab a few winks."

The two rogues were asleep at a Petrol stop when the Vespa arrived up behind them. Joseph and Emily parked the scooter a short distance down the road at a roadside diner and phoned for a taxi.

SEVENTEEN

Philippe arrived in London late Thursday and rented a Fiat for 24 hours. On Friday morning, he was at the storage facility before 8:00 a.m., an hour before the group would arrive. As he approached the gate, the guard took a look from his booth.

"May I have photo identification?"

He flipped through Philippe's passport. "What is the nature of your business, Monsieur Sauliere?"

Philippe got out of the car.

"I am meeting with an art dealer to discuss one of his works. His shipment will be arriving this morning and he will be expecting me."

"Who are you meeting with?" The guard was determined to trip him up.

"Mr. Samuel Wentworth. He has a delivery from Heathrow this morning."

Philippe's impatience was showing. The guard fumbled through the papers on his podium running his finger down the list until he located it.

"Since you don't have documents declaring your business, I must ask you for Mr. Wentworth's pass code, otherwise you will need to wait here for his arrival."

Philippe leaned toward the guard and whispered, "Virginia". The security guard was surprised, he didn't expect that. There was nothing he could do to prohibit Philippe from passing through, and the barrier was raised.

Pulling out his smartphone, Philippe thumbed through the scanned papers from Monique's manifest envelope.

The vault area should be in Section D door number DF498.

Section D's hall was stark, with cement passageways and locked grey metal doors. Philippe made his way through to scout for a hiding place, while avoiding security cameras.

Close to the section's exterior door was a manifold to a drainage system. He inspected the option, then waited. A truck drove in, and he dared not think it could be Monique and Alexandre.

As the truck passed, Philippe placed a bug, then lifted the lid and lowered himself into the drain, with the edge of the lid open. Inside was damp and smelled of dead animals.

It wasn't long. First, the hum of an engine stopping overhead, then familiar voices. Monique accessed the door to Section D from the digital panel on the wall and placed a wedge to hold it open.

Philippe edged the manifold cover a few more inches to get a bearing. The front end of the van was over him and he wriggled out without falling into camera range. He listened for their voices returning in the hall. Philippe was wearing leather gloves and took a cloth from his supplies, dousing it with chloroform.

Alexandre was the first out. Philippe applied an instant chloroform cloth over his face, and threw him down.

Then Monique stepped out. "What the heck Philippe . . .?" The cloth was over Monique's face before she finished.

"A bit of your own treatment."

But she couldn't hear him. Philippe placed them in the van, taped their mouths with duct tape, and fastened plastic ties on their wrists and feet.

He finished carrying the wooden pallets from the locker to the van including Wentworth's Dali, then dragged the two of them down the hall in burlap bags.

Philippe had been a student at L'École du Louvre, however the tuition was more than he could afford. In his second year, for extra money, he took an assignment to paint a forgery of a Picasso, then another. By the time, he was in his fifth year, he was in too deep with the Rouen auction house. He knew he had to make restitution for his secret criminal activity.

He found a niche out of camera range. The first in was Yves in the yellow Citroen, and within minutes the entourage arrived. The transmitter outside sent a clear reception to his earphone.

Mr. Wentworth pressed the digital fingerprint opening to Section D and was followed by Nigel Baker, Yves and Joseph. As they neared, Philippe stepped into their path.

Yves drew a revolver and yelled at Philippe to put his hands up.

"Who are you and what are you doing here?" Yves wanted his confusion to be seen.

"May I introduce myself? I am Philippe Sauliere. Agent Yves you know who I am! A confessed forger . . . but with remorse and a conscience. My intention was to intercept the thieves attempting to take the Cezanne. In your locker, Mr.

Wentworth, you will find two fiends from the museum at Epte and the auction house. Your Dali has been retrieved and is waiting in the van outside. Sir, your Cezanne has not arrived, as yet."

Mr. Wentworth interrupted. "Where is the Cezanne? It should have been delivered by an armed guard service. I saw it secured in Los Angeles. I am suddenly feeling like a pawn. Please explain, Mr. Baker."

Baker looked as surprised and at a loss. Joseph looked at Yves.

"We have intercepted it with some added safety precautions." Yves stated. "Let me make a phone call and see if we can locate the shipment."

Yves stepped away for the call. In minutes, the door buzzed and Yves released the security bar.

On a warehouse dolly, Emily rolled in the sealed pallet.

"Mr. Wentworth, we apologize for the ruse, but we were expecting the two cons in the locker to attempt a switch. But I see that was stopped."

Joseph turned to Philippe. "Now that we are all here, you should continue with the explanation. We are all interested in what you have to say."

Philippe stammered. "My family is unaware of my involvement in this scheme. As a student it was difficult to pay my tuition fees, and I chose to take painting assignments from the Rouen auction house. I'm sorry to say I fell into this trap, and I have a list of my works and where they were sent.

"I have another confession . . . a personal connection to the new forgery in the Frizon." He looked at Yves. "I was pressured to paint it on the promise it would expose the culprits. That was the only reason."

He slowly looked at each face in the circle. "If you will allow it, I have a serious proposal for this group."

Mr. Baker acted quickly. "Philippe, I believe we'll all be interested in hearing you out. But with respect, can I suggest we do it in a more formal venue? Possibly my office?"

Yves raised his hand; he would be glad to deliver Monique and Alexandre to authorities en route.

Wiltshire & Bradley's prestigious offices took the upper floors of a Westminster brownstone, including Nigel Baker's private penthouse office with a skyline view.

Baker and Wentworth were in conversation when Joseph and Emily arrived. Sandwiches had been arranged by the caterer.

Mr. Baker rose. "Miss Warner and Mr. Harkness, it's a pleasure." He enjoyed being the host. Wentworth then stepped forward properly, extending his arm.

Philippe arrived next, but still no Yves, and Mr. Baker was visibly annoyed at his tardiness.

"In the interest of time, please collect your lunches and we'll begin. I suggest Philippe take charge to continue." Nigel enjoyed the power of delegation.

Yves sauntered in with a nod and took his place.

Philippe began. "I've considered this for some time, and this is the group that should run with it."

Baker closed the office door as Philippe spoke.

"My proposal is for a foundation to be started, specifically to research and develop technologies to identify and sift out forgeries. Legitimate museums and galleries would welcome this." He glanced at the men. "And investors."

"In my opinion, the Frizon Monett rightfully belongs to my family, but they're not interested in millions, they just want their heritage restored. My proposal would sell the Monett through a reputable auction, with the proceeds to fund the foundation I've described. It sounds grandiose, but think of the possibility if we could improve the legitimacy and close down illegal operators.

Yves shifted in his chair.

"Late last night, Monsieur Robillard, was murdered in an alley in Lyon during the Bastille parades."

Wentworth and Baker were stunned, unaccustomed to such violence, but neither spoke.

Mr. Baker went back to the proposal. "Do you have a blueprint laid out to explain?"

"Monsieur Baker and Monsieur Wentworth, you both have the reputation and experience to put together a Board of Directors. I'll humbly offer my knowledge of the forgery market as a member."

He reverted to Baker's query. "I've considered some ideas to begin to develop technology, but it will need specialists."

He stopped to hear any response from the room.

Nigel Baker and Samuel Wentworth were spellbound, gaining instant respect for this young man from the farmhouse in Epte, Philippe Sauliere.

"Would anyone else like to step up?" Philippe asked.

Baker again spoke. "I am astonished at your boldness, Monsieur Sauliere, to make such a noble suggestion. I'll need to consider the repercussions but the concept is most commendable."

Wentworth nodded. "My first reaction, is that it is well-intended and extremely generous. The start-up funding would provide a sound threshold. Gentlemen, consider this seriously, you will never find a more generous starting point."

"And you, agent Yves."

Yves had been tight-lipped, but added some polite words.

Joseph and Emily left Wiltshire & Bradley after 2:00 p.m. They called the Vespa agency about the one-way penalty and took a taxi to Heathrow.

They hadn't spent time alone for almost two weeks without chasing someone or being chased. Emily snuggled her head on Joseph's shoulder on the flight, as he planned tomorrow's pursuit.

EIGHTEEN

They landed in Paris late but still took the Metro. Climbing the hill, he stopped her in front of le magasin d'horlage, the window lit up with its display of mantel clocks.

She laughed. "No, I won't need one again for a while. If I hadn't been so persistent in Rouen, we wouldn't be involved. But I do appreciate your thoughtfulness." She leaned into him.

On the crest, they saw Marie's shop was still open.

"Well, my wandering minstrels. Out adventuring again? While you were away that man came again looking for you. He was more anxious than last time and left a phone number."

Marie retrieved a crumpled paper from her apron.

"Did he give you his name?" Joseph asked.

"No. But still wearing that toque."

A couple approached Marie's cart, and Joseph and Emily excused themselves to the loft.

"*This* visitor is *not* from the gallery, Joseph."

He nodded. He fished in his backpack for a recorder. "Voila!"

"Can you put the phone on speaker so I can hear as well?" The phone rang six times.

"Yes, who is this please?"

"What do you want with me?" Joseph didn't introduce himself.

"Ah, Monsieur Harkness, I am glad you've returned safely from London. I have information relating to Charest if you would care to meet me at the top of Montmartre in artists' row in one hour."

The man didn't wait for a response but ended the call.

They looked at each other. "Did he sound at all familiar?" she asked. "Was there a lisp?"

They planned their positions. He'd get there early and post a transmitter under his table in the open, with Emily nearby. Halfway up the hill they separated. He found a patio close to the spot where the rifleman had shot his friend Daniel.

The man was easy to spot with a bruised eye and a slash over his brow.

"Monsieur Harkness?"

Joseph replied quickly. "Yes. I presume you're the man I'm to meet tonight? It's only polite that you introduce yourself."

"My name is Serge, but that is all you need to know."

He pulled up a chair over the concrete. "Please listen carefully."

"What I tell you can go no further than this table without my agreement. I joined the Tourneau and Charest operation a year ago under false pretenses. They were looking for a heavyweight to do dirty work, and I was on a mission to delve into their network deeply enough that they could be exposed."

"I'm all ears!" Joseph leaned in.

Serge continued. "You seem to be a good man, Joseph, interested in making wrongs into rights. I've been watching you and Emily, helping the Saulieres. Philippe is honest and can lead you on the right path; he never meant to deceive people but was told paintings would be duplicates for insurance purposes. He's a talented artist and I hope the day comes when he's recognized on his own merit."

Joseph nodded but was skeptical.

"My eagerness to expose the culprits led me to take my revenge on Monsieur Robillard. I discovered he ordered the assassination of my friend at the Rouen warehouse last year."

He held up the toque. "This was my colleague's. I recently found it stashed in Charest's office, and when I saw it I went after Robillard in Lyon to seek vengeance."

He looked at the ground in shame.

"Serge, what you tell me is a remarkable crime story, but I don't know why you've come to me. Now you've marked me as well with your revelation. We are both in danger."

"I'm sorry you feel that way. Everyone who tangles in the dark side comes to a point when they exceed their value and become a liability. That is what has happened to me, so I took care of their dirty work in Lyon. I don't mean to say Robillard didn't deserve what he got, he certainly did."

"Why not go directly to Interpol?" Joseph asked.

Serge's face was severe. "I'm afraid you wouldn't understand about Yves. I have personal reasons not to put faith in him. I have information about the complete system from forgers to buyers, to sellers, museums and auctions. Interpol needs it all."

Joseph wanted more about Yves, but Serge wasn't ready.

"Your agent Yves has protected you and I would rather trust you than him. I can't say more now, and I won't sit here and beg, Joseph."

There was an awkward silence. Serge was hoping for an ally. He stood to leave.

Joseph caught Emily's eye and signaled for her. He shook her hand with a forced smile, and took a seat again as they whispered.

"Serge, are you safe? If not, you are welcome to bunk in the loft tonight."

Serge's smile was no longer forced. "I'll accept your generous offer. As you Americans sometimes say, there is safety in numbers."

Emily cautioned. "Our landlady, Marie, has already been asking questions about you, so don't become visible. Climb through from the upper terrace, it is open."

She removed her scarf and laughed. "If you bump into a bloodhound, let him sniff this and he won't bark."

Serge didn't laugh. He worried about everyone, and now that included Marie.

Philippe phoned later that night. Joseph vacillated over revealing Serge's conversation and nixed the idea. Philippe was excited about the success of London meeting and Mr. Baker's enthusiasm. But he had a worry.

"Joseph, I'm concerned about Yves. He hasn't shown any commitment or interest."

"Yves is a tough one to figure out. I'm still learning." Joseph replied.

"Are you and Emily in?"

"For sure." Joseph hesitated. "I have an inside track on a witness who could add significant value to the project. I don't have his permission to reveal his name, but in principle would you support that?"

"Joseph, I have my faith in you. It's your decision."

They ventured to Rue Lepic to pick over delicacies for supper, selecting gruyere, baguettes and chicken crepes to serve in white wine sauce.

"Do we have red wine too?" Joseph relished an Argentina Malbec. Emily followed him to the shop before they started up the hill.

"What are we doing taking in a murderer, Joseph?"

"It's hard to convict Serge at this point. He seems definite in his belief Robillard was responsible for the agent's death, but that's still not justification for his actions. We need to know more, Emily."

"But are we becoming accessories now?" she asked.

"We should be cautious. I'll ask Serge more tonight."

At the loft, Marie's nightlight was out.

Serge didn't speak when they entered, but waved his hand to come and watch.

The reporter was on the streets in Lyon interviewing shopkeepers near a body in the alley. The coroner had taken care of business and departed, but the correspondent was digging for witnesses while challenging neighborhood safety issues.

The body had no ID, simply a heavy middle-aged man in a business suit. Engrossed with Bastille Day revelers, the crowd hadn't seen anything unusual on the street.

Serge's hand trembled as he described his attack on Robillard. Emily was disturbed by his distress and found the remote to turn off the report.

"What's done is done and can't be changed, Serge. Come, we are ready for supper." She laid the food out on the dining room table, with sparkling wine glasses.

Dinner was silent and limited to idle chatter about Paris in the summer. Serge showed polite interest but Joseph knew he was barely there. Joseph placed a second bottle on the table but it stayed corked.

They moved to the living room and Joseph braced for a long discussion. Serge fidgeted, reflecting.

"We are not here to judge you, Serge." Joseph encouraged. "You need to tell us about the operation and the forgeries."

Joseph started the digital voice recorder and placed it on the table. "Start at the point you were hired in Rouen."

"I came from the French countryside and worked on my father's farm while going to school. I went to university but fell into the same trap as Philippe did; I couldn't afford the tuition, and the best way was to paint forgeries.

"I was at the Rouen auction house, but the stress was overwhelming and eventually I quit painting. Charest had his claws into me, and I was so implicated I stayed doing various jobs.

"On the night the agent died, I was working in the warehouse. Charest didn't know I was in hearing range of the conversation. I was with the agent when he died. There are other details but I don't want to get into them right now."

Emily spoke with compassion. "That's okay, Serge, everything at your own pace. You don't have to answer to us for anything."

"I was proud of my first paintings and packed them up for shipping to Lyon. Once, I rode with Alexandre delivering the pallets to the wine vault. Robillard barked at us for being too slow, threatening us. Never gratitude.

"Maurice was a lookout and Alexandre a goon. But Monique; she was a real bull and kept us on our toes. Charest was intimidated, but trusted her. Tourneau barged into Charest's office regularly, his way of flexing his muscle; after every meeting, there was a shipment. Manifests were held in Charest's office, and one day I took digital photos. I have them here on a memory stick."

He pulled a chip from his pocket and placed it beside the recorder. A key fell too and he scooped it up.

"Robillard kept a log in the caves of buyers, sellers and transactions, guarded with a sophisticated alarm. It has everything you'd need to shut him down."

Emily rose and made some coffee. "We could all use a break right now."

Serge and Joseph relaxed and returned with a tray. She placed a bottle of Frangelico beside the cream.

The Tour de France was reaching its last legs. It had passed Bonneval, south of Paris, and was within a day of sprinting home and down the center of the Champs Elysees.

Paris was lit up like a Christmas tree in preparation for the cyclists, and Emily and Joseph headed to the Champs Elysees to join the evening revelers. Serge stayed behind at their loft.

"It's too early to eat, Joseph, but can we get a patio table and just watch the crowds. Let's try for a roof patio, it's easier to see."

They settled with a carafe of wine to take it in. A juggling clown passed on a penny-farthing bike, followed by acrobatic cartwheels and a fire throwing dare-devil. Bands played as children sang and danced on the street. Closer to the Arc de Triomphe, crews were building scaffolds and assembling benches for the winners' grandstand.

Leaning over the balcony, Emily was mesmerized by a face in the crowd. With binoculars, she zoomed in. It was a fashionably unshaven man with a pipe.

"Joseph! Look!" She handed him the binoculars. "Across the boulevard leaning against the lamppost."

Without speaking, he tossed some euros on the table and took Emily by the hand, pushing through partiers to the other side of the Champs Elysees.

Joseph kept his focus on the lamppost over the crowd. He was still there with his pipe in hand.

Reaching him, Joseph said. "Smoking's not good for your health. Is that cherry pipe tobacco I smell?" The man smiled.

"Daniel, we need to talk. What happened on the hill that night?"

"It would have been much better if you hadn't seen me. It's my day off!"

Daniel leaned in to whisper to Joseph, but instead he injected a paralyzer. Emily didn't realize it until Joseph collapsed.

Grabbing Emily roughly, Daniel said. "I hope you believe in angels, Emily. You are trusting in the wrong person, be on guard." He shoved something in her pocket and darted into the throng. He called back. "We'll meet again."

Over the noise, no one heard her pleas for help. She knelt over Joseph to help him up, and even cool water on his face didn't revive him.

I could call Yves. But that's foolish, he shot Daniel.

Joseph began to make noises.

"Come on," Emily said. "I need you to stand up. You've never needed coffee as much as now." She rubbed his cheeks and chest.

A nearby gentleman helped her dragged Joseph into a café.

"Merci, you are so kind to help us." She looked at the man to see if he was familiar. She was dubious about everyone at this moment.

Emily remembered every word Daniel spoke.

That we are trusting the wrong person? That we will meet again?

Joseph's squinted at her, his hand on his forehead.

"What happened?"

Emily leaned and gave him a kiss.

"What's important is you're alright. Are you strong enough to take the metro?"

"Not yet. My legs feel like I've been on a ship for a month."

Emily helped him to a chair; they would wait until he was back to normal.

Her hand felt into her pocket. On the back of a matchbook Daniel had written a note for her.

'7-22-11 Rouen, Garnier Obit'.

NINETEEN

Emily woke to the shower running and threw on her robe. In the living room, Serge had already folded his blankets.

She turned on cable news. The world was still at war and back home, Obama was still President and another election brewing. Locally, France had backed off an art tax, the Mayors of France were gathering forces against gay marriages, and the car maker Renault was embroiled in an industrial espionage scandal."

She turned the volume down. Most mornings she woke to thoughts of her sister in New York, and national and international politics meant little.

Life with Joseph was romantic and action-packed, but part of her wanted to settle to a simple country life. She sighed with a deepening exhaustion.

Serge came into the kitchen with a cheery greeting. He looked much better, clean-shaven, with a shirt and jeans borrowed from Joseph. He had emerged from the darker moods she'd seen when he arrived two days earlier. He started a pot of coffee.

Emily waited for the shower. Through the wall, Joseph whistled 'Que Sera Sera'. Every day was a new horizon for him that he faced with vigor, and she envied that.

"Come on Doris Day, I'm still waiting. Please leave a little hot water for me!"

Joseph turned off the taps and emerged with a towel around his waist.

"All yours, mademoiselle." He grabbed her and surprised her with a long kiss on her lips.

"Don't forget we have a house guest. Serge has been up awhile and brewed some coffee. It would be nice if you spent a little time with him while I get showered, do my hair, and get dressed."

"As you wish, Rapunzel."

After an intense conversation with Serge, Joseph called Yves. They spoke for twenty minutes and Yves was becoming more assertive, insistent on a meeting to hear the tape.

The reference to the dead agent sparked it, and it was personal to Yves. He prided himself on withholding emotions, but he wanted to hear Serge's account.

"Did he tell you about the murder of the agent?"

"It did come up briefly." Joseph replied.

There was an anguished silence.

"I didn't call to talk about that, Yves, but it's critical we find a way to take control of the Lyon vault. Were you able to make any inroads since London? I'm sure legal channels would be lengthy, but could we request it be sealed by the courts as evidence?" He hoped Yves was of the same mind.

"Leave that with me and I'll make inquiries at Interpol. Timing will be crucial and any police raids can occur simultaneously."

"Where and when can we meet?" Joseph asked.

"Philippe called me about a conference call on Friday. I'm not sure we should reveal everything about Serge. Let's focus on the Frizon and the system."

"Agreed."

Friday was windy and grey, the kind of day Emily liked to stay inside. They would take the Skype call from the loft. Emily and Joseph waited on the sofa and Serge paced to the balcony.

"Bonjour, Emily and gentlemen." Mr. Baker spoke first.

"Good morning, this is Samuel from California."

Mr. Baker had an announcement.

"Yes, I see we are all here. Joseph you have included a guest. Would you introduce him please?"

"Serge is a former accomplice in the forgery market, focused on finding justice. He gives his full support to our group mission."

"Without too much elaboration, I think what he has to say could be interesting." Yves said sarcastically.

"Thank you for including me. What I know will be helpful as I'm familiar with the operations of names you know: Monique Barbeau, Alexandre Duprés, Francois Tourneau, Jacques Charest, and Monsieur Robillard. Your discovery of the Frizon has just brought them to the surface and there's new work to do now. I can help"

Yves sneered at the comment, his mumbling heard over the call. He challenged again.

"You will need to persuade me first who rightfully owns the clock. I believe it belongs to the uncorrupted museum, although I admit to misleading Philippe otherwise." Yves was glad to change Serge's direction.

Emily entered their debate. "I'm afraid, Yves, you are mistaken in your conclusion. I've been withholding evidence until it is safe and the time is right. I have documentation and original papers held in my Swiss bank account in Paris that the Sauliere family is the owner."

The news shocked Yves, but he remained silent.

She continued. "I discovered the Frizon's feet would unscrew, with the cylinders revealing original documents that hadn't been seen for a hundred and fifty years."

Emily was in command. "Are you a little less confident now, agent?"

Yves was angry. "What documents? What are you talking about?"

"I never had one hundred percent assurance of your loyalty, Yves, so held it as my ace."

"How will we know for certain the Monett is an original?" Mr. Baker asked.

"I have examined it minutely many times inspecting every square inch, I'll know when I see it." Emily announced.

Philippe interjected. "If I may return to the situation at hand, it is urgent Robillard's art vault be sealed until the contents have been properly reviewed. Agent Yves, can you muster up the proper authorities to ensure this is done? Can we trust you not to interfere with the assets?"

"I pledge my commitment. You have my cooperation." Yves appeared to be coming on board at last.

Joseph said, "We need to discuss the future of Tourneau and Charest. They will know Monique and Alexandre's mission has gone afoul."

Samuel Wentworth asked that the next meeting be face-to-face. "If you all agree, there are sufficient matters for an actual boardroom meeting to resume this discussion, and the level of intensity is significant. May I defer to you, Nigel, to arrange a follow-up?"

"Certainly, but it's also time for us to bring in Scotland Yard."

They all signed off and Yves read through his new notes.

Emily took the laptop to the dining table and began a search for Garnier.

7-22-11 is a date. Could Obit be a death of a name Garner?

She was surprised how many Garniers died in July 2011.

GARNIER, George, 58, died 03-07-11, Chartres, France, survived by his wife and three daughters.

GARNIER, Estelle, 34, died 11-07-11, Lyon, France, long-time friend of Celeste and grandmother to two.

GARNIER, Roger, 32, died 21-07-11, Rouen, France, estranged from his family. Predeceased by his mother.

GARNIER, Roussell, 35, died 21-07-11, Rouen, France, died result of injuries.

GARNIER, Madison, 16, died 27-07-11, Tournai, Normandy, motor-cycle accident, leaves his mother, Helene, and sister, Marcie.

There were several announcements about Roger and Roussell but she was looking for a portrait. A faded photo black and white came up in a search for Roger Garnier. He was standing by a tractor with an older man at the wheel.

There were several articles that month in local papers about a body in a ditch, killed by gunshot. A man posing as his brother identified the body as Roger Garnier, but it went unclaimed.

Another July article speculated the murder may have been in Rouen. It was based on claims neighbors had witnessed a man with the victim's description in a small vintage car near the museum. Nothing was substantiated.

She called to Serge. "Serge, do you mind telling me about the murdered agent at Rouen. I know it took place about a year ago, but I didn't hear the full story."

"He was an Interpol employee who tripped himself. You have heard of him from your agent Yves. He was murdered by Charest at the warehouse. I tried to warn and protect him but he had been betrayed by someone he trusted."

"Do you know his name?"

"It was Roger. I'll have to think about the last name; it will come to me." Serge was evasive.

"Do you remember him driving a vintage red vehicle?"

"Yes. An old Isetta."

Searching the French Auto Club, she hacked into their membership.

Just as I thought. A 1965 red Isetta owned by Roger Garnier.

It was sold a year ago, the seller's address in a farming community outside Rouen. Emily jotted it down to follow up later.

Emily wondered if she should just say it, or hold it with her bundle of aces.

The night before the meeting in London, Serge met Emily and Joseph at Montmartre. He had taken a room at a boarding house in Rouen and hopped a commuter train to Paris.

The early morning flight to London had them at Wiltshire & Bradley with time to spare. Nigel Baker was already at work in his office.

"Come in, come in. Help yourself to coffee while we wait for the others."

"Is Mr. Wentworth joining us by phone?" Emily asked.

"As luck would have it, he had business in town for the week and he will be arriving shortly."

Philippe and Yves arrived next. Yves was carrying a large brown leather catalogue case.

"You, you . . ." Emily wanted a run at him.

"Just a minute, babe." Joseph said. "I'm sure he will have a really good explanation."

Yves ignored her and placed the case on the table.

He opened it and lifted out Emily's Frizon, wrapped in velvet. The back door was left open to expose the Monett. Some stood for a closer look and others leaned. They were all in awe.

Philippe addressed the table.

"Now that you have all viewed the Monett and the real Frizon, I'm proposing we work with an agenda." There was no objection.

"I need to offer my apologies for my part in the theft of the clock. From photos stolen from Joseph and Emily's loft, I studied and practiced, painting a forgery on the duplicate clock Yves provided. In the fleeting moments at the Citroen, I put the new clock into the velvet wrapping and stuffed the original under the trunk cover above the tire well, as Yves instructed." Philippe admitted.

"Yves, this is preposterous. May we see your identification?" Nigel Baker exploded.

Joseph turned to Yves. "Are you even really an Interpol agent?

"I am indeed an Interpol agent."

Yves pulled out an identification shield from his belt and showed it to the group. He didn't offer to pass it around.

"I have taken an oath to fight crime and inform police officials worldwide of underground crime, fraud and embezzlement. I admit, Joseph, I have not always been forthcoming, but with good reason."

Yves looked insulted as he thought his integrity was being challenged.

"Let's not dwell on Yves while we have critical issues to discuss." Joseph suggested.

Mr. Baker and Mr. Wentworth looked dubious but were ready to continue with the foundation's agenda.

Philippe circulated a proposed mission statement, and the next hour was dedicated to an open discussion of objectives. There were some minor amendments, but unanimous agreement to the direction.

He announced, "If everyone agrees then, we'll go forward with this draft mission. We'll start with a research program to explore new technology. A hundred percent guarantee is not possible in validating works, but we'll improve on what's available now.

"At the outset, I propose we nominate and appoint a board of directors beginning with Mr. Baker and Mr. Wentworth. Other additions will be discussed as we go."

Philippe looked at Joseph and Emily for their reaction.

Joseph looked at Emily. "We would be agreeable to that."

"Mr. Baker and Mr. Wentworth, would you work on the legalities to set up the foundation and incorporation?"

They were all impressed with the momentum.

Philippe stopped and looked for volunteers to continue in the preliminary process, ending with Yves. "Are you in on this with us?"

"That is likely my friend."

Yves consented, but a trust issue remained as Emily suspected he was protecting a lie of his own.

Philippe moved to conclude the meeting. "Good, we will make plans after the meeting. We have plenty on our plates for now. Can we meet again the same time next week? Perhaps Serge could prepare to share his knowledge of the forgery process when we meet next."

Wentworth, stated, "I'll stay in London until next week to work with Mr. Baker, so if it is okay with Nigel, this is a good place to meet again."

Emily asked, "Mr. Baker, do you have a secure facility to keep the Frizon until our next meeting?" She was still attached to her beloved clock.

"Of course, Emily. If you would accompany me to my personal safe and we'll secure it now before you leave. The only other people that know the combination is my dear wife, Eleanor, and my trusted executive, Lori James. After twenty years of marriage I have learned to trust my wife implicitly and Lori is above reproach."

Mr. Baker insisted on posting a twenty-four hour guard on the clock.

"As Philippe indicated, this might be worth $50 million. We can't afford to take chances.

"Joseph, I thought a representative of Scotland Yard would be at the meeting? Did you hear what happened?" Emily fretted back to Montmartre.

"Well that was my understanding too."

Serge sat across the aisle and was out of earshot.

Joseph whispered, "Emily, we need to keep Serge under the radar. His information can surpass his value to the police as a murder suspect. *Later* he could negotiate a confession in exchange for leniency, considering his cooperation in the case."

"Do you think he's safe in a boarding house in Rouen? If he gets in trouble, where will he go?"

Joseph nodded. "I'll ask him to stay with us a few days until we have a better picture."

Back at the loft they settled into the news channel until the phone rang.

"Hello Joseph, its Yves."

"What's up?"

"Can the four of us meet tomorrow? I'm in Paris for a few days. The George V in Le Bar at 6:00 p.m."

"I just need to check with my people. Hang on a sec." He knew Emily and Serge would be in agreement, and he confirmed it to Yves.

Serge and Joseph resumed their comfortable chatter.

"Joseph, you can see how widespread the theft of European art is, yet it filters away outside the news, sparing their criminal networks from exposure. Buying and selling takes place without records and those involved stay unnoticed."

Serge pointed at the TV. "Look, on the news! Another art theft in the Netherlands." Emily turned up the volume.

"They stole seven precious works . . . including a Picasso, Gauguin, and two Claude Monets."

Emily was excited. "I see Scotland Yard has taken over the investigation. That could make it easier if they get involved in our case."

Joseph nodded. "Need our ducks in a row."

CHAPTER TWENTY

At 5:00 p.m., Emily was dressed and ready. In a high society voice she teased, "How about kicking our heels at the George V, I haven't been to Le Bar in ages. It is so cozy and relaxing."

Serge played along. "The gentlemen have no objection."

The trio exited the loft and caught a taxi from St. Pierre to the Champs-Elysees. Behind them, a blue Renault weaved to keep pace and with a zoom lens Joseph saw the driver.

"Must be out on bail," he whispered to Emily and Serge. "Charest has sent his bull dog Maurice. He must be aware of your defection, Serge."

Joseph offered the driver a generous tip to lose him. The cabbie, a lean man with a cockney accent, responded with spirit and switched to the next lane with the pedal to the floor.

A high-speed political motorcade was ahead en route to the Hôtel de Ville, the municipal government building, and a motorcycle escort preceded them to hold back traffic. With gusto, the driver swerved in behind to join the entourage, accelerating past police whistles and their failed efforts to stop him.

In the commotion, Maurice was forced to a full stop to wait for traffic to resume. A police motorcycle took off after the taxi, but the driver was experienced with the streets of Paris and eluded him.

As the taxi jostled, Emily held Joseph's arm for balance, like a giddy girl on a Disney ride. It relieved some tension in the car, and again brought Serge to a smirk.

"Hey pal!" Joseph tapped the driver's shoulder.

"Stop somewhere near the George V, but not directly in front. Excellent job jockeying in traffic! Do you have a card, if I need you again?"

The man grinned, with most front teeth missing and others yellowed.

"Anytime, Monsieur. My enjoyment, here's my number."

They got out at the Louis Vuitton store and walked to the hotel, approaching the door on Avenue George V.

The doorman's uniform and manners were impeccable. "Bonjour, Madame et Messieurs. Welcome to the George Cinq, one of the world's finest hotels."

The foyer was opulent, with crystal chandeliers, polished brass, marble floors, and plush, overstuffed chairs.

A true Parisian palace, the hotel housed historic wine cellars. It was renowned as Eisenhower's home during the Liberation of Paris, and portraits of previous owners and guests furnished the walls.

The famous mahogany lounge was on the main floor and Emily requested a window table.

"Why would Maurice be on our tail, Serge?" Joseph hoped for a clue.

"I suspect they want me," Serge replied. "Some of their problems would diminish if I were out of the picture. But I'm looking forward to clearing my conscience with Scotland Yard. I'm not your regular murderer, I an equalizer. I believe in justice and I know I will serve time in prison."

Joseph knew Serge was sincere but it occurred to him criminals might commonly rationalize their motivations.

Yves was ten minutes late and came into the room out of breath, with his motorcycle helmet under his arm.

"Sorry to be late, but there was a motorcade, holding traffic . . . at every intersection."

Emily laughed out loud.

"Yves, you met Serge at our last meeting. He's from the Rouen auction house.

"We are appreciative that you have thrown yourself into the lion's den." Yves gritted his teeth with a compressed compliment.

Yves stepped closer to shake hands, and uttered words that didn't please Serge.

Serge's face was tight and severe, and Yves turned away.

Joseph and Emily watched the exchange, then the tension eased as Serge moved to the window. He stared to the street, then composed himself to continue.

Emily raised the big news item.

"This morning's headline was about the Kunsthal theft in Rotterdam. Scotland Yard says they detoured a sophisticated alarm, and speculation suggested they could have been involved with massive international debt. Those paintings would only be a minute fraction of the European black market, but the theft still endangers the integrity of respectable collections."

Yves nodded. "Emily, I enjoy your passion about art, so you might recall a daring gang robbery in Zurich in 2009, capturing millions of euros in famous pieces. And later, a Brazilian robbery in the night; these thieves are brilliant and may never be caught."

Emily's suspicions spiked again about Yves.

"You have a remarkable memory for details."

"That's part of my talent that got me into Interpol."

She thought his voice wavered and wondered if he were leading them off course, or just withholding Interpol facts.

Yves didn't detect her vigilance, and continued. "Last year several thefts took place right here in Paris."

"Yves, was Robillard involved in earlier thievery?" Joseph wondered if they were chasing amateurs while the main theft rings mocked them.

"Of course, they'd have something to do with it."

Emily thought Yves's behavior was erratic, possibly to throw them off a scent.

"We're to meet with them in London on Monday; should we now advance our meeting?" Joseph asked.

"Timing *is* critical to confiscate the Robillard ledger. Interpol will need to do the work across the borders. I'll coordinate with Philippe and my connections at Interpol."

Joseph and Serge spent the afternoon searching reports of art thefts. They dwelt on potential coincidences of perpetrators who could be involved at each robbery and compared alarm system technologies.

Emily needed a break from the intensity, and went out alone on a shopping trip. Inside her jacket pocket she carried an envelope, a birthday card to her sister.

It would have been futile discussing the issue with Joseph. They'd been warned not to have contact with the past and she was about to breach it.

The envelope was simple; no return address, and signed by her childhood pet name. Only her sister would know. The Hudson River would be beautiful this time of year and the autumn leaves spectacular in colors only God could create. She envisioned them and silently mouthed the words–amber, gold, crimson, burgundy, purple, sumac orange. Her throat felt a lump of emotion.

Past the Halle Saint Pierre museum, she turned right at the bank and entered the post office, looking to see that she was alone. The wicket had a line, and she waited to have her envelope weighed for overseas.

Emily used to be relaxed and free in Paris but now leaving the market area, she did habitual shoulder checks. She shouldn't expect to find anyone now, as the Frizon was safe in London.

Cigarette smoke twigged her senses, and the association made her think of Daniel's pipe tobacco.

A keyhole patisserie was ahead and she darted in and ordered brioche and jam with a tall black coffee. Glancing in the mirror behind the cashier, she checked the window reflections.

Emily opted for an outside patio seat sheltered by the overhang. She scoured the panorama.

The wine shop across the square had a large ceramic planter in front, and their walls were overwhelmed with ivy. A ruffled canopy was above the door and the fretted windows displayed their crates of vintage wines.

Behind the ceramic there was a movement. She watched it and nodded to herself.

Familiar . . . dark clothing, a tam, a cigarette.

"Give me a break! All I wanted was a half hour to myself." She spit the words out softly as she searched her memory.

It can't be Monique or Alexandre, they're in custody. Why would anyone tail me now?

She wouldn't recognize Tourneau or Charest. She wasn't amused by the interruption, but felt she could handle almost any surprise.

Emily dug for her cell phone to snap an image, but the man wasn't clearly visible even on a zoom.

Is this a set-up? The only reason for a tail would be to lead them to Yves . . . or even Serge.

She dialed Joseph giving him her position.

"Joseph, you can't leave Serge alone. If someone is following me, they'll know Serge is with us, a perfect opportunity to get rid of him."

Her manner was forced and Joseph knew she'd been pushed too far.

"Do you have the pistol I put in your bag?" He asked.

Emily was startled by his seriousness.

"Yes I do, Joseph"

He put his hand over the receiver and whispered to Serge, then came back.

"Em, you there?" He waited.

"Serge and I will come by the terraced roof way and take the guy by surprise."

They rushed from the loft hastily, picking up speed as they crossed yards and rooftop gardens to the streets behind.

Emily chortled seeing their silhouettes on the flat roofline above the shop. They descended to the balcony, and as the street momentarily cleared of pedestrians, Joseph rappelled down a clothesline cable landing on the man by the planter.

The noise brought a shopkeeper out with a broom, flabbergasted with two men scuffling on the ground, the taller man holding the younger one in a tight grip and pulling on his ear.

"Arrêtez! Arrêtez!"

The merchant waved his hands to stop the fighting in front of his store and as bystanders gathered, Joseph dragged the smoker to a narrow lane holding his face flat against the stone.

He screeched at the man, "What are you doing tailing my girl?" He flipped the man over to see his face.

"Well, if it isn't bumbling Maurice. Who sent you here?"

Maurice didn't answer.

"And what are you looking for?" Joseph knew the answer but wanted to drag it out of the squirming Maurice.

Serge approached Emily at the table. Her eyes were tired and she was ready to leave the patisserie. He looked at her kindly.

"Are you alright, Emily? Joseph and I can handle this, you go to the loft and we'll be along in a few minutes."

She took his suggestion and headed to rue de Saules. Seeing Marie and Toby at the flower shop put her at ease.

"Bonjour, Marie. A fine day, is it not? I brought you some pastries from the St. Pierre patisserie."

"Merci, Merci, you are too kind to an old lady."

Toby sniffed the corner of the box in Marie's hands.

Emily had to find ways to slow life's pace, and her time with Marie did that. She took a moment to notice the store's carts were in a semi-circle. She had never taken time before to appreciate these details that were important to Marie. Today the baskets were beautiful, bursting with chrysanthemums, asters, pungent calla lilies, orchids, gerbera daisies and roses.

She was marveling at the bouquets when Serge came up the hill alone. She excused herself to Marie and mounted the staircase to the loft. Serge went to the lane and up the back ladder, entering from the dining room.

"Where is Joseph?" Emily inquired with mild alarm wondering if she had put too much trust in Serge.

"He had Maurice arrested for violating his bail in the kidnapping case. He's finishing a police report; he'll be along in a few minutes."

"Serge, I was wondering if you would do some legwork. I found an address outside of Rouen, it's the seller of Roger Garnier's Isetta. It could be family. Emily handed him the address and the photo of Roger with the tractor.

Serge was blunt. "What if it leads to someone we know?"

Her eyes widened. "Then we will know. Be discreet and certain you are not recognized."

"Consider it done, Emily."

TWENTY-ONE

Rouen, France, July 2011
One year ago

Rene followed Dodger from Lyon to Rouen on the afternoon train. Dodger was at ease until the Paris stop when passengers crowded in around him. A fleeting look behind him put him on edge, but with a second look there was nothing.

Cloak and dagger life is too much. Interpol by day, burglar by night.

He snatched his leather bag and wormed between standing passengers toward the next car. Rene followed.

As the train rolled into the Rouen stations, Dodger took a leap from the platform to the ground below. Staying on the other side of the track, he was sure he had outwitted the tail.

Ignoring the pain from the hard landing, he skulked toward a lineup of 'take & leave' bikes. He knew the back lanes of Rouen like the back of his hand.

At the Rouen auction house, he ditched the bike at a fence line, and with no vehicles in the lot, he made the summation that the warehouse would be empty.

He picked the front door lock and removed his shoes to tip-toe down the hall. He had been here several times before while working for Interpol. They wanted evidence of Charest's involvement in the forgery exchange.

Listening, he heard other breathing, and backed up to the entrance. He found his shoes and looked for the bike.

It must have been Charest!

Rene stood in the adjacent alley. Dodger waited until long into the night for Charest to leave, and Rene waited too.

TWENTY-TWO

Rain was soothing against the glass patio doors, but the draft in the bedroom awoke Emily. The sky was grey and the cobblestone streets looked slippery. Her head ached and she poured a juice for herself.

She opened the shutters to listen to the bell of the sharpening man wheeling his hand-made trolley.

Coffee in the kitchen wafted to the bedroom, stimulating her to get going. Joseph and Serge were in the living room in front of the morning news.

"Is it raining in London too?"

Emily reached into the cupboard for Tylenol.

"It's grey but promises to clear this afternoon. Dress for the weather and we'll be fine." Joseph said.

Emily called from the kitchen, "What do you want in your omelets? The choices . . . mushrooms, spinach, tomatoes, shallots, peppers, leftover bacon? Oh, a good selection of cheeses."

Joseph got up to help. He pulled out his polished omelet pan. Handy in the kitchen, he fired up the burner.

Emily chopped fruit and sliced the banana bread as Joseph created his savory omelets. Serge made a second pot of coffee.

"Most impressive team work, fellas!" Emily enjoyed their initiative.

"Well, Emily, France has long been a country of protesters and women's equality has never been overlooked. We've been well trained." Serge kept the banter light.

Breakfast was ingested in twenty minutes. The St. Pierre bus was on schedule and using the unmanned train shuttle, they arrived at the Roissy Charles de Gaulle forty-five minutes before check-in.

The airport resembled a futuristic space station with fast trains tunneling through terminals, and finding their gate took twenty minutes, leaving them in a rush for the BA flight.

Paris to London was an hour and ten minutes, so short there was only time for newspapers and coffee before the pilot announced their descent.

From Heathrow they took a direct train to Paddington Station, and departed for Kensington. They didn't face any luggage delays as they had carry-ons and a light satchel.

Nigel Baker was waiting in the baggage arrival area. His limousine was purring at curbside, with the chauffeur holding a golf umbrella at the rear door. Whisking out into traffic, Mr. Baker pushed the button to raise the privacy glass.

Baker talked non-stop en route to the Wiltshire & Bradley office, relaying developments with Samuel Wentworth. His position on the Securities Commission gave him access to potential employee lists, with retired names more likely to produce a consultant looking for work. In preparation, he had drafted a Non-Disclosure Agreement for the new company.

Samuel Wentworth had applicable resources in California where technology and research was optimum. He located digital equipment and image editing software to evaluate authenticity and forged aspects of a painting. Advanced technologies of X-ray fluorescence were ready for RFP bids.

By the time the rest of the group arrived at Wiltshire & Bradley, Nigel had presented a clear picture to them.

Joseph inquired if they discussed it with Yves yet. Baker shook his head, but confirmed Philippe had been apprised.

Yves arrived late with two guests. "Emily and gentlemen, I would like to introduce Capt. James Macdonald and his assistant Sgt. John Newman, both from Scotland Yard."

Yves and the two men circled the table greeting each player.

"I'm sorry, Serge I don't recall your last name." Yves said.

Serge's face was red, and he shot back.

"Yves, do you really want to do this now in front of Scotland Yard? For the moment, we will keep this our secret, agreed?"

"It really isn't an issue to delay our meeting." Yves said. He fumbled with humiliation, and the others looked to each other trying to diffuse the awkward moment.

He gestured for the Scotland Yard men to begin. Capt. Macdonald stood to address the table.

"It's my pleasure to meet each of you. With the arrests at the London storage facility, we have become more attached to this case."

"I commend you all for your courage and commitment in tracing this forgery racket. Some of you have put your lives in danger, however, we ask you work with our office to limit future personal risks, in the UK. Agent Yves, I give my condolences to you for the loss of your partner last year."

He didn't see Serge's menacing scowl at Yves.

The Captain stopped as Serge rose. Yves sat back on his seat.

"Excuse me, Captain, I need to make something clear."

"Go ahead." The Captain found his chair and encouraged Serge to speak.

"The Interpol agent who was murdered last year in Rouen was my acquaintance. I am Serge Bouet. Captain, I'm afraid you will not like my background check. Agent Yves has known who I am from the moment he laid eyes on me. You will see I have turned a new leaf, otherwise there wouldn't be any reason to come forward and put myself in jeopardy."

Serge reached into his pocket and stepped across to Yves, placing an item on the table under his palm. He closed his fist around it and looked at Yves.

Everyone's eyes were on it as he pulled his hand back to release a silver ring with a raised triangle emblem and a blue sword.

"I believe that belongs to you now, *Yves*." The sarcasm on the agent's name couldn't be missed, and Joseph watched Emily.

The room stayed quiet, waiting for Yves's response.

Yves faced the Captain.

"Sir, this should become evidence with Interpol in France. The last time I saw this ring was on the hand of Monsieur Robillard." Yves didn't look at Serge.

Serge started again. "As you wish, Yves, but they *will* find out this ring is part of a set."

He looked at the Captain.

"I took this from the finger of Monsieur Robillard when we met in an alley in Lyon. There are three rings with this same emblem and sword. Do you have one, Yves?"

The Captain asked for a brief recess. Newman had noted everything on his iPad. They returned to the seats and MacDonald spoke.

"Serge, we did prescreen you before today and were informed of your involvement with Mr. Robillard. With the nature of this investigation and your information, we understand from French authorities those charges are postponed for the moment. But I do admire your courage in stating your background."

The meeting resumed to discuss suspected art frauds in the UK that could have been related to the operation. With so many inconsistencies, the discussions were postponed until each of them could be interviewed independently.

In his summation, the Captain advised he would work with French and Interpol authorities.

Preparing to adjourn, Emily spoke up. "Captain Macdonald, could I meet with you along with Philippe, to discuss documents I found in the Frizon that relate to the clock's ownership. You should be aware of this." Yves's head turned to Philippe.

The Captain, Philippe and Emily moved into Nigel Baker's private office.

"Henri and Madeleine Sauliere are Philippe's parents," she explained. "They know of my findings hidden in the spines of the clock. These documents will restore their good name."

Emily wanted knowledge of the certificates to be on record with Scotland Yard, not solely with Yves's contacts at Interpol. She explained the risk she and Joseph faced. If the Epte museum found out, they'd be ruthless to destroy the documents.

Captain Macdonald scribbled notes and thanked her. He held the door, handing them his business card with direct line access.

Yves accompanied Macdonald and Newman to New Scotland Yard's building for his follow-up.

Captain Macdonald handed Yves a numbered ID pass and started to register his name in the security log.

"Agent Yves, we can't continue unless you give us your full name. You know we require an Interpol security match of the photo taken as you entered our front door."

Yves whispered it to Macdonald, who entered in the building registry and wrote it in the day log he kept in the breast pocket of his uniform.

They took the elevator to a floor with multiple cubicles and soundproof dividers, and Macdonald retrieved a file from his desk.

"We'll go to a training room as I have something you should look at."

He led the way to a corridor with a dozen meeting rooms in a row, all with window views.

"In here." He opened the second door.

A player was lowered from the ceiling with the touch of a switch, already loaded with footage from selected museum and gallery robberies. Macdonald paused it on several occasions to point out two people that he suspected were involved in more than one heist.

"This one here." Macdonald used a pointer. "He is Frans Hillier, a well-known cat burglar. He drops from the ceiling by a wire, bypassing the laser beams. French born, but now resides somewhere in Tuscany. He's beyond our police jurisdiction, until we have an international warrant. Hillier is also in the security footage of a robbery at the Museum of Art in Paris in 2010. A number of paintings were taken there, including a Picasso and Matisse. Our profile of him indicates he likes to work alone."

Yves made his own notes. "Will you be giving me some photos?"

Macdonald didn't like the disruption "We'll continue for now and talk about details later."

"The next man involved in more than one heist is Liam Nuus, who can fairly be described as both radical and dangerous. He was involved in the theft at the Zurich museum of a Monett, Degas, a Cezanne and others. It's our experience that these thieves are contracted by people who have a collateral obligation in amounts well into the millions. Thieves are usually paid in diamonds or gold, an untraceable commodity."

He ran through each robbery image again, this time zooming on freeze frame shots. "Yves, please look at these and let me know if anyone is familiar to you."

Yves tensed, but made no comment when the theft of the Seefeld villa went up. The slide stayed on the screen for thirty seconds and he perused it, hoping faces were unrecognizable and that Macdonald wouldn't examine it further.

As another next image flashed, Yves commented as an attempted diversion. "I assume Swiss Bank accounts are used to transfer money offshore. These aren't local capers, but international trades of extraordinary value, with extremely high stakes."

He was relieved the Seefeld burglary passed without closer analysis.

"Interpol will be the organization to lead the way here." Yves said.

Captain Macdonald was looking over the top rims of his glasses, scratching his bald patch.

"These thieves blend back into society without arousing skepticism, their own families unaware of their moonlighting while working at normal day jobs. It will take hours of detective work tracing and infiltrating these circles. This isn't a Jack and Jill tactic. This is a manhunt."

Yves interrupted, searching for a foothold.

"Please slow down, Captain Macdonald. What areas of surveillance have been covered by Scotland Yard? Where did you leave off, and where is Interpol to pick up?"

"Of course, I'll give you the full briefing, starting with the UK robberies and our knowledge of known cross-border connections. I'll set up a meeting for Scotland Yard to come to Lyon. First, Interpol must seize the Robillard notebook."

Yves complied. "I'll make some calls and have an answer about Lyon before I leave this morning."

Macdonald shut off the video. "I'll take a closer look at the photos of the museum thefts, it's likely some would match the Interpol data."

Yves nodded.

TWENTY-THREE

Philippe approached the family farmhouse at Epte, reminded what a beautiful sight it was with its lush landscapes and leafy crops divided by bold strips of cornfields and sunflowers.

Henri was in the driveway, tinkering under the hood of his 70s farm truck. It was rusting at the wheel wells but served its purpose. Madeleine was on the back kitchen stoop hanging the washday laundry on a long double reel from the house.

They were surprised to see Philippe and stopped their work.

"Bonjour, Papa et Mama. It is a wonderful, sunny day for hanging the linens."

He greeted his father with a kindly touch on the back, and his mother held his face in her hands, kissing both cheeks.

"What brings you back home so soon?"

He asked, "Aren't you going to offer me some home baked goodies and a coffee first?"

She returned her handful of pegs to the basket at her feet and wiped her hands in her apron.

They pulled up chairs in the kitchen, and Madeleine brought in home-made bread and jam from the larder. A tea towel covered the loaf to prevent it from becoming crusty, and Philippe took several thick slices while it was still warm.

"Please tell me . . . I need to ask you, has Monsieur Tourneau been around to the house since I was last here?"

His mother glanced at his father and Philippe knew the answer. "We never invite him," she said. "He just barges in and harasses us about the Monett."

Madeleine bit her lip nervously, feeling vulnerable that she couldn't deter Tourneau. "He wasn't here long and we had nothing to say to him."

"I need to go and have a talk with the man." Philippe decided.

"I have much to tell you. Please listen to me carefully." He took a gulp of coffee.

"Remember the couple from Paris, and the story of a Monett clock? I saw the Frizon for myself and it is true. You already know about the scrolls she found belonging to the Saulieres. They will be returned to us, but what is in question is the future of the clock."

Philippe slowly described the proposed foundation. "I hope you will agree with me, Papa and Mama . . . we should donate the clock to the foundation, for sale at auction. You will receive a percentage right off the top and then an annual modest income dividend check from the foundation. All you'd need to do is attend a routine annual meeting. Papa, you will be comfortable for the rest of your life. You and Ma can travel or do whatever you want.

"In exchange, they will retrieve Angelique's portrait, believed to be in the hands of Monsieur Tourneau. There will be a public exhibition. I suggest we'd loan Angelique to a Paris museum to be appreciated." He knew that any other way would bring pressure to his parents, beyond their ability to cope.

Philippe sipped again, and his eyes looked up for his parents' response.

Henri and Madeleine went outside to talk. Returning, Madeleine came and hugged Philippe with tears in her eyes. He would have their full agreement and support.

An automobile rumbled in the lane and she jumped up.

"Mon dieu, Monsieur Tourneau is back again!"

"Papa, may I borrow your rifle for effect?"

Philippe reached to the rack over the door and lowered it.

Tourneau stomped up the stairs and across the porch. He was livid and shouted through the screen door.

"Philippe! I heard you came from the train station, I want to talk to you. Put that thing down."

He was belligerent, his anger out of control.

Philippe kicked the door open with his foot and lined the rifle barrel to Tourneau's head. He dropped his left hand to his pocket and turned on the transmitter that Joseph had given him.

"You are trespassing, Tourneau! We are filing a restraining order against you."

Tourneau look surprised but persisted. "You are making things difficult for yourself, Philippe. I have people that will cut you down before you make it to the court house."

Madeleine inched her way back to the hall and dialed 112 for local police assistance. Tourneau didn't see it, or he would have abandoned the fight.

"Three witnesses here! And you've made a death threat to us." It took self-control for Philippe to refrain from blurting about the scrolls.

Tourneau eyed Philippe and the situation, considering a rush. "The Frizon belongs to the museum, and you *will* return it. If not, one day soon you may find that a member of your family has met with tragedy."

"Tourneau, you're out of time. You are hereby under arrest for death threats, harassment, propagating forgeries, and your involvement in Robillard's scheme. I'm sure the police will have a longer list."

Two police vehicles pulled onto the property, sirens bleeping intermittently. Tourneau turned in dismay.

"You won't get away with this, Philippe. You won't! There are other people." His threats faded as an officer thrust his hands behind his back.

"Is Agent Gervais with you?" Philippe asked the officers.

A detective stepped forward.

"Monsieur Gervais, you should be receiving evidence from Interpol and Scotland Yard about Tourneau of the Epte museum. I also have a new tape and witnesses to today's conversation. Tourneau has just threatened our lives. There must be no opportunity for bail in this case." Philippe was succinct.

Gervais was already aware. "You are Philippe Sauliere then. I finished the report and admit your work is admirable. Now we have Tourneau!"

Some fight was still left in Tourneau. "It's entrapment . . . Monsieur, you can't arrest me!"

Gervais continued with Philippe. "It wasn't a planned confrontation, the man can't seem to stay away from us. You do know he is tightly connected with the auction house in Rouen, don't you? With court approval today, a raid is about to take place there within the hour. Would you care to observe it?"

"Sorry Ma! I'll be back for supper."

The first car left with Tourneau, and Philippe joined Gervais's car to Rouen.

Philippe directed the detective up the metal staircase at the auction house. A second police car and a Ducato van arrived at the loading dock with sirens silent, then Yves in an unmarked Renault. The policemen wore bullet-proof vests and protective shields, forming a procession on the stairs.

Philippe suggested Charest was likely in his office, past the hallway joining the warehouse to the showroom.

The tactical unit separated and advanced quickly toward the connecting door. Gervais was on their heels, followed by Yves.

A laborer, who Philippe didn't know, was removed quickly from the warehouse without resistance. In a burst of force, the office door was kicked open, exposing a startled Charest struggling to get out of his grand leather chair. He reached to his desk for a gun.

"Go ahead, Charest! Try to get a shot off, and we'll put one between your eyes. Give us the excuse."

Yves and Detective Gervais advised Charest of his rights and cuffed him. "You are charged with the murder of Roger Garnier, and numerous counts of forgery and illegal transport of stolen property."

Charest was caught off guard and raised his brows at mention of the dead Interpol agent.

"You have no proof I killed Roger Garnier!"

He yelled toward the front of the building. "Therese! Call my lawyer."

A young female desk clerk peered down the hallway.

Detective Gervais approached Therese, asking if there were others in the building. Everyone was accounted for except a driver, who was expected within the hour. She was asked to come to the station to make a statement.

A police guard stayed on site until a crew arrived to secure the paintings and files, and his logs and manifests.

Police cars were dispatched immediately to the Epte museum, finding only a security guard and a laborer in the yard. Pallets in the basement were removed to dry storage along with Tourneau's files, and the building and contents were sealed to await the audit team.

Tourneau and Charest were taken to separate rooms at the Vernon police station for interrogations. Under the pressure they respectively protected their personal interests, but generously incriminated the other.

TWENTY-FOUR

Joseph and Emily heard the same day about the Charest and Tourneau arrests and the raids.

In celebration, Joseph arranged to surprise Emily with a late dinner reservation at Le Meurice Hotel, overlooking the Tuileries Garden.

He asked Emily to wear her blue Channel dress for a special evening out, then popped out to a cigar shop for an English language newspaper. Absorbed in the news, he sat at the corner with his coffee while Emily fussed with her hair at the loft.

Joseph passed a fine jeweler, stopping at their elegant display of drop diamond earrings. He hadn't purchased jewelry or flowers for Emily since this whole affair began. They boxed the earrings, and he whistled up the hill with a bounce in his step. At Marie's basket, he selected twelve perfect roses.

They had time and freedom again at last, and Joseph wanted to resume their courtship. He was happiest being with Emily and not on a case with Yves.

He bounded up the staircase. She was breathtaking to him, standing in the living room waiting for his return. Joseph felt an odd sensation, and his eyes began to sting and pool. He took her into his arms and kissed her. He hadn't taken time to feel this way since last Christmas, and the subsequent months wasted away.

Enthralled in the exquisite dinner at Le Meurice, they were a couple again. Music floated up from the grand piano, and he looked into her eyes, feeling they were again reuniting.

Emily quietly enjoyed the moment.

But it would be an awkward time to share her burden with him. She longed to feel fulfilled and had felt this way for so long.

Emily told Joseph of her inquiry to Le Cordon Bleu cooking school, with a campus where she could train to be a pastry chef, then continue with gastronomique schooling. Or an alternative could be the Equis Institution outside Lyon where she had dined with Yves.

Taken aback by her need to stretch her wings, it hit him. She had given up too much to be with him. In New York she'd been an aspiring artist on the doorstep of award winning recognition when she encountered Joseph.

His life threw them into a dalliance with crime and deception as they brought down Sanderson's law firm.

Emily had never said she was unhappy, but Joseph knew she longed for new ways to express her talents, and that she pined to see her sister.

Her blue eyes sought his encouragement as she spoke and waited for Joseph's reaction.

"Joseph, we're a pair. You are my best friend in the world. I can't do something like this unless you support me to follow my dream. If it can be the Paris option, I'll only be gone six hours a day for four days a week."

She laughed. "Think of the pastries I could make for you."

He liked the bribe. "I don't care about the pastries, but I don't want to lose you."

"Joseph, you'll never lose me, you're my number one priority. But I need to accomplish something on my own. You don't want me to be dependent on you for the rest of my life, do you?"

"Actually, I do. I want to take care of you, keep you safe and show you how much I love you every day."

"Can't we do both?" Emily was touched by his sensitivity and had much to ponder.

Leaving the Le Meurice, Joseph stepped out to the valet area to hire a taxi. He stood erect and focused across the street. It was dark, and the man nearby struck a match.

"It's our friend, Daniel. I wish we could get him to stay put and explain the mystery that surrounds him."

Emily was no longer shocked easily.

"What are we going to do?"

"You stay here. I'm going back into the hotel and out the parkade entrance. I can get across the street without drawing his attention."

"I don't like this, Joseph. Remember your last encounter?"

"I remember. I have a score to settle."

"Be careful . . ." Her words faded as he was already on his way.

Joseph planned to take him from behind, near the limos on the boulevard. Daniel surprised him, stepping out as he approached.

"Hello, Joseph. I told Emily we would meet again."

"What the heck is going on?"

"It's complicated. Why don't we join Emily for a night cap?" Daniel was nonchalant.

The pair returned to the Meurice and took a table in the corner of the elegant lounge.

"Daniel, I'm glad to see you again. But you have me totally befuddled." Emily spoke softly.

Daniel opened up to them. "When I was young, my mother ingrained a lot of scripture in me. Might be hard to believe when you see me now."

Joseph wasn't ready to accept a phony plea for acceptance. "How can you say that? Your life has been a fraud since we've known you?"

Daniel continued, "Mull over these words. 'There is an appointed time for everything, and a season for everything under the heavens'. You did not find me by accident, Joseph. You both need to work on patience."

Emily wasn't grasping Daniel's words at all.

Joseph asked. "When we met you at Montmartre, you were taken out before our eyes by a sharpshooter. Yet, you are here before our eyes."

"You are aware of Agent Yves. He has led you and misled you. My mission with Interpol is to follow Yves and to ask for your help to reveal the truth."

"What is 'the truth'?" Emily needed it in simple terms.

"You see people the way they want to be seen. Many people lead double lives with ease and without suspicion."

Joseph asked, "Are you saying that someone like Yves is living a double-life? That's not possible, he is a devoted agent focused on rescuing the art world. Granted, his ethics are a bit different."

"I am not here to dissuade you, but I need your help." Daniel lit his pipe.

"Lay it out, Daniel." Joseph was tiring from the long introduction.

"There's a man named Robert Garnier, who worked with another cat burglar who used the con Dodger Garnier."

"You're not making a lot of sense."

"A year ago, a lone thief broke into a Paris museum and wriggled through some vent tubing that would be impossible for a regular size man to fit. He went out a window and was caught on camera, but was never found. Nor the paintings.

We believe he connived with Robert to secure the paintings. Robert did some freelance work for Charest in the past, and knew the layouts of the auction house and its warehouse."

"I'm not seeing where we come in." Joseph said.

"Emily and Joseph, I need to ask you to adopt a double-life. We've concluded Dodger is the lithe thief and Robert stashes them, possibly at the Rouen warehouse. You are close to Yves and we would like you to work that angle for any information leading to the other two."

"Implausible, Daniel," Emily pleaded. "We can't stretch ourselves that thin!"

"You have transmission equipment, Joseph? Use your eyes and your ears and you will see this differently."

No one spoke for a few minutes.

"We don't promise anything." Joseph gave in.

"Good, and neither will I."

The case of the Frizon's title was reviewed by the French court, ruling that the clock was in Bouleau's possession for safe-keeping on behalf of Charles Sauliere.

Bouleau was brought before the judge and questioned on how he became custodian. In the hearing, he was no longer the innocent old man, and on persistent questioning he changed his story, confessing he knew of the Monett.

Monsieur Bouleau said he'd inadvertently spoken of the Monett years earlier at the Rouen auction house, causing thugs to raid his store looking for a canvas Monett, with no idea it was in the clock.

He presented a questionable scenario that his nephew pushed him to sell the clock to avoid being targeted again. He said the nephew had insisted if the painting were exposed, their family reputation would be clouded and labelled as robbers.

But Bouleau waffled with inconsistent testimony. When he refused to provide the nephew's identity, the judge levelled a contempt charge. He was ordered to return the 1000 euros to Emily, and had thirty days to come forth with the nephew's information. The Rouen police department started his file.

Emily was satisfied finding that the clock would be returned to the Sauliere family. The museum catalogued the portrait of Angelique and the court agreed it would also transfer to the Saulieres, to be held at the museum pending a permanent exhibition site.

Joseph and Emily took the Eurostar to Vernon the following Monday. Walking hand in hand, Emily slowed to add wild gladiolas and periwinkle to the bouquet she was creating for Madeleine.

Madeleine Sauliere insisted they stay at the farm overnight to discuss the exhibition. Not so much the hors d'oeuvres and refreshments, but the color she should wear to blend with the pastel portrait of Angelique.

Philippe was in the field on his father's tractor. Even before the door opened, Joseph anticipated the warm aroma of freshly baked bread, and he wasn't disappointed. Emily donned an apron and stood alongside Madeleine who was fixing a Chicken Chasseur. Mushrooms, shallots and tomatoes were already in the pan and Emily added the wine, brandy and Lyonnaise sausages. A roasting pan of winter vegetables and roasted garlic potatoes was in the oven.

Over the meal, the Sauliere boys told a hunting story of the time they came across a 200 kilogram boar. Philippe was animated and waved his arms.

"Shrub bushes get overrun with boar in the fall and farmers can bag as many as they want." His eyes rolled. "Oh, the meat is such a sweet delicacy, like pork but the color of beef. These animals are robust and capable of killing a man; their heavy tusks are fair warning. This one had no fear and came too close to the farm."

Felix jumped in and took it over. "Stefan got the rifle, and Philippe and I went to the barn for pitch forks. We chased it to the back field and Stefan fired, hitting her in the head. But it only angered her and she charged. Stefan wasn't fast enough with the old gun for another shot."

Philippe stood, shouting the best part.

"Felix was close enough he thought he could jump on her back and hold on to her tusks. He leaped and landed on her back but her girth was so wide he couldn't right himself."

The boys were all standing now. "The boar just ran in circles to shake Felix off. Stefan got the rifle in focus but the risk of shooting Felix was too great; she changed directions faster than Felix could swing, and he slid off to the dirt. Stefan and I distracted her and Felix ran for the house."

Madeleine added, "Felix, show them your scar." The kitchen rocked with laughter.

"Took me three months before I could sit down comfortably." Felix pretended to rub his behind. "But her big head is hanging over the fireplace so I have the last laugh."

"Thanks to Felix, our freezer was full of sweet pork ribs and roasts for the winter." Philippe said.

With the table cleared, Philippe sat with Joseph and Emily and his parents to discuss the exhibition.

"Of course, the Sauliere family including my father's uncle and his family will come from Normandy," Henri said.

They all threw in names as Philippe wrote. Baker and Wentworth, Serge Bouet, Captain Macdonald and Sergeant Newman, the Mayor and dignitaries in Vernon and Paris, the new manager at Epte Museum, Detective Gervais, and the Dean from École de Louvre. It went on and on . . . heads of galleries, museums and schools, and the media.

Emily added, "Don't forget the art collectors who had originals stolen by Robillard."

"We could try to get lists of patrons from some galleries and museums; the more people that view the Frizon Monett, the greater the interest will be at the auction," Emily suggested.

Philippe announced his coup.

"We have a prestigious salon at the Musée du Monde near the Tuileries Gardens. It's a plum for them to exhibit both the Frizon Monett *and* the new presentation of 'Angelique Sauliere'. They will be in bulletproof glass, with the scrolls on the wall with wired security. The first Friday will feature a spectacular black tie gala for the Who's Who."

This was a proud moment for Philippe in front of his parents. The Sauliere were polite but quiet, but Joseph detected they needed to hear more about how it would affect them.

Joseph expounded. "A respected house will conduct the auction of the Frizon on site ten days after the exhibition closes. A legal document is being drawn up assuring you of a percentage and an annual return."

Madeleine glowed. "I haven't seen Angelique's portrait yet but I know it will be beautiful. The Musée du Monde has been so kind and generous and I understand they've offered to hang 'Angelique' in their gallery on loan for an indefinite time."

Emily reached across and touched Madeleine's shoulder. "Henri and Madeleine, you'll be the stars of the Gala. Madeleine, we'll shop at the Haute Couture fashion houses on the Champs Elysees. You'll have the gown you always dreamed of." The idea was a hit with Madeleine.

They played a French card game called Milles Bourne into the evening, laughing and sharing stories until Emily could no longer hold back her yawns.

She excused herself to retire and Joseph followed a polite distance later.

TWENTY-FIVE

Preliminary hearings for Jacques Charest moved quickly. Based on the strength of evidence Charest was denied bail, facing a charge of homicide voluntaire for premeditated murder in ordering Serge Bouet to kill Monsieur Robillard. Serge had a secondary motivation but his date with the court would be postponed to deal later with his own fate.

Tourneau and Charest were arraigned for multiple charges of fraud and forgery, and Monique Barbeau and Alexandre Dupres faced prosecution for kidnapping, transporting stolen goods, and fraud.

The court had heard Serge's testimony against Charest, and gratefully documented his knowledge and evidence of forgeries sent over the years to unscrupulous dealers and auctions.

The death of Roger Garnier remained unsolved, but the Judge grilled Serge on his knowledge. He declared Garnier had worked in the museum before attracting Charest's suspicion. Serge attempted to warn him, but he insisted he was close to blowing the lid off the forgery operation and needed more time.

On the day of the murder, Serge overheard Charest instructing an unknown person that Garnier had to be removed. Although Serge was at Roger's side when he succumbed, he didn't see the shooter. The shot was from the doorway.

Another wave of charges named certain Charest employees, with further evidence of conspiracy to defraud.

Yves was at the Paris court hearings, and since the meeting with Daniel, Joseph was more acute to Yves's reactions and movements. He saw him flinch when the topic included Roger.

At the name, Emily also flinched. "Joseph, the clue Daniel gave me on the matchbook led to a farm address for the deceased Roger Garnier. Serge was to check it but I haven't heard anything yet."

"We'll call Serge," Joseph said.

Joseph was puzzled why Yves chose to remain in the back section of the courtroom. "He's an unusual man. He is always in charge, whether it's subtle or vocal. I wonder why it's subtle today."

At the end of the session, Yves left quickly, down the wide staircase to the boulevard. His yellow Citroen was at the curb.

"Come on Emily, we need to follow him. Our rental is down the street."

The pair scurried to the car and took pursuit. Yves was skilled at high speeds and narrow lanes, and it was challenging to keep him in sight.

"Do you think he knows we are following him?"

"It's hard to say. Do you have a map? Can you see what could be ahead?"

Yves spun onto the 8th Arrondisement and stopped at an apartment building near the river. Yves ran into the building and they waited in the car. Emily snapped pictures of the street and building.

An hour later, Yves came out with a roll of paper in his fist.

He asked, "Should we check this out, or keep on with the chase?"

"Do you have your pistol in your bag?"

"Always! I'll let you out to check the building and I'll head for Yves. There's a bar at the corner, I'll meet you there."

Without further discussion Emily hopped out of the car. Nervously, she composed herself and walked into the apartment lobby. A resident directory was on the wall.

Ah, ha, Robert Garnier, 3B.

It was a four story building without a lift. She climbed to the third floor and loitered outside 3B on the pretense of waiting for a friend. Ten minutes passed and she was ready to leave. The unit door burst open and a man, oblivious to her, ran past and down the stairs. He didn't seem to notice her.

Confident she hadn't blown her cover, she continued toward the corner bar.

Her cell rang. "I've lost Yves, so I'm coming back for you."

"Joseph, I'm at the bar and so is the man from the apartment building. The dead agent was Roger Garnier, right?"

"Yes, that was it."

"This man is Robert Garnier. Too close to be a coincidence."

The loft phone was ringing as they came up the stairs. Fumbling with the key, Joseph ran in for it.

"Hello. Who's calling?"

He heard panting and gasping.

"Serge . . ." The voice trailed off.

"Serge, Serge! Are you still there?" The call went dead.

Joseph turned to Emily.

"Do we know where Serge is, or what his phone number is?"

"What's the matter, Joseph?"

"It was Serge. He couldn't to tell me anything but was definitely in distress."

"Call Philippe! He'll know how to reach him."

Searching her bag, pulled out a ragged notebook with Philippe's number."

Joseph called and briefed him.

"I'm sorry, Joseph, I don't where Serge would be. The last address I have is a boarding house several blocks from the auction house. It's above a used book store."

"Thanks, Philippe, but Emily and I will go there now."

"Absolutely, Joseph."

Joseph turned to Emily. She had picked up the cue and was filling a backpack.

"Toby?" she asked.

"Let's get a start without him and see how things pan out. If we don't have any luck, you could get him tomorrow."

She nodded, and stood ready at the door.

Joseph took ammunition from the desk drawer and packed two pistols and a transmitter.

Few words were spoken on the train.

Hiring a cab at the train station, they stopped in a shopping area and went on foot for the bookstore.

"There it is, Joseph." She pointed to a three level building in need of repair.

Next to the shop entrance, a door led to the upper apartments. The directory inside listed 'Serge Bouet' in Unit 4B.

Joseph went ahead to the second floor. The door was ajar and he called through the opening.

"Serge. It's Joseph."

He waited, then shoved the door with his foot.

"He's not here," he called back. "It looks like the last thing he did was call us."

Emily picked up the dangling handset and tried the redial option. It rang to their Paris number. Beside the phone on the desk, a note pad had a half-torn sheet.

"It looks like Serge was writing something that was removed."

Emily held the pad up to light bulb, feeling the impression on the paper. With a pencil from her bag, she rubbed the graphite over the indentions.

The exposed letters read: *'Char – Rene – Seefeld'*'

"The only thing making sense is that 'Char' might mean Charest," Emily surmised. "But he's behind bars."

"But he could still have men lurking around," Joseph said. "We should get to the auction house; it'll be sealed up and monitored, but we can't rule it out. Maybe Serge was there."

The auction building was wrapped in yellow police tape. Walking to the back, they stopped at fresh mud tracks on the steps inside at the back.

Emily went closer. "The tracks don't come out. Either he wiped the mud off inside . . . or more likely he's still in there."

Joseph's finger was on his lips and leaned his ear to the door. He reached to the back of his belt for his revolver and slowly turned the knob. It released.

"Odd this isn't locked." He whispered.

"Careful, Joseph."

Lying on the warehouse floor was Serge, his mouth gagged and his wrists and ankles bound.

Joseph crawled over to Serge.

"Are you okay?" The body was limp and Joseph rubbed his arms hoping for some response. His hand was wet and sticky.

"It doesn't look good, Emily. Looks like he's been shot." He looked toward the hall.

"You stay here with Serge. Do you have a pistol?"

She nodded and reached into her jacket.

Emily froze when the eerie sound of a pistol hammer clicked in her ear. A hand covered her mouth but she managed a whimper.

Joseph turned to see a man standing at the rear door with his arm twisted around Emily's throat and a gun to her head. The man was lithe, wearing black pants, sweater, and a balaclava over his face to disguise himself.

Joseph stood up with his hands raised over his head in surrender.

"Step away from him." The gunman gestured for Joseph to move into the open, away from Serge. Put your guns on the ground!"

A moan eased from Serge's body.

Joseph smelled propane gas and heard hissing tanks from the offices and across the warehouse.

"You won't shoot. The whole building will blow with you in it." Joseph challenged.

The man replied in a disguised voice. "You have about five minutes. If you value your life, you will go immediately! Take the kid with you."

"I'm sure I recognize the voice. Is it you Yves?"

Joseph took two steps forward and surprised the man with a foot karate chop, kicking the gun across the floor.

"Run now, Emily! I'll be right behind with Serge."

By the time Joseph dragged Serge down the back stairs, Emily had hotwired a car from the alley. He pushed Serge into the back seat, and the car propelled from the alley spitting dirt.

A thundering blast blew out the back door and a section of cinder blocks, followed by a cannonball of flame and debris. A shard of metal ripped into their car hood and a rod impaled the engine.

"Don't stop, Em!" He shouted.

The car was slowing down.

"It's the engine."

"I'll call for an ambulance. Don't get out of the car with all the debris flying."

A black mushroom cloud rose to the sky as nearby residents flooded to the scene to witness the spectacle.

Serge was rushed into surgery suffering excessive blood loss, and Joseph and Emily waited for three hours in Emergency. During the wait, detectives interrogated them and required a statement.

"You folks are lucky to have escaped the warehouse."

"We went looking for Serge and found him with a bullet wound. The shooting had taken place before we arrived. The smell of gas was heavy and we took off seconds before the building blew." Joseph stated.

Emily felt guilty for not admitting to her suspicion of Yves. She wondered what made her protect him.

"Did you see anyone else in the building?"

"There was a guy not far from Serge when we came in the back door. It wasn't much of a conversation as we smelled the gas. He was dressed in black with a balaclava so we didn't have a chance to recognize him."

While they were talking with the officer, a doctor arrived still in green scrubs.

"Monsieur Harkness?"

"Yes, we are friends of Serge Bouet. Is he okay?

"Surgery went well. The bullet went into his shoulder missing major organs and arteries. He is in recovery and should be able to go home in a day or two."

The doctor turned to the detective and handed him an envelope.

"Here is the bullet. I presume you'll need it for your case."

"Yes, thanks, we will send that to ballistics."

The detective resumed with Joseph and Emily. "The fire is still burning, but in the aftermath of the explosion, we're finding many shreds of canvases. It will take forensics months to match up the puzzle. Also, a leather artist's tube on the ground with the initial 'R', do you know what that means?"

"I expect it meant 'Robillard', an art thief who was murdered in Lyon weeks ago."

"I'd like you to look at these photos and see if any of this makes sense to you."

The detective passed his iPhone to Joseph loaded with images taken on the spot.

The photo that alarmed Joseph had three partial canvases protruding from half an artist's tube. They zoomed and Emily immediately identified two of the pieces, Cezanne's *Boy in Red* and Monett's *Poppies*.

"Zurich!" Emily announced.

"What do you mean?" the detective queried.

"When we went to find Serge, we recovered a note. One of the words was '*Seefeld*'. There was a masterful art robbery there some years ago. These paintings were among them, and a specialist would know if they are originals or forgeries. Looks like they were stored in the warehouse and someone was making a get-away with them."

Emily bit her tongue fearing she had implicated Serge.

"Was anyone else seen fleeing the building?" Emily asked.

"Yes, a security camera at a utility pole in parking lot gave us a grainy picture. It shows the three of you escaping, followed immediately by a man who went to the alley."

"Curious . . . could I have a look at the footage?"

"The two of you need to go to the police station to look at mug shots of previous burglaries."

"We'll go, but first I need to see Serge."

They were only allowed minutes with him, and he assured them of his impending recovery. He was distant and troubled and refused to discuss the warehouse.

"Serge, let us help you." Emily offered.

"We know about Seefeld."

"You *can't* know about Seefeld. I'm not a thief. I had nothing to do with that!"

"We know you didn't do it, but you know who did."

"Emily, I've already put both of you in danger. I can't say more; it is best you don't know about the warehouse. At a later time I will be able to tell you."

"Anytime you need us, you must call." Joseph patted Serge's arm.

Across from the hospital a man watched with binoculars fixed on the front door.

TWENTY-SIX

The exhibition at the Louvre was called 'Late Raphael', highlighting astounding Italian Renaissance works and drawings by Guilio Romano.

For Emily, it was a dream to be able to spend time here. A magnificent edifice, it dated to the twelfth century housing royal guests and became a museum in the 1800s. It was now a mecca for artists, students and tourist.

She wanted Joseph to understand her passion and couldn't comprehend why it wouldn't be in everyone's blood.

"The Renaissance is my favorite art period, Joseph. I could spend days here."

He tried to sound convincing. "I'm sure I'll enjoy it too, but I wasn't thinking of the whole day." She pursed her lips and nodded.

"You'll change your mind when you see these. We'll bring the iPad and do our own audio tour."

"In that case, I'll be sporting."

She took his hand. On the way they passed L'Orangerie and she talked and he listened about the murals of Claude Monet's Water Lilies.

"Emily, can you believe this? When we were in New York, Paris was the place we only dreamed of, and now we're here in the world's most romantic city, with history on our doorstep."

The crowds were thick as they worked their way to the Pyramid entrance. "It's amazing Philippe got to study here," Emily said. "His work is incredible, but when the press releases the whole story, what will happen to his five years of study?"

A myriad of signs at the entrance pointed to the selected works and collections. At admissions, Joseph asked about membership and the Patron's programs, but his effort for names didn't succeed.

"I am sorry, Sir, everything is online, and on our site you'll have ample choices for donations and support. You'll understand we must protect our members' privacy." A line was building behind him. "Do you wish to purchase day admission for the exhibits?"

"Yes, two adults please."

Emily tucked her arm in Joseph's elbow, and he handed the woman his 24 euros.

Inside, he lamented, "That didn't go as well as we hoped, but I understand the privacy issue. If I were a member, I'd expect the same. Over there . . . Starbucks! We'll stop and plan our route."

Nigel Baker phoned to arrange another meeting. Wentworth was already back to California, and had proposed another Skype conference.

Baker was concerned about Serge's injuries, hoping he'd be well enough to attend.

"Joseph, are we in danger? Is there a threat to the members of the foundation?"

"I don't think so. It appears the explosion was intended for the warehouse, and unfortunately Serge was there at the time. But he is recovering well." He glossed over the fact that Serge was dragged to it.

In his manner, Baker asked. "Shall we set the telephone conference for Friday?"

"Fine with us."

"It would be reasonable for each member to put in a $10,000 US loan contribution, to fund opening legal fees and the related costs for set-up and consultants. The auction funds from the Frizon won't be available for at least another month."

"We will take care of our end, Nigel." Joseph assured.

Nigel had been unable to reach Yves and asked Joseph if he'd advise him of the meeting.

Joseph dug for his wallet and searched for Yves's direct number. It rang seven times without an answer.

"I'm wondering, Emily, should we go to Lyon and find Yves? Or if you'd rather stay here, I don't mind going it alone."

"I don't see any reason why I shouldn't go with you. We've been a team for the past year and that's the way it should remain." Emily was unsure if he had another motive. Do you have an objection?"

"That's what I hoped you would say." It was awkward and he was embarrassed; he hadn't meant to sound abrupt.

"When should we go?" Emily asked.

"Well, this is Wednesday and the Skype meeting is Friday. So we don't have time to waste. How is now . . . ?"

Joseph was in mid-sentence when Emily pulled her overnight bag from under the bed.

Emily made a face and he laughed, the tension gone. She added, "By the way, has anyone talked to Serge since he left the hospital?"

"I'll give him a call to be sure."

Joseph dialed Serge's number in Rouen, then hung up.

"No answer for Serge either? I wonder if the two are connected in some way." Emily mused.

"Definitely ill will there. Serge distinctly had a grudge . . . did you see that too?" Joseph replied. "Something to do with Roger Garnier and his last words."

"Will we ever know?" Emily asked.

"Serge was angry enough that he won't hold back for long; he wants to get even.

Joseph was partial to his worn satchel, and packed it with a minimum of clothing, listening equipment, and lenses. His shirt pockets were filled with his tools.

In Lyon, they returned to the coffee shop that Yves had recommended to Emily when she was the lookout for the Robillard rendezvous.

She had a poutine and Joseph a Monte Cristo sandwich, each with a fresh dark roast mug.

From their vantage at the patio table, they had a direct view of the Interpol building. Raising the camera, Emily focused on the front door and took a few pictures to justify her tourist look.

Smartly dressed men and women in suits passed through the revolving doors, but no one with a turtle neck sweater like Yves.

Joseph dialed Yves's cell again with no answer. It occurred to him that Yves could be at the office, and he pulled out his Interpol contact number where he'd first reached Yves.

After the sixth ring a voice answered, but it wasn't Yves.

"Hello, I am calling for agent Yves, is this the right number?" Joseph inquired.

After a lengthy pause, there was a muffle and another voice came to the phone.

"Who is calling please?"

"My name is Joseph Harkness. I've been given this number to contact an Interpol agent by the name of Yves."

"What is the nature of your business with him?" The man voice continued to interrogate him.

"We have a business relationship, and I must speak to him urgently." Joseph was insistent.

"Where are you now?" The odd questioning went on.

"As a matter of fact, I am at the café across the road from the Interpol building. May I come in to speak with you?"

"What makes you think you've connected with Interpol?"

"I already explained, this is the Interpol number I was given, that I used to contact agent Yves. He is my assigned contact." Joseph was becoming exasperated.

"Stay where you are, I will come to you."

The line went dead.

Emily watched the door through the zoom lens. Twenty minutes later a man in a shirt, tie, leather jacket and sunglasses came through the revolving doors. He looked across to the patio and his focus remained on them.

"Joseph! That's our man. He's heading our way."

Within a minute he was close. Joseph whispered, "I'm not liking this situation. Something peculiar is up."

"Bonjour, Monsieur Harkness."

The man put his hand forward in a formal greeting.

"Bonjour, Monsieur . . . but I'm afraid we don't know who you are."

"I presume the lovely lady is Emily Warner."

He tipped his hat. "I am agent Yves Deslorme, how can I be of assistance?"

"What are you doing answering agent Yves' phone?" Joseph wasn't ready to be pleasant. "Where is he, is he okay?

"I'm afraid you will need to answer my questions first. What were the circumstances when you first met agent Yves?"

"I can answer that point blank. He beat the dickens out of me after he shot a friend of mine at Montmartre. Now you owe me some sort of an explanation, for the cat and mouse game you're playing with us."

"As I said, my name is Yves Deslorme. The man you refer to as 'agent Yves' was a con man who stole my cell phone and has hacked into my personal computer and downloaded a number of strategically delicate files. Could you enlighten me further in respect to the contact you had with this man."

Joseph and Emily exchanged shocking glances.

His first concern was the number of times he'd left Emily in Yves's protective care. Then there was the possibility of losing the Frizon forever.

"Did you ever see an Interpol shield?" Deslorme pried.

"In the beginning, he showed me something official looking . . . yes, I'm certain he did. I didn't feel I needed to question him. I am not at liberty to give you further information about our background."

Joseph quickly re-sorted details in his mind of his first introduction to Yves.

The man was pointed. "If I may be candid, you have been duped. We've needed to run interference where Yves allowed himself to become involved in the forgery operation. Captain Macdonald of Scotland Yard has recently been in touch with our offices and I believe I am up to date with the status of the cases. Interpol's cooperation is ongoing through appropriate channels. It goes to say, of course, that agent Yves's participation in your foundation will not happen."

"Joseph has asked you several times. Is he alright?" Emily interrupted Deslorme speech.

"I will confirm your Agent Yves is being illusive but he will soon be apprehended. I believe you have now met another of our agents who has been spotting you, Daniel Boisvert. There are serious security reasons why I cannot tell you if Yves is dead or alive."

Joseph continued to prod. "I have another friend who is also missing. Do you know about Serge Bouet?"

"I can't comment on that due to pending legal matters. Back to the telephone number for our con man, how did you come to have my phone number?"

"If you don't know that, then I won't need to explain. And if I have a need to call you again in the future you will certainly be informed of the reasons." Joseph was angry and dismissive.

Agent Deslorme rose. "In that case, I don't see I have anything further to discuss. I have enjoyed our chat. Perhaps another time. This is far from over; the forgery ring is ongoing under our surveillance. You can contact me or Daniel, if ever in trouble."

He tipped his hat at Emily, and walked back toward the Interpol building at Lycée du Parc.

They waited until he was onto the street.

"That's the last thing I expected." Emily said. "I totally trusted Yves. We need to call Captain Macdonald. What if this new agent Deslorme could be a fake too?"

"We'll see Macdonald on Friday in London, but this can't wait till then."

"What about Serge?" Emily asked. "We should try him again."

She continued to talk as Joseph dialed. "I trust Serge told the truth; he didn't have any reason to lie to us. Besides, he put himself in jeopardy by coming to us . . . perhaps going to Yves put both of them at risk. Someone was prepared to place Serge in the explosion."

There was still no answer on the line, and Joseph shook his head.

"On a hunch, Emily, we should check Le Jardin Hotel; see if anyone is registered there as Simon Walker!"

"You might have something."

In the taxi to the hotel, their minds grappled about what had happened and what could face them when they arrive.

The story of Yves left them humiliated and violated.

"Could Simon Walker be agent Yves, or could he even be Serge?" she asked. "What are you thinking, Joseph?"

He didn't answer right away as he was focused on the hotel as they pulled in. "Wait in the lobby and I'll talk to the desk clerk. I'm not sure if he'd remember me."

"Are you packing today?" she asked.

"I almost didn't, but had a last minute change of heart." He slapped his hand against his jacket pocket.

They got out across the road and Joseph went ahead. It was an executive hotel with a polished reception counter manned by two men.

Joseph didn't recognize either clerk from his stay with Alexandre. A minute later, Emily entered the lobby, loitering at a brochure rack as Joseph approached the clerk.

"May I have a key to the room for Simon Walker please?"

The clerk was startled by Joseph's request, and cleared his throat to stall. He withdrew his wallet, realizing he hadn't yet offered the 100 euros.

"Is he expecting you, Monsieur?"

The clerk watched the money as it was laid on the counter.

Joseph answered, "Mais oui! He told me to ask at the desk for the key, that I should come up."

This time he wasn't given a traditional key, but a plastic card that the clerk swiped with a code. He was sent to the twelfth floor to the room at the end of the hall.

TWENTY-SEVEN

Emily waited for an elevator on the ground floor and Joseph ambled beside her.

"Twelfth floor, please." Emily was closest to the elevator panel.

He leaned and whispered. "I got the impression at the desk, someone is in the room."

Other people got on at the mezzanine. A boisterous man monopolized the ride telling his wife about the noise from the next room, determined everyone know the issue. Emily was first off on the twelfth, and Joseph struggled past the man to break free.

The doors closed and they walked silently down the hall.

"Joseph, what now?" she asked.

He raised his finger.

"Whoever is in the room is not expecting us unless the desk called up. From experience, they're not likely to answer a knock at the door. So we'll let ourselves in with the key."

"It has to be Yves!" Emily's voice was almost silent at the door.

Joseph nodded and readied his revolver. "We don't know if he is alive or dead. Stay behind me outside the door until I give you an all clear."

The key slid in triggering the green light, and Joseph turned the handle, easing the door's weight against his shoulder.

"It's okay Joseph, you can come in." The familiar voice called boldly across the room in the darkness and it took a moment to adjust to the dim light.

"What the Sam Hill is going on, Yves?"

Joseph's revolver pointed at the silhouette by the window.

"Well if it isn't Punch and Judy! Come in. I've been hoping you would figure it out."

Yves's speech was slurred from too much Scotch whisky, and Joseph gestured to Emily it was clear to enter.

Joseph couldn't hide his irritation. "Yves, if that is your real name," he scorned, "go back to the beginning and try us with your best story." His gun was still out.

"I appreciate your candor and I guess we will start with our chance meeting on Montmartre."

Yves sat again to face them.

"We're ready, please start!"

"I really was an Interpol agent then, and I was protecting your friend from Montmartre, helping to put him into a junior undercover role. He was a recruit who had applied in New York to our international department and I was following him. But he deviated from the plan and exposed his real identity to you.

"To put your mind at ease, the assassination was a ruse! I used a rubber bullet and the apparent victim is still alive. The first ambulance was an Interpol vehicle to remove him from the scene, ensuring that anyone would be convinced of his death, and clearing his way to become an operative."

Emily threw in two cents. "Thanks for telling us about Daniel." She played along. Maybe, Yves doesn't know about Daniel's reappearance and the irony that he is now on Yves's case.

Yves raised his head to Joseph. "I must say, I didn't expect you to be so skilled in tracking me through the lanes and staircases in the dark that night. You are a worthy opponent and you did get in some pretty nasty punches. I was bruised for weeks.

"I was backup for the Interpol agent, Roger Garnier, in the project to expose Robillard and Charest. I was the one the dead agent called before he was murdered. Roger gave me the date and time the next forgery would be exchanged in Normandy. He thought he'd become invincible, that they'd never find out his identity; then he turned gutsy and tried to rob Charest's safe. He whispered a dying message to Serge that I expect somehow included my name. Whatever it was outraged Serge."

Joseph interrupted him. "What about Deslorme? Is he legitimate?"

Yves continued, "I was versed in the case before you became involved, and I couldn't believe how you fell into my lap. It was a coincidence that I was in agent Deslorme's office when his cell phone rang. I thought I would do him a favor, but instead it was the two of you. Like baiting a horse with a fresh carrot, I couldn't resist.

The real agent Yves Deslorme only knew me as a recruit. You've already met him, or you wouldn't be here right now. Am I right?"

Emily nodded.

"What did he tell you about me?"""

Emily answered, "He basically set the record straight and stripped you of your authority."

"And rightly so," Joseph added. "Don't ask me my opinion of you right now, Yves. You wouldn't like it."

"Fair enough. The Robillard-Charest case was always Deslorme's and he was kept informed along the way by police surveillance. Don't think he got short changed."

Joseph changed the tone. "The foundation has a meeting tomorrow in London, by Skype. I'll give them your apologies. I hope they are not set back by trust issues."

Yves put his hands in the air with a sneer.

Joseph went on, "Do you know where Serge is? He gave testimony to the police about Charest, but has been out of touch. What do you know about the explosion at the auction house? I don't have proof, but I suspect you were there. If I'm not mistaken, your eyebrows are singed and that gash on your cheek is fresh."

Once again, Yves shrugged, then answered.

"If you had done your good deed in putting away the crooks like Serge did, and then had to answer to a murder charge, would you be answering all your calls?"

Joseph did not let up. "I know little about him. Do you know where he lives, any of his friends, a known hangout? Anything?"

"I'm here to tell you about my covert involvement, but Serge is entirely another story and I don't choose to go there right now." He stopped.

"Do you want me to continue?" Yves was now annoyed, having lost control of the matter.

"Please, go ahead Yves." Emily said diplomatically, noticing the roll of paper taken from the apartment the other day.

"It was my plan to get close to Robillard's vaults in his caves, and Joseph, you opened the door perfectly for me by penetrating his activities. But pompous Charest kept demanding a bigger piece and became more resentful of Robillard. Charest never noticed I was watching him.

"I knew he'd find a way to dispose of Robillard without dirtying his own hands, and it wouldn't have been difficult to coerce Serge into being the monkey in the middle and take the fall.

"Charest purposely left the dead agent's toque in sight in his office, knowing it would incite Serge against Robillard. He is a passionate Frenchman with a belief in righting wrongs, and ensuring the guilty pay. Those are admirable qualities.

"With such a noble concept of putting the Monett up to fund a foundation to monitor forgeries, I knew I had to see it through. Baker impressed me from his Robillard dinner meeting that he showed guts. He will be a good leader and I'm sorry I won't be at the London meeting."

"That is certainly understandable." Joseph acknowledged.

"Emily, I apologize for being deceitful but it was the only way I could make the switch in Lyon. It was my first intention to benefit personally from the clock, but the trust on your face made me do the right thing. Thank you for helping me to remember there was once some good inside me."

Emily answered, coaching him, "At the rendezvous, guilt was written all over your face, and I knew what had happened. I kept faith in you, and having overruled the greed, you saved your own life. I see a good agent in a confused man and I hope you have the opportunity to become respectable again. You haven't stolen or murdered anyone, just a misdirection."

"My dear, naïve Emily. I crossed the largest international policing organization and was blacklisted. They don't take 'sorry' for an answer, and your faith in me makes me ashamed. I ran interference and kept you safe; that should have been the job of agent Yves Deslorme, so I don't have regrets. Whatever disciplinary action they deem suitable, I will accept. But I need time to sort myself out. Interpol is where I want to be so I will plead my way back into their good graces, all in due time.

"Joseph, if you find yourself wanting thrills and adventure, please let me be the one to bring you into Interpol for an interview. They'd give me brownie points for that."

It was a carrot, dangled in front of Joseph. Emily studied his face for a reaction but he didn't blink.

Before leaving Simon Walker's room, Emily asked for a glass of water. Taking a glass from the refreshment tray on the sideboard, she flipped open the roll of paper.

Joseph isn't going to believe this. His double-cross living is ridiculous.

TWENTY-EIGHT

It was two in the afternoon in London, but only 6:00 a.m. in Los Angeles. Nigel called Samuel Wentworth and woke him to discuss a matter an hour before the Skype meeting. Their routine morning calls were becoming lengthy as their friendship grew, both men realizing the benefits of their business relationship.

In the preceding week, Nigel Baker made gains in identifying potential consultants specialized in fraud and security detection, carbon dating and x-ray diffraction. In the same time, Wentworth and his California accountants developed a model of financial projections for the business plan. The two men discussed the three o'clock agenda.

Nigel Baker's secretary had sent confirmation texts ahead of the meeting, but Yves's text did not go through, and Serge did not reply.

Philippe Sauliere connected first, then Joseph and Emily.

Joseph chose words respectfully about Yves's resignation, but was less confident what he should say about Serge.

"Yves did an excellent job to bring us to this point safely; he won't be able to make an ongoing contribution. I tried to reach Serge and didn't get an answer; we trust he is safe. If he's not on this team, it will be a loss."

Philippe quickly came to Serge's defense. "Joseph, I might be able to find him. When I'm back in Epte, I will do some sleuthing. He has a miserable flat where he lands when he's feeling sorry for himself. My guess is that he is lying low. He has always faced his responsibilities."

Baker agreed. "I hope you can find Serge."

"Well then, to the meeting at hand. Samuel, I see you're online. Philippe, Joseph and Emily have already connected, but unfortunately Yves has withdrawn and Serge Bouet is out of contact. We hope to correct that soon."

He read directly from his agenda.

"We are ready to begin. Samuel and I sent out a Request for Proposal after the last meeting to recruit a qualified organization as a research partner. I've received presentations from five companies, addressing the RFP scope of work and costs, and I've emailed them to each of you with the profiles, strengths and weaknesses.

"The Institute of Art has separately delivered a proposal to outsource our research on authentication, and an accredited security company in Devon has submitted specs on their advanced software developments."

Nigel paused and Philippe spoke up. "We shouldn't overlook students at the greatest museums in the world, right here in Paris. For employee hires, it would be a PR coup to have involvement by a graduate student."

Joseph nodded. "Nigel, these HR resumes don't include any names from London or Paris. Have we overlooked local talent? As Philippe suggested, bringing a Paris contact would add strength."

Wentworth's voice was forceful in volume. "I've prepared a shortlist of employee applicants, and my assistant has started gathering references. I concur with Joseph, we should find a local candidate if possible. Philippe, you might be in the best position to dig for a recruit."

Baker closed the topic, ready to move the agenda forward.

Joseph interrupted, "I believe you mentioned, Nigel, you had prepared a Non-Disclosure Agreement. Could you send us the draft? We'll need it for RFP discussions."

The finance agenda item had to be a deferred, pending completion of the business plan, under Wentworth's control. An initial startup contribution of 10,000 euros from each member was agreed, to be repaid when the Frizon funds were released.

Nigel Baker announced that Capt. Macdonald and Sergeant Newman were now with him in the office.

The Captain took over.

"Besides the initial arrests, Scotland Yard's investigation uncovered a competing ring responsible for other international crimes. We've identified some masterminds who ordered the forgeries, but there's pressure on the court system and the backlog could take years to bring the offenders to trial."

"One step forward and two back. Overall, we have done our best job and we can't ask for anything more." Joseph laughed.

"Right you are." Capt. Macdonald said.

Joseph said, "The detectives assigned to the Rouen explosion reported a substantial number of paintings were destroyed in the fire. They came from a hidden shelf in the ceiling but Charest claims not to have known about it. From the ruins pulled from the fire, Emily identified a Cezanne and a Monet. And looking back over the major museum thefts in Europe in recent years, there is another abominable criminal factor at play."

"Joseph, I have a copy of that report, and it concerns me greatly. The Zurich authorities should be advised of it and I'll take care of that."

Before Joseph or the Captain could speak again, Nigel interrupted.

"I'm sorry, gentlemen, we've run past our intended time for today. We've reviewed all the material for this meeting ando I suggest we adjourn."

Some were displeased with Nigel's abrupt ending.

"Joseph, as we left Yves, I found he had a drawing from the 8th Arrondissement and flipped it open. It's a floor plan for one of the Paris museums. Why would Yves have it?"

"Emily, do you remember the building shape? Would it help to sketch an outline of anything you remember?" He rummaged for paper, then speculated. "My suspicion is that it might be the Musée du Monde. Can you bring something up on the laptop about the museum?"

She googled a tourist guide of the exhibits. There was no question, it matched her recollection of Yves's drawing.

"There's a newspaper article of a robbery at the museum last year and there's an ongoing investigation about faulty alarm systems." Emily said.

"Perhaps we should visit the Musée du Monde tomorrow morning and add a few stake-outs at the 8th Arrondissement of Yves's comings and goings." Joseph suggested.

They waited for the museum to open at ten a.m. and requested permission to photograph the main exhibits. The head of security was curious about their request and quizzed them.

They provided ID and a contact at Interpol, Yves Deslorme. After a discreet phone call they were granted access.

Joseph took charge leading Emily to the main exhibit hall. A group of art students surged upon the featured pieces, a Degas, Matisse, Van Gogh and other impressionists Emily recognized.

Blending with the group, Emily noticed the man from the corner bar. It was Robert Garnier.

She whispered. "Don't look at him. We'll take note of the paintings he stops at, then follow him when he leaves."

Robert saw them and slipped out the emergency exit and they were right behind. He pulled his old blue Renault to the street. Joseph had seen it before.

Joseph ran to the taxi by the curb. He pulled his wallet out and handed the driver 1000 euros and his phone number. Emily hopped in, leaving the driver standing on the curb with his mouth agape.

Robert was still in his sight and Joseph tore onto the busy street. "Buckle up!" he shouted. They sped past the Arc de Triomphe, determined he was not going to back off. Traffic ahead suddenly slowed and then stopped with congestion, and Joseph looked for a detour.

Without warning Emily, Joseph yanked the steering wheel to the right, his tires screeching with smoke as the car spun ninety degrees, bouncing over the sidewalk, and up a paved pedestrian walkway. They slowed through a courtyard at the top and pulled to the empty street behind.

They were waiting at Robert's apartment when he arrived, and Joseph had a gun in his face before he shut the engine off.

"Robert Garnier, I have some questions for you."

"Not saying a word."

Joseph hauled him out of the Renault and roughed him up threatening him to come up with the truth right away.

Emily called Daniel and explained the situation.

"Have Joseph make a citizen's arrest charging him with assault. You can hold him for a while and get some information, then stage an escape to let him go. I'll meet you back at Le Bar in an hour."

Emily's phone rang. It was Serge. She was relieved to hear from him.

"Emily, I checked out the farm. The name on the mailbox is 'Garnier'. It's an old stone building in poor repair. The same tractor was in the field as in the picture, and the old man. Beside an old fallen-down barn, there's a new large cement garage, three times the width of a normal garage."

"Fantastic job, Serge. We'll plan on an old-fashioned country stake-out."

"Count me in." Serge made excuses and hung up.

Daniel sauntered into the lounge with a folder under his arm.

"Hello, Daniel. Thanks for meeting us." Emily said.

After ordering a round of drinks, Joseph was anxious to settle into business.

"Daniel, it appears Robert Garnier is planning a museum robbery in Paris sometime soon. He was casing Musée du Monde this morning. Emily saw the papers in Yves's room and he's obviously in cahoots with Robert."

"This does make sense. I've been monitoring them for their next move."

Emily relayed her phone conversation with Serge.

"It's time for us to split up," Daniel said. "Joseph you'll take Yves, I'll take Robert. Emily, keep sleuthing with your research; you'll maintain coordinates. I anticipate something else related to the farmhouse may arise. Try voters' lists and property deeds."

Joseph objected. "Hold on, Daniel. I don't like you giving Emily orders."

"Oh, so it's just you."

Joseph saw the irony and burst out laughing. "We'll rendezvous at Montmartre tomorrow afternoon and drive to the Rouen property. If the two boys are involved in art thefts, I'm suspicious about that stone garage."

"I promised Serge he could help. He's already in Rouen. Are we like the apple dumpling gang?" Emily asked.

TWENTY-NINE

For months, Joseph had been working on his own scheme but continued to hold back.

The time was now right. He could look into his old identity if he dared to break the rules of the witness program. He dialed and waited for his New York lawyer, Martin Sproule, to pick up.

At first Martin was concerned something had gone wrong, but the call quickly turned to a light banter all was okay. In Albany, the Thomas York Chauffeuring company was prospering under the new management and Thomas's share equity was healthy.

But it wasn't for business reasons he phoned; it was to ask Martin to arrange for Rachel's sister, Amy Redmond, to briefly join Emily in France. He would surprise them with enrollment at the Paris Cordon Bleu cooking school for a three month course.

Martin cautioned against the boldness of such an offer, but had empathy for Rachel's painful separation from her family for the past two years.

"Martin, could you arrange a temporary ID for Amy? The Redmond name might trigger attention in New York or Paris."

"It isn't my line of business, but I'll see what I can do. Call me tomorrow morning on my secure line about 9:00 a.m."

Amy Redmond removed her coat and placed her coffee on her desk in the Albany regional library branch. She had worked there for eight years as Librarian and lived within a close walk.

Martin was taken aback how much she looked like Rachel. Same color hair and similar eyes, but Amy was shorter and looked a few years younger. Her glasses rested mid-point on her nose as she looked over the frame as he approached.

"Miss Redmond?" Martin inquired.

"Yes, but how do you know my name?" Amy was startled.

"I am strictly a messenger. Is there a private place where we can discuss a matter of critical sensitivity?" Martin kept his voice low.

She didn't know where it was leading. "I am about to restock the History stacks down this hall. Come with me if you'd like, it's the last bank on the right."

She nodded in the direction and finished loading her trolley, then took her time to the History aisle.

"I'm here on behalf of a mutual friend. This person requested you join her in Paris for a three-month cooking course at the Cordon Bleu school. You have little time to decide to pursue this, and once I leave here today, you will never see me again."

Amy's jaw dropped. "This is preposterous!"

"That it may be, but you can guess who I am representing. If you decide to go, you'll be on a British Airways flight to London tomorrow night, then connecting on Air France."

He handed her a sealed brown envelope.

"This is your new passport and your return ticket. Make believable excuses here for your imminent absence, and remember, you'll be out of contact for the duration. You won't have a fixed address, nor will you be Amy Redmond for the next three months."

Martin began to look at his watch.

Amy was flustered and tears welled in her blue eyes. Martin felt sorry for her; he knew it was too much to absorb in five minutes.

Martin looked toward the door.

"I must leave now. The choice is yours. If you choose to go, you will be met by a sign at the Charles de Gaulle airport for Amanda Mitchell."

He shook her hand. "It was a pleasure to have met you." He paused at the exit turnstile, knowing he left Amy trembling and fragile.

In slow motion, she watched him through the doors. In just five minutes her life had changed. Finding the junior librarian, she asked her to cover and grabbed her coat.

She walked to the corner facing the cool north wind, oblivious to the chill. Realizing the decision had already been made, she had to act quickly. She would feign a family emergency, requiring a leave of absence.

She ran back and located the administrator. "I'm sorry to leave you so suddenly, but these circumstances are beyond my control." She wasn't sure it sounded believable.

"Go ahead, Amy, do what you have to do. We'll wait until you come back. But keep in touch."

Amy removed her bag from the security cabinet and left through the back door. Scurrying toward her car, she was in a fog. She drove directly to her apartment; it was so easy, the passport and her tickets were in her hand.

In half an hour, her bags were packed, and she had time to curl up in the armchair by the fireplace. With Rachel's picture in her arms, the tears rolled deep tears, tears of joy.

The next morning, Amy phoned her parents to explain she was going on an eco-adventure and would be out of contact for several months. She gave the same excuse to her neighbor and phoned her boss to the confirm approval for her leave.

At 4:00 p.m. her buzzer rang. She couldn't be delayed and had been about to call a taxi.

"Hello. Who is it?" She called through the intercom.

"It's your taxi, Ma'am. I was ordered to take you to the airport."

"Do you mind coming up and helping me with my bags?"

Relief and excitement swept over her.

Amy was unable to sleep on the BA overnight from New York to London. A window seat had been booked and she snuggled against it with a pillow and blanket. In what seemed like moments, she woke to the clatter of morning coffee, received a petite dejeuner of croissant, cheese and fruit. She wasn't hungry but she thought it would ease her nerves.

The plane touched down early in London, and an attendant confirmed her Air France gate and that her bags had been checked through to Paris.

Joseph woke early and dressed in the dark to take care of his business. It was mild and breezy in Paris and he took a jacket. He hadn't told Emily of his plans and kissed her gently as she slept, holding back any hint of excitement. She opened her eyes and sat up, questioning him with her look.

"You are sometimes too curious," he retorted. "A man sometimes likes to surprise his lady. I'll be back in a couple of hours."

"Love you," she called as he took off down the stairs.

Emily dressed warm and walked to the grand staircase on Montmartre, sitting for a slow coffee and brioche. She thumbed through a fashion magazine, and at a boutique on the rise, she treated herself to a Givenchy silk scarf and a vial of Chanel perfume.

Joseph arrived back at the loft behind her. She knew by his grins he was up to mischief. He tempted her to a ride across town to show her something important, and called for a taxi to meet them at the corner.

"She was curious but trusting as they rode, but eventually gently pushed. "Joseph, are we headed toward the airport? Are you taking me to London, or what?"

"You'll see."

She no longer seemed to be amused, and he reached for her hand.

The cab stopped at Terminal 2E and Joseph took the driver's card and tipped him to wait nearby, that he wouldn't be long.

Inside Arrivals, he borrowed a cardboard sign from the transportation coordinator, printing the words 'Amanda Mitchell'.

He turned to Emily. "Here, can you stand here and hold this up, I need to check on something."

Joseph stood back among the passengers. He'd never met Amy and wanted their first recognition to be between the two of them only. Tears welled in his eyes as he watched Emily faithfully holding the sign, just because he had asked her to.

Emily was at the bottom of the escalator when Amy appeared. Emily looked twice at Amy, then at the sign and she knew in a flash. They locked eyes and all their arms went in the air, screaming and crying, hugging and jumping. It couldn't be more obvious they were sisters.

Joseph stepped in to pick up the dropped luggage.

Emily grabbed him and took his face between her hands. "You dear, dear man." She planted a loving kiss on his lips.

She looked at the sign for prompting. " . . . Amanda, this is my . . . Joseph. Joseph Harkness." She knew Amy could never know about Thomas York.

She lowered her volume to a whisper. "I'm no longer Rachel, I'm now Emily Warner. It is so wonderful to finally see you."

"If this is your doing Joseph, then I know . . . Emily has been well taken care of. May I have a hug too?"

"One more thing, ladies. You're both enrolled at Cordon Bleu's cooking school, starting on Monday. For three months, you'll be pros!"

Emily was about to kiss him again. "Joseph! Our taxi! Think he's still waiting?"

A pang of hurt stabbed at him, realizing he'd need to share Emily for three months; their private time would be at a minimum. Admonishing himself for that thought, he looked at how happy Emily was. He would never forget this moment.

The cooking classes were intense hands-on demonstrations in the most elaborate of French kitchens.

Emily and Amanda found a two bedroom suite near the school, ideal for them to reunite in privacy. It was like the old university days, with two classes a day and five days a week.

She could still spend two nights a week at the Montmartre loft with Joseph. On the first weekend, she demonstrated a new gourmet plate to him, and he noticed the change already in her, how much happier she seemed to be with her sister here and her renewed self-confidence.

Yves disguised himself as an elderly man, with grey hair and beard over a fine black silk suit and striped designer tie. His eyebrows were thickened by a touch of glue and grey powder. A monocle was his finishing touch, a must for inspection of art. He forged a Foreign Press badge guaranteeing his entry to the Paris Gala, and took a deep breath of confidence.

The reception line had broken up when Yves arrived after 8:00 p.m. and he blended into the crowd unnoticed.

The audience of socialites and dignitaries buzzed in anticipation of the unveilings. Along the window, three accomplished sketch artists demonstrated their talents.

Except for sanctioned photographers, photos were forbidden. Press kits were provided to the media and all other guests received stamped souvenir prints that could not be copied.

Emily was radiant in a discriminating pink sleeveless crepe dress, with a low draped back that hung off her curves, and tiny pearls hand-sewn onto a shear overlay. Her auburn tresses were pulled up into a pearl beaded clasp, showing her elegant long neck and the drop diamond earrings, Joseph's gift to her.

Yves watched her stride across the room, confessing to himself he was jealous of Joseph.

He kept moving, edging his way into the crowd, fearing scrutinizing eyes. He hadn't yet returned to Interpol to plead his case for a second chance, but had spent the last week at the hotel.

The exhibition hall was imposing but sparsely appointed. The featured works were under ceiling spotlights, draped in red silk to await the ceremony. The mystery behind the cloaks only added to the evening's excitement.

The first unveiling was announced at 8:30 p.m., a grand historic moment, with guests gathering close in adoration, realizing they were witnessing this event. The hush of the crowd broke quickly to an extended applause as the crimson cloak was lowered by Madame Sauliere, revealing to the world the extraordinary portrait of Angelique.

Twenty minutes later, the room's attention was drawn to the covered Frizon. The Mayor of Paris removed the red cloak, and the room went quiet, with only gasps and whispers at the sight of the gold clock. For this moment, Diplomats and common folks mingled together, briefly forgetting their class distinction as they pushed tight for a closer look.

The glass case was raised on a platform and rotated slowly to reveal the Monet. The initial awe changed to applause and celebration.

At nine o'clock, the scrolls were revealed as a surprise to everyone. Reporters and critics gathered close, some declaring them to be illegitimate, that the confirmation and questionable spelling of Monett did not translate to any relationship to the great artist. Others were astounded by the possibilities, and either way, the Saulieres were proud.

Festivities started again, with the central grand piano filling the hall with the music of impressionists Ravel and Debussy.

Emily found Joseph and motioned with her head.

"An older man with a heavy grey beard has been staring at me and when I make an eye connection, it's like looking into his soul. Do you see who I am talking about?"

Joseph scanned the heads looking for the gentleman.

"I see him, and yes he was looking at us."

Emily whispered. "I have a strange inkling it could be Yves. His intense look grabbed my attention."

"What would he be doing here?"

Emily laughed. "He deserves to be here, otherwise we wouldn't be here, looking at the original Monett in the Frizon."

"Maybe I'll slip over for a chat."

Joseph disappeared into the throng. Yves saw him coming and tried to avoid it but Joseph outfoxed him.

"Hello, Yves . . . nice you were able to make it. We all hoped you would join us." Joseph extended his hand.

Yves chuckled. "Well, Joseph, I thought my disguise was better than that. What gave me away?"

"Emily. When she looked at your eyes, she saw into your questionable soul and knew it was you."

"Smart girl, your Emily. She looks ravishing tonight; you're a lucky man."

"Believe me, I know how lucky I am." Joseph warned. "Yves, let me introduce you to some of our guests."

"Joseph, that's not possible. My archrival is here and an introduction on this occasion wouldn't be received in favor. I still haven't thrown myself into the lion's den. I'm here for simple curiosity, to see the portrait and the Sauliere's celebration. They are very proud of Philippe."

With uncharacteristic passion, Yves asked, "Please walk away and let me savor the evening? I promise I will get in touch. And give my best to Emily." He sauntered to the back, his hands clasped behind him.

Philippe scrutinized every guest, looking for Serge to arrive. The gala was scheduled to end at 10:00 p.m., and fifteen minutes before closing, Serge entered the room. The crowd had become sparse, and most dignitaries and press had departed. As hosts, Nigel Baker and Samuel Wentworth also saw him.

"Serge, it is good to see you." Nigel was eager with his handshake, followed by Wentworth. Joseph and Emily came right over, but didn't mention that Yves had been present.

"How can I get in touch with you, Serge?" Joseph asked.

"I'll find you in the next few days and we'll have coffee on Montmartre." Serge smiled slightly and turned as Nigel Baker tapped him on the shoulder.

Nigel felt a fatherly urge toward Serge and took him aside. "Serge, I know you will be facing a difficult time when the murder charge is laid."

Serge winced at the mention of it.

"I have a team of excellent lawyers and would be honored if you'd allow me to offer any one of them for your defense. I also understand from Capt. Macdonald, he has asked for leniency on your behalf."

Serge was torn between this genuine kindness of his friends and the overwhelming circumstances of the evening.

"Thank you, Sir. I have no choice but to accept your generous offer, but for now I would like to relish this evening with my colleagues. Can we talk at a later time?"

"Of course, son." Nigel stuffed a business card into Serge's pocket.

The gala was grand in Parisienne terms, its success beyond any expectations, with tangible buyers for the Frizon Monett.

The Sauliere slipped away back to quiet country life, leaving 'Angelique' on long term loan to the museum.

THIRTY

L ondon's prestigious Soutees Auction House featured the Frizon Monett on the cover of its catalogue and with newspaper ads in New York, London and Paris.

Philippe attended the advance preview the day before the auction, to observe any notable visitors. A metal scanner was at the entrance with two armed guards and the Frizon was secure in a bulletproof glass case guaranteed by the security consultants.

A Greek billionaire and his aide walked past the other items and directly to the Frizon. His examination with a magnifying glass was meticulous, and he dictated numerous observations his aide transcribed into a notebook. Before the Greek man left, he requested a meeting with the auctioneer.

An American accent was echoing from the entrance, and Philippe jotted his description. He was a large man with little discretion as he summed aloud the faults of the Monett and its potential to be a forgery. He was distinctive, over fifty, hefty, clean-shaven with bulging eyes and a polished head. Philippe discounted him as a serious bidder.

A pair of French gentlemen arrived, deep in conversation, both splendid in the finest bespoke business suits and crisp white shirts. They stood back from the glass case discussing observations from a distance before approaching the display. Philippe overheard certain words of their discussion including mention of Angelique Sauliere. Philippe hoped the Monett would stay in France.

Nigel Baker entered with Samuel Wentworth, delighted that Philippe had appointed himself as the official observer. Philippe gave them a quick review; there were no concerns.

The auction was advertised to start at 11:00 a.m. with Soutees' doors open an hour earlier for registration. Bidders were in the building at ten, representing diverse buyers from North America, France, the UK, Russia, Spain, Greece, and the UAE.

The Frizon was listed third in the catalogue.

Overnight the room had been transformed from a showroom to theater seating, with rows of plush chairs from wall to wall. Sections at the front were reserved for those with bidders' cards.

The podium and clerk's desk faced the auditorium.

Philippe and his parents took seats in the last row for the best vantage. Joseph and Emily arrived without Amanda, and slipped in beside the Sauliere. Nigel Baker and Samuel Wentworth took seats on the opposite side at the back.

The event had multiple security cameras, and Yves Deslorme's attendance was in an official observation capacity. From the viewing room he scanned the room repeatedly on the monitors.

The elderly man with the heavy grey eyebrows from the Gala entered and took a standing position against the back wall. He felt eyes from the last row and avoided looking in that direction. He knew who they were.

Deslorme's camera focused on the man twice; there was something familiar he couldn't pinpoint. His professional curiosity brought him down to approach the man, but he was already gone from the spot. A glimpse of his jacket leaving the building was as close as he got.

Right at 11:00 a.m., Serge came in and took the single remaining seat at the side.

The gavel sounded and the room listened. The auctioneer announced bidding would be in US dollars. He read the rules audibly, but everyone with cards already knew the routine.

Two unknown masters came up for bid before the Frizon, in both cases with prices higher than the scuttlebutt predicted. Baker and Wentworth silently nodded approval.

At 11:20 a.m., the room became silent again as two apprentices carried the Frizon to the front with white gloves. They placed it on a table covered in dark blue velvet beside the podium, enhanced by a ceiling spotlight.

The room waited in anticipation for the velvet to be pulled away. A murmur of voices spread across the floor when the auctioneer called for an opening bid of $50M.

The bidding started in $2M increments, then $1M, with bantering between the Greek billionaire, the two Frenchmen, the American and a Russian gentleman. At $50M it stalled with the Russian still in. Some bidders looked around to inspect their competition, but the two Frenchmen in front stayed calm and unfazed. The American went to $51M and the bidding again became frenetic, including a new telephone bidder. Silent paddles continued to rise stopping again at $65M.

The auctioneer finally lowered his gavel the third time and pointed to the Frenchmen, drawing polite applause that the now famous Monett had been sold.

Under armed guard, the Frizon was removed immediately and transported by an armed security vehicle to an undisclosed location in the north of France. An armored vehicle was waiting at the curb.

A number of spectators and bidders left at the next intermission.

As the room cleared at the end, Serge mustered the courage to approach Yves Deslorme.

"Monsieur Deslorme, I need to meet with you as soon as possible. I have important information." His torment was obvious to Deslorme and they agreed to meet the next day.

The proceeds of the Frizon, after commission and another ten percent to the Sauliere family, left the foundation with $53.5M, more than they had anticipated.

Office leases could now be signed and employees hired in Paris and London. Nigel, as an instrumental working leader would oversee London, and Philippe with his technology consultant would organize Paris.

Serge knew he'd be tried for the murder of Monsieur Robillard. In spite of promises of leniency, he was aware he would face years in prison in a cement room with only a portal to daylight. Grateful for Nigel Baker's offer to provide a defense attorney, he planned to go directly to London to discuss his case.

His story would discredit the absconding Yves and the revered agent Roger Garnier, lost in Rouen last year.

The Interpol elevator opened to a large lobby and Yves Deslorme was waiting.

Serge gave testimony for the next three hours. He reviewed previous thefts and photographs, recognizing the same three men on more than one occasion.

He couldn't bring himself to reveal the last words from Roger Garnier that haunted him.

THIRTY-ONE

Rouen, France, July 2011
One year earlier

R oger Garnier finished his overnight stake-out of the auction house. He was bloated from too much coffee and his clothes were tainted from the stale cigarette smoke. He cranked the car windows down to breathe the fresh morning air, then turned over the engine on his mini red Isetta. As it rolled to the road it objected with a quiet backfire sputter.

Roger had been playing both sides of the auction circuit. Working under the guise of an Interpol detective he was closing in on the forgery operation at the Rouen auction house.

During his stake-out the night before, he watched Charest and the others leave the auction house, then he broke in and disarmed the system making his way to Charest's office.

Sitting on the floor beside the office safe, he unfolded a pouch of instruments to attempt to crack the vault door. With a flashlight and sound monitor, he worked his way through the combination.

Sweat dripped from his forehead. At 4:00 a.m. Roger heard the final pop in the combination and the safe opened. His mind was on the job and he didn't hear the shuffle at the front as Charest entered the building. Charest knew what needed to be done but wanted someone else to do the dirty work.

Roger quickly photographed the manifests and transfer papers and placed a hearing transmitter under Charest's desk. He cleaned up after himself and returned to the car.

Charest stood at his office window for an hour and watched the antique Isetta until it left. It had been parked too long in the alley behind the delivery docks, and the constant dim glow of cigarettes confirmed his suspicion.

In the morning, he searched his office for any clues of the thief, and bending down by the safe, he saw the bug under his desk and incriminating chips of mud on the floor.

Hours later, Charest faked a call to Monique, ordering her to come to the warehouse to pick up a shipment of forgeries. The other end of the line was dead, but all he wanted was to set the bait.

"Monique, today's Paris shipment is being postponed until tonight. Be at the warehouse about 10:00 p.m."

Roger heard the invitation, and after meeting with Rene he returned to Rouen with the intention of being at the warehouse before ten. He parked the Isetta further down the alley, without using his headlights.

Rene felt unsettled about it and followed Roger to Rouen. He couldn't risk being connected to the Zurich museum theft. He parked a block from the auction house and walked to a back dumpster in the parking lot to watch for activity in the building.

Creeping to Charest's window, he placed a transmitter against the glass and stood outside to listen.

"There is a little red car on surveillance in the back alley. Bring the driver to me!" Charest ordered Monique. "He is definitely nosing around here."

"Did you want him roughed up a bit?" She was eager to please at a time like this.

"I'll take care of that in here. Just get him."

Rene looked toward the Isetta. He didn't have time to warn Roger, as two shadows emerged from the delivery dock and crept up beside little car. The driver's window was open to allow Roger's smoke spirals to drift out.

Monique raised her gun and ordered Roger to get out and put his hands on the hood. Maurice was on the opposite side with his pistol.

Monique grabbed Roger's jacket and slammed him hard to the hood of the Isetta.

Across the parking lot, Serge arrived and saw the commotion around the Isetta, watching helplessly as Roger Garnier was being beaten.

Charest was a bully and prone to deal with things irrationally but this was the first time Serge feared serious danger. Earlier in the afternoon, Serge overheard Charest talk about thwarting a suspected thief. He would trap the man into a confession about a high profile theft.

"Hands over your head. Maurice take his revolver." Monique demanded.

"Who are you, and what do you want with me?" Roger feigned innocence.

"You know who we are. You've been sitting here watching us the last two nights." Monique said.

Roger struggled with his balance as she shoved and kicked him toward the building.

"You're his puppet, aren't you?" Roger knew it would infuriate her.

She whacked him across the cheek with her revolver leaving a bleeding gash.

"Don't get testy with me!"

Serge, unarmed, waited by the dock for the door to begin to close and crept up catching it before the lock clicked. He was able to see and hear from behind a stack of pallets.

Charest stood in the middle with an empty chair.

"Bring him here." He commanded.

Roger was thrust into the chair, his hands behind his back and his ankles tied against the chair legs. Charest circled him and scratched his own chin with his revolver.

"Who are you and who do you work for?" Charest asked.

Roger was silent.

"Don't toy with me. We searched your car, Monsieur Garnier. It will be less painful for you if you come clean." Charest's face was red with rage.

"What do you want with me? I've done nothing to you."

"You fool, you brazen fool. Last night, I stood just feet away from you when you broke into my safe. I know what you took. Now I ask one more time, who are you working for?"

Rene picked the lock on the side door and inched his way down the hall. He stopped at the door leading into the main warehouse and listened to Charest's interrogation.

"You know, Monsieur Garnier, I'm looking at your drivers' license and I believe I have seen your picture somewhere before. I never forget a face, it will come to me."

Charest stormed back to his office and rifled through a stack of files. He stopped at a newspaper clipping and returned to the warehouse.

"Ah ha, Monsieur Garnier, here it is! You see I am envious of my competition and I keep detailed files on the thieves that outfox me. For instance, the Austrian villa robbery in Zurich. Here are security photos of the three men who hijacked the museum in daylight and took the Cezanne and Van Gogh. See here."

His fat finger pointed to a grainy picture. "This is you!"

"I don't know anything about that." Roger pleaded.

"Do us both a favor and lead me to your accomplices and I might save your life." Charest offered.

Roger refused to talk further. With his fists clenched, Charest battered at Roger's head until he was barely conscious.

"Monique, bring the sodium pentothal. I believe our visitor will be ready to talk."

Rene was powerless to overtake the three of them and protect Roger. He recalled the day they barged boldly into the villa. It was supposed to be a one-time deal then they would go straight. His mind flashed selfishly to his fledgling Interpol ambition, then to the dreaded possibility of being imprisoned.

The high exhilaration and success of their heists had left them on a tight wire. Working security during the day and with thievery by night, they were hooked.

They were unable to turn in the stash from the heist. Roger had assured Rene it was safe in the rafters, and he and Robbie brought them in during the night.

The serum was injected into Roger's arm. He was weak from the beating and didn't offer resistance. Charest rubbed the injection site to activate the serum and after a few minutes he began with his questioning.

"Is your name, Roger Garnier? Yes or no?"

"Yes." Roger mumbled.

"Were you involved in the Zurich robbery of the Cezanne and Van Gogh?"

"Yes." He tried to focus but his eyes were blurry.

"Give me the names of the other two."

"My brothers, Ren . . ."

As Roger struggled to tell the truth, a shot rang. Charest's head snapped around to see the door close. He jumped up, and shouted for Monique and Maurice to take chase, then looked pitifully at the dying man, and walked back into his office.

Serge was stunned seeing Roger's head drop. He couldn't leave him sitting there dying and he stepped out from behind the pallets to help.

Roger struggled to speak while Serge cradled his head. "Roger, it's Serge. Who did this?"

Leaning close to Roger's lips, Serge heard him whisper. "My broth . . . Rene . . . Seefeld. Air vent."

His body relaxed and his eyes closed and there was no longer a pulse.

Serge avoided the wrath of Charest and left through the back door before anyone returned or knew.

"Could Rene have shot his own brother?" the words rang in Serge's head.

The dying man's message was haunting.

THIRTY-TWO

Serge was on point in Rouen waiting for the go-ahead from Joseph to go to the Garnier farmhouse.

Joseph had picked up a rental to drive from Paris to Rouen, and Emily navigated with a map. Daniel was in the back.

Joseph looked in the mirror toward Daniel.

"I've mulled this for a few days and I'm skeptical about their new cement garage. It's early to jump to conclusions but if we can check their hydro bill, we might find their garage is humidity controlled."

Daniel replied, "I'm with you on that. I've been following Yves on orders from Internal Security, and just like your own snooping found, it appears Yves and Robert may be planning another one. The scrutiny of several major thefts had between one and three thieves, and signs point this way."

Emily was curious and still partially believed Yves's innocence. It had to be a mistake.

"Daniel, do you really believe that Yves could be a cat burglar at night?"

"My opinion ruminates over both Yves and Robert."

She was edgy and continued to question him.

"Do you have the authority for us to breach the garage? Then what? If there is a warehouse full of stolen art and forgeries, what do we do?"

"Yes, I do. We'll stop in Rouen to arrange for equipment to temporarily seal the door. It is my responsibility to organize back-up."

"Emily, can you call Serge and ask him to meet us at the police station." Daniel requested.

"You don't think he'll be nabbed on the murder charge?"

"*Outside* the police station." They laughed. "But I'll make a phone call to be safe."

"Daniel, do you expect violence?" Emily asked.

"Follow my lead, I trust the judgment of the three of you."

Serge was driving a pickup truck and parked in the neighbor's driveway, asking them to safely leave the area.

A squad car following sans siren and parked near some high shrubs.

Joseph pulled up behind the police car and they all got out to discuss the tactics of the raid.

Serge and two policemen would take the house, Joseph and one detective at the garage, and Daniel on point outside with the remaining officer. Emily would stay at the vehicles, with binoculars and cell phone.

A blue Renault was near the shed, and Yves's yellow Citroen was there.

There wasn't any visible movement and Daniel gave Serge the green light.

Running toward the house along a row of heavy bush, Serge and the police officer ran to the back kitchen door.

"Police! Open up. Robert Garnier! Open the door and put your hands over your head. If there is anyone else in the house, come out the front door."

From the car, Emily saw a curtain move upstairs, and phoned Daniel.

Joseph and another detective approached the garage. It had multiple locks. They tried shooting the lock open but it resisted.

Daniel came around from the back of the garage positioned on his knee. The fields were high with tall grass, an advantage to use for cover, but also for escape.

Emily called Serge. "An upper window over the back kitchen just opened and a man is climbing out!"

"Got it!"

A foot chase ensued, with Robert well in the lead toward the dilapidated barn. Serge was a hundred meters behind, having trouble over the rough terrain and stumps. He fired his rifle in the air, but Robert kept going.

From the old barn, a diesel tractor roared and barreled through the side wall, shattering the boards to the ground. The tractor charged at Serge, and two policeman fired at Robert but he evaded them and continued to the field.

Joseph was about to assist Serge when the garage door was yanked open with a barrage of bullets.

Rene started firing randomly and Daniel and Joseph retreated.

"Get off my property! You're trespassing."

"Rene Garnier, surrender yourself!" Daniel demanded.

Emily was now out of the car. She scanned the garage with the lens, finding a trap door at the top facing the old barn.

She called Joseph. "Babe, there's a trap door on the north roof. I'm not sure if it's used for getting in or out under the current circumstances . . . hold on . . . I see a rifle protruding. Serge is in the line of fire! Get him out of there!"

"Serge, twelve o'clock, get down!" Joseph yelled.

Serge dove into the tall grass, but the police officer was grazed but still mobile.

Joseph listened at the door that was shut again. There were sounds of tinkering and hammering close to the door. Meanwhile the trap door rifle fired routinely in the air.

"The scoundrel has the rifle rigged to distract us."

The tractor continued out of range toward a fence line that accessed the range road.

Joseph heard the cell phone ring in the garage, then someone shout. "If we have to, we'll take the girl. They won't shoot in her direction."

The wounded officer used the low belly crawl to reach his vehicle and call for more back-up. Bleeding, he collapsed on the front seat of the patrol car.

Emily crawled through the ditch to reach him and affixed a tourniquet.

In the background there was a hail of gunfire.

Two police vehicles screeched from the road forcing the tractor back to the field.

With a bull horn, the officer demanded, "Mr. Garnier, get off your vehicle or we will be forced to fire."

Robert raised himself into a standing position with his arms stretched wide, the tractor veering back toward Serge.

He challenged them to fire. "We live and die as brothers! You'll never separate our bond of the sword."

Serge was within range with his gun raised. He called to Daniel. "Are you going to take the shot?"

Robert began the volley, and Daniel's return fire struck the feisty thief in the chest. Slowly he slumped over the steering wheel of the tractor as it puttered to a stop.

Joseph checked the open garage door. Rene was on foot somewhere not too far. He darted a look toward the car and Emily.

He couldn't see Rene's face in the distance but saw him holding Emily's head by her auburn pony tail with a pistol at her temples. Rene's attention was briefly deflected watching Robert's demise.

Rene yelled out. "No! You idiots, he was the one good! Joseph! Let's play fair. An eye for an eye!"

Tears rolled down Rene's cheeks.

Joseph was pacing wildly.

Daniel put his hand on Joseph's shoulder to help him calm down.

"Take it easy, Joseph. Emily is a strong girl, you know she will talk her way out of this."

Joseph found an ironic smile.

Emily spoke softly with pity. "Please, lie down here on your stomach and put your hands behind your head. You won't be hurt."

He spit on the ground. "Aren't you the good saint?" He yanked her head back and ran the mouth of the pistol down the length of her neck.

"We know you didn't mean to shoot Roger," she pleaded. "He would not want his death to come to this. Make your life worth something. Let me talk to Joseph?"

He reluctantly nodded in agreement.

Joseph's cell rang; it was Emily from the field.

"Joseph, Yves wants a way out. Talk to the police, there must be some way. Don't shoot him."

Joseph turned sharply to Daniel. "That's Yves! Rene and Yves are the same person!"

Daniel nodded. "We've suspected it for a few months. My orders are to bring him in safely and we have some latitude to negotiate."

Yves listened to Daniel on Emily's cell.

"Do as Emily says, Yves. As long as you co-operate, you won't be hurt. Emily, hang in there, you are a strong woman."

Speaking calmly and quietly, Emily coached and comforted him. "Yves, you must drop your gun and place your hands on the back of your head."

"Just give me a minute to think," he said.

"No, the longer you take will make the police edgy. Do it now. Come on, I'll stay with you. Behind your head now and then on your knees."

Emily gently took the gun from his hands and tossed it.

She spoke back into the cell. "Yves, is on his knees. Joseph, please come and help me."

Joseph and Daniel ran across from the garage as a police vehicle moved in. Joseph didn't even look at Yves.

Emily was enveloped in Joseph's arms while Daniel and the police detective took over the arrest.

Yves turned back with his hands in cuffs behind his back. "Joseph, you are a very lucky man. Thanks Emily for saving my life once more."

An ambulance siren wheeled in to rush the wounded officer to hospital, and a coroner was called for Robert.

Within minutes a SWAT team arrived with a fleet of security vehicles. On a desk in the garage, Rene's inventory book catalogued all the building's stolen masters, with a total value in the billions of dollars.

"Too close a call, Joseph." Daniel said. "Looks to me like Robert was giving Rene a chance for a getaway."

The intensity caught up with Emily, with a wave of emotion her tears poured out. Wrapped in Joseph's jacket, she clung to him.

Yes, they're right. I am a strong woman. But was this too much?

THIRTY-THREE

Emily slept while Joseph fixed a breakfast at the loft. He had already been to the newspaper store for the latest broadsheet issue of Le Parisienne. The front page featured the take-down, with no pictures.

GREATEST ART RECOVERY SINCE THE WWII VAULTS
Paris, August 3, 2012– A police raid on Thursday brought an end to a major international art theft ring. The trio of Garnier Brothers had eluded police for the past ten years, and are believed to be responsible for theft of dozens of paintings of the great masters. Rene Garnier, the ringleader, was captured at a farmhouse near Rouen. Robert Garnier, his brother was killed in an exchange of gunfire. A third brother Roger Garnier had been killed in 2011, and homicide charges have been laid against Rene Garnier in his death.
Rene Garnier has been remanded at La Santé prison pending a hearing of evidence against him in five museum thefts and the death of his brother Roger.

Photos of museum thefts involving the three men contributed in the investigation, including a 2009 robbery in Zurich.

Forensic investigators and detectives have descended on the farm to catalogue the collection and establish if they are originals. A repatriation project will use sophisticated microsystems under development by a foundation in London and Paris, under the leadership of Nigel Baker and Philippe Sauliere.

Serge Bouet's previous meeting with Yves Deslorme had provided evidence that had already been used in cases against Charest, Monique, Alexandre, Maurice. It could now be used against Rene as well, and Interpol was grateful.

They summoned him again for more about the murder of Roger Garnier. He had nothing to hide and restated the events.

"Monsieur Charest trapped Roger at the warehouse, trying to photograph forgery manifests. He was tied and interrogated, when Charest got some photos from his office incriminating Roger in an unrelated robbery. Charest became belligerent demanding names.

"I witnessed it from a stack of pallets. Roger refused to answer and was beaten. Charest injected him with sodium pentothal, expecting Roger to answer Charest's questions and give up his partners.

"Roger was under the serum influence, speaking the word 'Rene' when a shot came from the office hallway. The shooter fled, and Roger lay dying on the floor when they left to chase the shooter. I went to help him.

"Roger died wearing a silver ring with a raised emblem and a blue sword."

With a pencil, Serge scratched a crude drawing that the panel accepted as evidence.

"Charest gave the ring to Robillard as a trophy for Roger's death, and later I removed it from Robillard's finger.

"When I first met Rene in London, he was wearing an identical ring, one of a matching set of three. He was using the name Yves, but my suspicions were confirmed.

"Roger's words 'air vent' didn't make any sense, but when I realized the three brothers could be art thieves I connected them to Seefeld. This summer I went to the warehouse and checked out the notion that some art could be stuffed in the vent. From a shaft above the rafters, I had just pulled out a leather artists' tube when Rene found me. We grappled and I took off for the door. His bullet caught me in the shoulder."

Yves Deslorme thanked him and reminded him they'd be in touch.

Out of respect, Joseph and Emily travelled to Rouen and attended a humble memorial service for Robert. Yves wasn't there, but his elderly father sat by himself and a cousin spoke about their early days.

As they left, Daniel surprised them, standing at the door.

Joseph smirked. "Daniel, you've been a haunting shadow and a helpful friend. Will we see you again?"

"I'll take the high road and you the low, and we'll see where life takes us. Remember, Emily, to watch for angels."

"I'll recognize your pipe tobacco anywhere."

THIRTY-FOUR

On the seventeenth of August, he wheeled his rental car through the countryside in the North of France to the quaint village of Le Wast. He wound down a cobbled lane to a blue shuttered building.

A distinctive brass plate was on the door, 'Basil et Pascal Pasquier, Collecteur'.

Josephine, the amiable patron of the first floor shop saw his car drive up and came outside to greet him with a warm hug, then he ventured up to the third floor garret.

Two high artisan desks sat before the windows opening to a view of the azure sea.

A man came out from a small office to welcome him, then a second man joined him, both dressed in fine gentlemen's attire. The men shook his hand warmly and embraced him; they were always glad when he came.

There was chatter in German from the artisan desks in an alcove, where two skilled student craftsmen were working.

On a cotton sheet, gilding brushes were laid out, and under halogen magnifying glasses, the men worked in precision applying gilding gold leaf paint to the crowns of two identical 1725 Frizon replica clocks.

Two more unpainted clocks sat on the floor, also modelled explicitly to the specifications of the famous Frizon.

"Have the gold plates arrived, Basil?" Daniel asked.

"Mais oui!" Basel answered. The armored truck came yesterday. We will be ready soon with the first clock. Two seasoned impressionist artists will arrive today, one from Paris and the other from Switzerland."

"I have good news," Daniel announced. "The Greek bidder from the auction has agreed to take our first Frizon Monett for $68 million US, and the Russian will be next. Disguises are necessary for all of our dealings outside this room in future." He threw them fake IDs.

"Gentlemen, our timing to release our new Frizon Monetts is impeccable. Each sale will have a condition of privacy and confidentiality, not to be resold for three years. If we're careful, at fifty million or more a clock, a billion dollars is not unrealistic for us."

Pascal drew out three wine goblets and uncorked a fine Bordeaux.

Daniel raised his glass to the men.

"Ah, we celebrate our good fortune in France!"

The End

PREVIEW OF

ROGUE
COURIER

**BOOK THREE OF
THE THOMAS YORK SERIES**

ROGUE COURIER

SHIRLEY BURTON

ROGUE COURIER
BOOK THREE OF THE THOMAS YORK SERIES

The suspense intrigue heightens for Thomas and Rachel in the third in the series.

In their Paris identities, Joseph and Rachel take a high risk assignment hired by the wife of a missing international courier, leading to a drama beyond what they'd faced in New York.

Planted clues drive Joseph on a chase from Paris, to Amsterdam and London in pursuit of critical evidence. He is intrigued by messages clearly intended for him, but they pull him deeper into a web.

The international courier's loyalty is not clear, and Joseph and Emily follow the puzzle pieces to the world's diamond capital where a covert mission unfolds involving missing diamond inventory.

The courier's life becomes tangled in a conflict between the man who controls his livelihood and a ruthless South African diamond dealer. The consequences of greed and temptation change the lives of the three men.

Emily's life is in danger as she works to find evidence to resolve an estate matter for a suspicious death, but runs into life threatening opposition from the victim's relative.

Please join me for ROGUE COURIER.

Reviews appreciated on amazon.com and goodreads.com. Comments always welcome at shirleyburtonbooks.com.

About the Author

Shirley Burton lives with her husband in Calgary, Alberta, Canada, with a view of the magnificent Rockies. Inspired at a young age to write stories for children on her street, she became driven and motivated to write, starting with research for a ten-generation family saga.

"There comes a time in life to take the leap into writing. It's that time for me. I hope readers will become as attached to my characters as I have."